She Don't Play Fair

She Don't Play Fair

She Don't Play Fair

Clifford "Spud" Johnson

www.urbanbooks.net

Urban Books, LLC
78 East Industry Court
Deer Park, NY 11729

ISBN 13: 978-1-60162-554-0
ISBN 10: 1-60162-554-5

First Printing July 2013
Printed in the United States of America

10 9 8 7 6 5 4 3 2 1

Distributed by Kensington Publishing Corp.
Submit Wholesale Orders to:
Kensington Publishing Corp.
C/O Penguin Group (USA) Inc.
Attention: Order Processing
405 Murray Hill Parkway
East Rutherford, NJ 07073-2316
Phone: 1-800-526-0275
Fax: 1-800-227-9604

She Don't Play Fair

by

Clifford "Spud" Johnson

Chapter 1

Special had a satisfied smile on her face as her third orgasm subsided. She gently pushed Keli (pronounced Kee-Lee) away from her and pointed a perfectly manicured finger at Dewitt, her rented stud for the evening, and signaled for him to come to her. After enjoying the pleasures of Keli's feminine tongue she now wanted her sexy Caribbean stud to come fuck the living daylights out of her. She needed this; she needed it bad. She was trying to rid herself of demons. Thoughts of Papio's handsome face stayed with her day in and day out and it was slowly driving her insane. That's why she decided to bring Keli with her to Aruba. Aruba, a beautiful island in the Caribbean Sea north of Venezuela. Was it far enough though? Could this beautiful piece of earth in the Caribbean help her stop the demons from haunting her? Or would it only offer her temporary relief? She didn't know those answers but she was damn sure going to find out.

Keli was lying next to Special on the huge bed inside of their villa as Dewitt mounted Special and gave her what she craved: dick! Special wrapped her legs around his waist and tried her very best to help him drive his long, thick dick deep inside of her love walls. Keli kept herself busy by kissing and gently sucking on Special's firm breasts. The heat they were generating made the air-conditioned villa feel as if they were outside in hundred-degree heat. The sex was incredible and felt damn good but it just wasn't working. Special could not for the life of her get Papio's face out of her head.

Dewitt's condom was filled with his seed so Special eased him off of her, got off of the bed, and went into the bathroom. She felt dirty, not because of the sex she just participated in but because of the wrong she committed against a man who really and truly loved her. She wasn't built for all of that lovey-dovey shit; her life was all about her. All about getting that money and living the good life. Fuck the world and everyone in it was her motto. At least that's what it was until that fine specimen of a man called Papio entered her life.

Ain't this a bitch. Here I am on a beautiful island in the Caribbean, getting my freak on with two fine mothafuckas—Keli with her sexy chocolate self, and Dewitt, a big-dick Caribbean stud—and I'm stressed the fuck out about a sound business decision that had to be made. Papio was good to me, true, but the money was what it was all about. A bitch like me is $8 million to the good and it's only going to get better. I gots to shake these weak-ass thoughts. I ain't got time for that shit; there's way more money out there to be made, Special said to herself as she stepped into the shower stall and turned on the hot water.

As the hot water began to soothe her body, Keli came into the bathroom and joined her inside of the shower stall. She silently took the soft sponge from Special's hand and began to wash her body. Special sighed and relaxed while Keli's hands roamed all over her body. Before she realized what was happening Keli was on her knees and Special's right leg was gently placed over

Keli's shoulder. Keli's tongue worked her magic quickly and brought Special to another very satisfying orgasm.

"Come on, baby, let's go get some rest; we got a flight to catch and some money to go get."

"I know that's right, honey," Keli replied as she finished showering. When they stepped back into the bedroom Dewitt was no longer there.

"Did you tip the man good, K?" Special asked.

She went to the bed and snatched the soiled sheets off of the bed and tossed them onto the floor. Keli stepped to the linen closet and grabbed a fresh set of sheets.

"Mm-hmm. I gave him another five hundred dollars and told him that we'd give him a holla the next time we came out this way."

"Good. Now come on and get in this bed and hold me tight, baby, maybe then I'll be able to get a peaceful night's rest."

Keli stared at her for a moment and then asked, "Papio?"

Special openly admired Keli's chocolate, thick, five foot seven inch solid frame and sighed. "Yeah."

"Why are you still tripping off of what you did to that nigga? You said it yourself: it had to be done."

"I know but I can't seem to get that pretty nigga's face out of my damn head. I mean even when we're getting our freak on I see that pretty-ass face of his. I hear his voice in my sleep and I wake up sweating straight tripping the fuck out."

"Damn, like that?"

"Yeah, girl, like that. I never thought it could happen to me, but, girl, I fell in love with that nigga big time."

"It's a tad bit too late for that revelation, don't ya think?"

Special stared at her lover/friend and partner in crime for a minute. "Yep, way too damn late. Let's crash; we gots to be well rested for this move out in Denver."

"Are you sure that fat fuck Jolly ain't playing games again, Special? I mean you know how he gets down. Fat fucker probably thinks if he gets us way out to Colorado he might be able to get some pussy or some shit."

Special cuddled closer to Keli. "Now you know better. Jolly may be on some freaky shit but he knows not to fuck with me when it comes to my money. I'll have his fat ass wearing a thong if I found out he was playing games with us. He's on the up and up. I could hear it in his voice. He has a nice and easy move laid out for us."

"I'm with you, Special, so if you say it's good then I'm good. But if Jolly does decide to play some games please let me sleep his fat ass."

"Don't worry, K. I will," Special closed her eyes and tried to get some sleep. But just as she expected sleep eluded her. Thoughts of Papio again consumed her mind. That morning in Dallas kept replaying over and over inside of her head.

Everything had worked to perfection, everything except for those two coldhearted-ass Seneca Indians tripping out on her by flipping the script when they told Papio that after they got their money back from his man they were still going to kill his mother. There was no way in hell she was going to stand there and let that go down. Mama Mia didn't deserve no shit like that and there was no way she could be a part of something so cruel. Special knew she was a cold bitch but she wasn't that damn cold. She could cross Papio but she couldn't do that to his mother. So once she realized that Paul and Jon weren't trying to hear her and her pleas to spare Mama Mia's life she didn't think; she reacted. She pulled out her pistol and shot both of them in the head. They were dead before their bodies hit the carpet.

The decision had been an easy one for her to make; she had their money already for setting up Papio so fuck it. The next decision she made was the hardest she ever made in her life. Shooting Papio wasn't necessary; she could have easily left without shooting him. *Damn it, Papio! I asked you to let me make it and you wouldn't! I had to do it. I had to!* Those were her last thoughts as sleep finally overcame her.

Special and Keli arrived in Denver, Colorado, focused as ever as they strolled confidently through the airport. They had discussed their plans during their flight from Dallas/Fort Worth to Denver and felt that they were well prepared for whatever lay ahead of them. As usual, whenever they were together heads turned. Both men and women gave them appreciative stares as the two beautiful women stood waiting for their luggage to come out of the carousel. Special, five foot four with her jet black hair hanging past her shoulders, looked as if her golden skin were actually glowing from her time spent in Aruba. When she smiled at a few good-looking men as they passed her the small gap in between her front teeth seemed to enhance her beauty instead of taking something away from it. A five-star chick for real, even casually dressed in a pair of capris and sandals with a baby tee on, Special was truly special indeed. A Serena Williams clone was what one could say to describe Keli. Thick and chocolate. Sweet and edible. Plain and simple, she was one bad bitch.

They caught a shuttle to Hertz rental and rented a Dodge Charger. With Keli driving, Special pulled out her cell and called Jolly, her contact in Denver.

Jolly smiled when he saw Special's number show up on his phone. "What's good, Special? Tell me you're in town. Better yet, tell me you're in town with that fine-ass Keli," Jolly said, laughing.

Special sighed as she relaxed in her seat while Keli turned on to the freeway headed toward their hotel.

"Yeah, we're here, Jolly. What time are we hooking up?"

"Where are you staying?"

"None ya. Look, let's get to the business, Jolly. We don't have time for the bullshit so don't start, okay?"

"Bullshit? Damn, all I wanted to do was see where y'all was at so we can hook up from there and get to the business. Don't be like that with me, Special. This is a serious lick I got set up here. No bullshit, a nice chunk of change for all involved. But we gots to be on point for every phase of this move. Shit gats to go down just right in order for it to pop off righteously."

"I'm feeling that. I'm not feeling any of the extra shit you're known for bringing to the game, Jolly. So understand this: the first time either me or Keli gets the impression you're with the bullshit we're out. If we decide to bounce we're taking a chunk of your fat ass with us. Understood?"

"That's cold, Special."

"I'm a cold bitch. Now, where and what time are we hooking up, Jolly?"

"Remember Bernard's?"

"That club you used to hang at on Sundays, yeah, I remember that spot. I thought it got burned down years ago."

"It did. Do you remember that IHOP that was right down the street from there?"

"Yeah."

"Meet me there in a hour, cool?"

"Cool. We're hungry anyway. Should have known your fat ass would want to meet at a restaurant."

"That's cold, Special. I know, don't say it, you're a cold bitch! One hour." Jolly ended the call.

Special was laughing as she closed her phone.

"What kind of shit was he popping?" Keli turned the car into the parking lot of the DoubleTree Hotel.

Special shrugged her shoulders at her partner. "The same weak shit his fat ass always tries. We're good though, *mami;* we meet in a hour."

"You still feel good about this, Special?"

"Yeah. That fat fuck got some good shit ready to go down. I can hear it in his voice. We're good. Time to get some more money."

Keli gave her a bright smile. "You already know I'm with that shit."

Chapter 2

After checking into their hotel and changing clothes Special and Keli were back inside of their rental car headed to the meeting with Jolly. Special was wondering exactly what Jolly had in store for them. Normally whenever she dealt with Jolly the money was good, but it always came with a bunch of extra shit that she was in no mood to deal with. Fucking Jolly wasn't happening this time; she'd been there before and just the thought of that fat fucker on top of her made her feel as if she would throw up. The excitement in his voice told her that he had something real good for them; that alone was a plus to her because it gave her the advantage she needed to keep that fat pig at bay. If he needed them that bad he would be on his best behavior and everything could be good. If he still chose to act she would let Keli handle his fat ass.

At a red light Special looked to her right and saw Papio smiling at her while sitting in the driver's seat of a gold 2009 Corvette.

"What the fuck?" She slid down in her seat, immediately trying to hide.

"What?" Keli asked.

Special slowly peeked over the bottom of the window to confirm what she saw. She sighed when she saw it wasn't Papio smiling at her in the 'Vette, but a youngster who could have easily passed for Papio's little brother.

She knew Papio was an only child, so she grinned at the young one and gave him a finger wave as the light turned green and Keli drove on.

A few minutes later when Keli pulled into the IHOP parking lot, Special noticed that the youngster in the 'Vette had pulled into the parking lot as well. "Looks like we got a young'un who thinks he can get his mack on, K."

"Yeah, I peeped him when he first got on us a few lights back. You wanna make it happen with his young ass? Looks like he might be worth a little something."

"No time for the weak shit, we got to see what's up with Jolly first."

"Might as well get a line on his young ass, we might have some time before we head back to L.A."

Special smiled. "Why not? Let's see how the young'un gets down and take it from there."

"Gotcha," Keli said as she put the car in park and began to touch up her lip gloss.

They were both looking scrumptious as they got out of the car and walked toward the entrance of the restaurant. They took their time walking through the parking lot so the youngster could get a good look at them. The youngster hopped out of his car and quickly stepped to them. When he saw how good both of the ladies were looking he made up his mind that he had to have one of them. His mouth was literally watering when he smiled at Special.

"Excuse me, can I have a moment of your time please?"

Special turned toward the young man and hit him with her killer smile. "Sorry, babe, but we're running late for a very important business meeting. Maybe another time." The women entered the restaurant.

Mesmerized by all of that ass both ladies possessed the young man became even more determined not to let them get away from him. He followed them inside the restaurant.

"I understand business is business, *mami,* and I respect that. But you must give me the opportunity to add some pleasure into your life. All work and no play is a waste of life," he stated confidently.

His usage of the word *mami* hit Special right in the heart because Papio used to call her that so much. She sighed and smiled at Keli. She then took a moment to let her eyes roam around the restaurant until she spotted Jolly sitting in the back, stuffing his face.

"There's Jolly. Go get at him while I speak with this young man for a minute," Special instructed Keli.

"Do you want me to order something for you?"

"Yeah. Whatever you get is fine with me. Make sure you get me some grape juice though."

Keli gave her a nod and stepped toward the back of the restaurant where Jolly was eating.

Special turned her attention to the young man. "Okay, Mr. Pleasure, give me a reason why I should give you a opportunity to interrupt my business."

With a confident smile on his face the young man said, "First off, *mami,* my name is Rico. And I'm a man who can give you the very best of everything while you're in my town."

"How do you know I'm not from your town?"

"Because you have a look of elegance and I know all the elegant women in this town."

"Okay. What makes you think I want or need anything from you while I'm in your town, Rico?"

"You may not need anything from me, *mami,* but I promise you will want everything I have to offer you."

"Let's kill the mack talk, young'un, and get straight to it, like I told you, I have some business to take care of. What's on your mind? You trying to fuck? If so then you gats to know that I'm no ordinary around-the-way girl, and since you already figured out that I'm not from Denver you should know that I won't be in your town for too long. So make your move and I'll tell you whether or not we're with it."

She waited for Rico to come back with his best shot. Instead he was silent.

"Well." Special smiled. "Yeah, we—me and my girl—we come as a packaged deal, Rico. Don't tell me that may be too much for ya, young'un?"

Rico laughed. "Funny, *mami*, real funny. Okay, it's like this: I'm definitely trying to fuck and since it's a double move I'm really with it. When can we make this happen?"

"Give me a number and I'll get at you after I've handled my business. It shouldn't take more than a couple of hours."

"Come on, *mami*, I'm not trying to let you shake me. I'm trying to make this happen for reals."

With a serious look on her face Special told him, "Listen, Rico. I don't play games, especially when it comes to my business. Me dealing with you, though it may give me some pleasure, is still business for real. Business because in order for you to achieve the best feelings you've ever felt in your young life you will have to pay top dollar. As long as you're ready to spend then you will win and I won't shake you. So, what up?"

Rico gave her his cell number and said, "I'll spend whatever. Money ain't shit to me. Ask your man Jolly about Rico."

Special was impressed. "Ah, you're observant, young'un. I like that. Let me get with Jolly and I'll hit you when we're through, cool?"

"Cool. But you haven't even told me your name."

"Does it matter, Rico? We're still going to do some business right?"

"For sure, but I still want to know your name."

She gave him a kiss on his cheek and said, "That's sweet. But you need to remember this, young'un, sweet niggas always finish last in the game. Spend your money and have some fun. There's absolutely no time for feelings. Keep it business, baby. Now, let me handle my business here so I can handle you later."

Rico had a smile on his face as he shook his head. "You're one bad female, *mami*. Do you and I'll be waiting for your call later."

"That's what I'm talking about, young'un. I'll hit you up later." She stepped toward the back of the restaurant where Jolly and Keli were talking.

"What's good, fat man?" Special sat down.

"Money, a whole bunch of it. So I need your undivided attention on this shit, Special. There's no time for you to be fucking with the local dope boy and getting all distracted and shit."

"Aww, Jolly, if I didn't know better I'd think you were jealous. Don't worry about Rico Suave. I got him. You know how I get down: business first. What you got for us?"

"Bullshit. That young wetback ain't no good, Special. Watch his ass if you choose to fuck with him."

"Understood. You know me, Jolly. If there's anyone who needs to be watched, who do you really think the watcher should be?" Special stared at Jolly, her eyes ice cold, demanding, showing no weakness whatsoever.

"Now, let's get to this business, and don't fuck with me, Jolly, my time is money, don't fuck with my time, fat boy."

Keli sat back in her seat and watched her girl work, impressed to the max. She loved how Special handled business; she also loved the ends she always made whenever she fucked with Special. She had a feeling that this was about to be another big payday.

"All right, it's like this: I got a line on some serious money to get. But before I get into it I have to give you ladies a little history lesson, so pay close attention."

When neither of the women spoke he gave them a nod of his head and continued. "Today the currency of the United States is the US dollar, printed bills in denominations of one dollar, two dollars, five dollars, ten dollars, twenty dollars, fifty dollars, and one hundred dollars. At one time, however, it also included five larger denominations. High-denomination currency was common from the very beginning of US government issue in 1861: five-hundred-dollar, one-thousand-dollar, five-thousand-dollar, ten-thousand-dollar, and $100,000 bills. The high-denomination bills were issued in a small size in 1929, along with the one dollar through one hundred dollar denominations."

"So, what you're telling us is that you have a move set up for us to take some high-denomination bills?" asked Keli.

"If you will let me finish I will get to that. Now, may I continue?" Jolly asked with a frown on his face.

Keli gave him a slight wave of her hand and sipped some of her orange juice.

"Today there's approximately 165,372 one-thousand-dollar bills in circulation. 342 five-thousand-dollar bills and 336 ten-thousand-dollar bills are also in circulation. I mean, actually still being used! But they're worth way more than the actual sum. The five hundred dollar bill, which has William McKinley on it, is equal to $6,220 today. The one thousand dollar bill, which has Grover Cleveland on it, is equal to $12,440.55 today. The five thousand dollar bill, which has James Madison on it, is equal to $62,202.73 today. The ten thousand dollar bill, which has Salmon P. Chase on it, is equal to $124, 405.46 today; and, last, the $100,000 bill, which has Woodrow Wilson on it, is equal to $1,591,521.20 today."

"Hold up a sec, Jolly. I was with you with all of this until you got to the $10,000 bill. I know William McKinley, Grover Cleveland, James Madison, and Woodrow Wilson were presidents, but who in the hell was Salmon P. Chase?" asked Special.

"At least you're paying attention. Salmon P. Chase wasn't a president, he was the secretary of the treasury and chief justice of the Supreme Court. Now, may I continue please?"

"One more question."

Jolly gave a long, exasperated sigh. "What, Special?"

"You said that these bills are now worth way more than their normal sum and that there were 342 five-thousand-dollar bills, 336 ten-thousand-dollar bills, and 165,372 one-thousand-dollar bills. But you didn't say how many $100,000 bills are in circulation. What's up with that?"

"I didn't say anything about that because I don't have any information on any of those bills."

"So why even speak on it then?" asked Keli.

"Because I wanted to give you the complete rundown on this move, because there just might be one or two and, if there is, I want you two to be able to recognize it if you saw it when this shit is going down."

"That makes sense."

"May I continue?"

"Sure," Special said.

"Thanks," Jolly said sarcastically. "I've come into some serious information locating several of these high-denomination bills. I have a buyer for whatever bills we can come up with from the information I've obtained. Due to the rarity of these bills, collectors will pay considerably more than the face value of the bills to acquire them. The buyer I have on deck is willing to pay ten thousand dollars for each five hundred dollar bill, fifteen thousand for every one thousand dollar bill, $65,000 for a five thousand dollar bill, $130,000 for every ten thousand dollar bill, and a cool two million if there's any $100,000 bills. Are y'all feeling me now?"

"You're fucking right we're feeling you! Now, tell us how we're going to be able to get our hands on those bills," Special said with excitement in her voice.

Jolly smiled at her. "There's this freak bitch I know who's married to this rich clown who happens to be in the collector business. Specifically speaking, he collects high-denomination bills. This clown is a super freaky geek who gets off major on watching his wife get freaked and fucked by men or women. Though she loves the dick she's not really feeling all of the extra shit he puts her through. Since he made her sign an airtight prenup she's stuck until she finds a way out. This move right here is her way out with a nice piece of money so she can keep it moving. She's agreed to give up the numbers to the safe in order for a decent split. I spoke with her the other day and she told me her husband is having a birthday party this weekend and it would be the perfect time to make this move. So I told her that she would have to be willing to have one more freak party for him, with some female friends I have who can make all of the right moves concerning the high-denomination bills."

"She's with it?" asked Keli.

"Neither of you would be here if she wasn't with it, Keli." He gave her look as if she were the dumbest person on earth.

Before she had a chance to jump over the table and strangle the life out of the fat fuck, Special asked a question. "How many bills does this fool have?"

Jolly shrugged his massive shoulders. "That's the big question, because, though she knows he has several of them, she doesn't know exactly how many or which ones are in his possession."

"So that means we might come out of this shit with some crumbs then huh?" asked Special.

"I doubt it. She is positive that he has more than twenty-five bills, so either way there will be a profit out of this."

"You said ten Gs for the five-hundred-dollar bills, fifteen for the one-thousand-dollar bills, sixty-five for the five-thousand-dollar bills, $130,000 for the ten-thousand-dollar bills, and two mil for the $100,000 if there are any right?"

"Right."

"What's the split?"

"We split it all three ways evenly."

"Three ways? What about the wife?"

Jolly stared at her for a full minute without answering Special's question.

"Aah, scandalous-ass Jolly strikes again, huh?"

"You know damn well I'm not giving no square-ass ex-stripper from Georgia that kind of loot."

"Yeah, what was I thinking. Does she know about us?"

"Nothing. All she knows is that you're some female friends of mine who's willing to put this down."

"All right. What does the husband do to be able to afford all of those high-denomination bills?"

"Does it matter? All that matters is he has them and we're about to take them from his ass."

"It does matter, Jolly. I want to know who he is and what he does because I'm not about to risk robbing a mothafucka who could be connected to some high-powered people who could come back and have us all smoked. So, what does he do, Jolly?"

"He's what they call a theoretical physics professor, and please don't ask me what that is because, baby, I don't have a fucking clue."

"When is this part supposed to take place and where?"

"Friday night at this ballroom in downtown Denver. That's when you two will be introduced to the husband because you'll be personally invited by his wife. The freak shit will go down the next night because we want to let him choose you two. That way it won't look obvious after everything is all said and done."

"How do we make our move?" asked Keli. "Strong arm or what?"

"Nah, it's going to be smoother than that. Once the freaky shit gets started our boy likes to pop a few X pills and snort a few lines of coke. He keeps his private stash inside of the safe. Wifey dear is going to sneak some of this potent knockout shit my man got me and switch it with her hubby's private stash. After a few snorts of this shit he will be flat on his ass within thirty minutes."

"So all we have to do is get freaky with his wife for like thirty minutes and once he's outta there we make the safe, get the bills, and step?" asked Special.

Jolly's fat jowls shook as he laughed. "Yep, that's it and that's all. Are you in or what?"

Special stared at Keli. "Are we in, K?"

Keli smiled. "You better believe it!"

"Now, Jolly, tell me some more about Rico."

Jolly groaned. "Come on with that shit, Special. Leave that kid alone and focus on the real money."

Special gave a slight shrug of her slender shoulders. "Come on, Jolly. It's Tuesday; we might as well make some more ends until Friday night when the real deal starts. Tell me what the young'un is working with."

"Coke, Purp, X, and every other kind of drug around. He's a dope boy supreme who is connected to some nasty Mexicans on the north side of Denver called the NSM. He's connected and tough and he has the town on lock. He's also the man I got the knockout shit from. So if you fuck with him be careful, and don't fuck with any of his shit if you get in the mood to get a little high. If you do get in the mood, get at me and I'll hook y'all up with what you want."

"That's sweet, Jolly, you sound as if you really care about us."

"I do. I can't have shit happening to either of you until after this big lick is done."

"Sweet, yeah, Jolly, you're one thoughtful mother-fucker," Keli said sarcastically.

Chapter 3

It had been over six months since Special had shot Papio in both of his legs and left him bleeding with two dead Indians in the bedroom of his home in Plano, Texas. He wanted her dead big time, and no matter what he was determined to make sure he killed her conniving ass. Just thinking back to all of the shit she put him through that day made him even more upset. He thought about enduring all of that pain until Doc-Tee, his illegal doctor from Oklahoma City, arrived to patch up his wounds. He thought about having to send for his main man Twirl from L.A. to help him get rid of the two dead Indians who had come to take his life. Special shot him then made her fucking escape while he lay in his bed, bleeding like a stuck pig. *That bitch did me dirty, and if it's the last thing I do I'm going to get her punk ass and get every dollar that bitch has. Crossed me out for a punk-ass $4 million; ain't that a bitch,* he thought as he sat back on his bed and watched as the one woman who really loved him got dressed and ready for work.

He had put Brandy through a lot of bullshit over the last year or so. Yet here she was, still right by his side. *I finally fall in love with a woman and I choose the dirtiest bitch in the world to fall for. When all the time I had a true five star right here with me from the be-gin. She's older yeah, but she's still a five star and totally fucking loyal. I'm never letting her get away either, fuck that shit. Brandy is the one I should have been with any fucking way,* he thought as he eased off of the bed and grabbed her from behind and gave her a kiss.

"Mmmmm, what was that for, daddy?"

"Just because you make me feel good. Because you have stayed by my side through a bunch of bullshit and remained true to a nigga. Because you hold me down without question. But most of all, because I don't ever want to lose you, Brandy."

"Whoa. Hold up, let me check your temp because you got to have a fever telling me all of this stuff, mister."

He smiled at her. "See, here I go trying to give you some of that square shit you crave and this is the reaction I get huh? All right, then let me fall back and keep it gangsta."

As he tried to walk away Brandy grabbed his arm and turned him back toward her. "Daddy, you know I've been waiting for you to tell me those words ever since we first hooked up. It goes without saying how much I love you and want to be with you. You know you mean the world to me. I want all of your love but I don't want it like this."

"Like what? What are you talking about, *mami?* You tripping for real."

"No, I'm not. Papio, ever since you got shot all you have been doing is stressing about how you're going to get that woman back for crossing you the way she did. You talk about her constantly, you even talk about her in your sleep, daddy. Don't let the hatred you are trying to make yourself have for her make you feel as if you love me all of a sudden, because both of us know better. You care about me and honestly I'll accept that for

the time being. Why? Because my love for you is genuine and hopefully you'll realize this and love me like
I deserve to be loved. But don't you dare try to make
yourself love me because that woman has become an
obsession of yours. That's not right nor is it fair to me."

"You're tripping, Brandy, that shit don't make no
sense. I hate that bitch and I'm going to make sure I get
her ass for that shit she did to me."

Brandy smiled sadly at the man she loved, the man
she met at the Federal Correction Institution El Reno
where she worked. She was the case manager when
Papio received his immediate release papers from a
thirty-year sentence. She fell for him instantly. She
risked everything for him without really caring about
her safety or future. She put her job in jeopardy by taking his Jamaican friend, Kingo, marijuana whenever
he told her to, and went as far as risking her very own
freedom when he had her drive a minivan full of stolen
money and drugs from a heist he pulled in upstate New
York. She knew without question she would do whatever he told her to do. Why? Because she loved him
with all of her heart, even though she knew he didn't
feel the same way about her.

"I understand your anger toward her, daddy, it's so
plain to see. Whenever you do catch up with her you
won't be able to hurt her; you love her too much."

Papio laughed. "*Mami,* you've been with me for a
little over a year now and you still don't get it, when you
cross Papio you're out. Period. Mani crossed me and she
was let go without a backward glance. I don't play that
second chance shit at all. You gats to know that for real."

"This may be true, but you've never felt as strong a
love for Mani or for me as you do for Special."

"Kill that shit, Brandy, for real; you're sitting here pissing me the fuck off. Here I am trying to tell your ass that it's you I love and you're trying to tell me you think I'm loving a bitch who shot me and was about to leave me for dead! You are really fucking tripping. But check it, Kingo once told me that real love balances and that it gives a man what's necessary to make things go smooth in life. I didn't feel him back then when he told me that corny shit but I do now. You, Brandy, you balance me. Don't worry about that bitch Special because just as sure as my name is Papio that bitch will be dead as soon as I get my hands on her. Believe what you want, just never forget exactly how cold I can be."

She stared at him for a few seconds and realized that maybe she'd been wrong; the hatred in his eyes told her that he was really going to cause that woman some serious pain.

"I love you, daddy; no matter what, that love will never go away. I told you from the start that I will never cross you and I meant that. To hear you tell me this makes me feel real good about us, but it also scares me 'cause I don't want to be hurt by you, daddy. I would never be able to get over that."

Papio reached out and grabbed her hands. "I've kept it real with you from the be-gin, *mami,* and I have no reason to switch up now. Remain true to me and it will continue to be all about us. I admit I've been tripping because I was off my square. I haven't made any moves since I got blasted. But all of that shit is over with now. It's time to get back to work. A nigga gots a hundred million to clock and I'm determined to reach my goal this year. So hold me down, *mami,* hold me down by continuing to love me."

She smiled lovingly at him. "Now that's my daddy! I was wondering when you were going to get back to being the Papio I fell for in R&D that morning."

He smiled. "Yeah, whatever. Check it, when you get to work, get at Kingo and tell him to give me a call. I need to get at his peoples, plus we need to holla. If you can, get him into your office and let him use the phone to get at me."

"I won't be able to do any of that this week, baby. The regional bigwigs are in town for their yearly walk-through of the institution, and you know how it is during these times; everyone is on pins and needles trying to make sure that everything is in perfect order."

Thinking back to when he was incarcerated in federal prison Papio nodded his head. "Yeah, I know how it is. Okay, tell him to give me a call on the wall phone."

Papio walked Brandy downstairs to the garage and watched as she climbed into his BMW and went to work.

After Brandy left he grabbed the phone and called his main man on the West Coast. When Q answered the phone Papio said, "Wake up, white boy, your man is back in the game. We got some money to get. You ready?"

With there being a two-hour time difference from Oklahoma City to California, Q had been sound asleep. But when he heard Papio's voice he woke up instantly and smiled. "Dude, you don't know how glad I am to hear your fucking voice, man. I was just telling Twirl the other day how worried I was about you. He told me you needed some time to get your mind right and that you would bounce back. I wasn't so sure about that though. Love is a bitch huh?"

"Check it, what's done is done, Q. I got a goal to reach and I've wasted enough time bullshitting. It's time to get back to the grind. I'll be West by the weekend. Line some shit up for me. It's time to work."

"Gotcha, dude."

"Good. Give Twirl a call for me and let him know that I'm back!"

"Will do. Anything else?"

"Yeah, I need you to put all of your ears in the street to work for me. I gots to have that bitch. Find her for me, dog."

"I'm on it. Later, dude."

Papio hung up the phone with Quentin and sat back on his bed and began to think about what he was going to do. His plans consisted of getting that $100 million so he could retire from the life and live the rest of his days as peaceful as possible. But before any of that could happen Special had to die.

Tired of stressing on Special, Papio called his mother. "Good morning, Mama Mia."

"*Mijo?* Is that you, mi *mijo?*"

"*Sí, Madre,* it's me."

She gave a soft sigh. "Are you okay, *mijo?*"

"*Sí,* I'm fine. I'll be home this weekend, so don't make any plans, we're going to do some catching up okay?"

"Catching up? You stay gone from me for more than six months and you say we have catching up to do. You will get slapped across your face first before we do any catching up! I can't believe you don't even call me, Papio! What were you thinking?"

"But, *Madre,* I had Q call you to let you know that I was okay."

"Bah! You are so wrong for doing that to me, *mijo.* We talk more when you come home. But, tell me, where is Special? Why haven't I heard from her either?"

It was his turn to sigh. "I'll explain all of that to you when I get home, *Madre*."

"Don't you tell me you run that girl away, *mijo*. She was the perfect one for you."

"We'll talk this weekend, *Madre*. Bye for now. I love you."

"I love you too, *mijo*. Bye," said his mother as she hung up the phone.

Papio walked downstairs to his state-of-the-art indoor gymnasium and began to work out. He got on the treadmill and started at a slow pace and gradually worked his way into a faster rhythm. As he walked the treadmill he was letting his mind drift all over the place. Thinking about his 3,800-square-foot home in Oklahoma City, as well as his expensive homes in Plano, Texas as well as California, plus all of his toys. His brand new Aston Martin and all of the money he acquired illegally over the years. He had well over $30 million saved in an offshore account being maintained by Q, and he had seventy more to get in order to reach his goal of one hundred. He took too much time off tripping about what Special did to him. *Yeah, it's time to get back to getting this fucking money,* he thought as he began to walk even faster on the treadmill. His legs were strong and so was his mind. That bitch had made him show weakness, and he knew that if there was one word that was not related to Papio it was weak. *I'm about to get this fucking money and get that bitch at the same time,* he said to himself with a smile on his face as sweat slid down his neck. Papio was definitely back in the game.

Chapter 4

Special woke up the next morning listening to Keli as she was walking around their room singing that song "Birthday Sex" by Jeremih. The first thought that came into her mind was of Papio. She had to smile because the memory of him making love to her on her birthday last year was so vivid in her mind right at that moment. She wasn't even that mad anymore about the $10,000 she lost to him because he had made her tap out. She shook her head and thought, *ugh!*

Keli saw that Special was awake. "That youngster has been blowing up your phone with calls and texts all damn morning. Why didn't you get back at him after we left the restaurant yesterday?"

"Fuck that young nigga. No way was I going to be jumping through any hoops for his young ass. We're going to play his ass nice and right while we're waiting to put this other move down."

Keli smiled. "I know that's right. So, what's on the agenda for the day?"

Special returned her lover/friend's smile. "Shopping! I thought we'd let Rico Suave spend some of that easy-earned dope boy money on us today. I mean after all we do have a fly party to attend. I don't see why we should spend any of our money on getting fly."

"I like."

"I figured you would. What's even better about this move is after we let the young'un spend his ends on us we'll bounce back and make Jolly's fat ass reimburse us for the money spent for our outfits for the birthday party."

Keli burst into laughter. "Brilliant, absolutely brilliant! That's why I love fucking with you, Special, you keep a bitch on point in every way."

Special shrugged. "Just trying to make sure we don't miss a beat with this shit, K. I'm in it to win it at all times. Now go on and get showered while I get at the young'un and set everything up for the day."

Special grabbed her cell and called Rico. When he answered the phone she said, "I see someone is like really into sweating a woman huh? You make me wish I wouldn't have broke down and gave you my digits, young'un."

"Damn, Special, why you shake me like that? I thought we were going to hook up last night."

"Shit changes, baby. It's all good because we got all day and night to do us, that is, if you're still interested."

"Kill that; you know damn well I'm still interested. What you wanna do? Whatever you want you got, just as long as you hold up to your end on this shit."

Special laughed. "Young'un, we're going to blow your mind as well as your little wee-wee."

"Baby, ain't nothing little about Rico."

"Is that right?"

"That's right."

"So you're telling me you're a Pussy Monster, Rico?"

"A pussy what?"

"Never mind. Look, we're getting dressed now so give us a hour or so and meet us at that same IHOP we met at. After you feed us we can take it from there. I'm in the mood for a little shopping, you cool with that, young'un?"

"I'm cool with whatever it takes to get you and that chocolate sexy friend of yours in my bed."

"That's what's up. Bring plenty of stacks, these mommies got expensive taste."

"I got you, baby. See you in a little bit." He hung up the phone.

After Special hung up the phone she made another call, this time to the West Coast. She had a smile on her face when her godfather and main connection as well as money man answered the phone. "What up, Poppa Blue?" she asked when he answered the phone.

"What's up? Waiting on your ass to get at me for the last week is what's up. Why haven't you checked in with me, Special?"

"Been on some vacation shit as well as trying to get my mind right."

"Still tripping off of that fool you blasted huh? Figures, your ass was always a sucker for love, just like your mama, God rest her soul."

"You know you need to quit with that shit, Poppa Blue. What you got for me?"

"Where are you?"

"Denver."

"Denver? What the fuck does Jolly have up his fat-ass sleeves?"

"A nice something-something could bring in a few tickets if it goes like he says."

"That's cool, just make sure you watch that fat bastard."

"Always. What's up?"

"Two strong-arm moves that pays well on some jewels out in Bakersfield. Something very appealing and new that should change the game."

"When?"

"Next week."

"How much?"

"Six hundred G each, 1.2 easy."

"All right, I'll hit you as soon as I'm done out this way."

"Good. Now we have some other things to talk about, Special."

"Don't go there right now. I'm not trying to deal with that right now. I mean everything is good right?"

"Yeah, everything is good, but sooner or later you're going to have to face shit."

"I know, just let me work okay? I mean it's not like everything ain't everything. Hold me down, Poppa Blue, pleeeeaaaseeeeee?"

"Always hate when you get at me like that. Your damn mama used to do the same thing, God rest her soul. Bye, girl, hit me when you're through out there. Tell Jolly I said to get at me," Poppa Blue said and hung up the phone.

Damn, every move I make has to be exact from this point on. I can't afford to make any mistakes, she said to herself as she shook her head from side to side. She climbed off of the bed and went into the bathroom to start getting herself dressed for the day.

After enjoying a nice breakfast at IHOP, Special, Keli, and Rico went shopping at Aurora Mall. The ladies enjoyed a couple of hours spending Rico's money on every name brand outfit they could put their hands on. Gucci, Prada, Louie, Jimmy Choo, and more. By the time they were ready to leave the mall Rico was horny and anxious as hell. Special knew that getting him for as much as she could was going to be as easy as taking candy from a baby. *This young fool is too good to be true,* she thought as she watched as he continued to stare at Keli's thick frame as they walked out of the mall.

Rico loaded all of their bags inside of his Cadillac Escalade and got into the driver's seat of the SUV with a smile on his face. "So, are we ready to go make it happen now, ladies?"

With a smile of her own on her face Special told him, "Not yet, young'un, we got to hit up the Cherry Creek mall for a hot second and then we can go to your spot and make it do what it do, cool?"

"Whatever, but don't be having me in that damn mall for another three hours, a man does have his limits, Special. What else do y'all need anyway? Y'all already bought every top-named designer in the fucking mall."

"Actually we didn't, Rico. I mean we did tear this bitch up but there's a few items that we missed. We got the Gucci, Louie, Jimmy Choo, Prada, and whatnot, but we need the Nine West, Givenchy, Cole Haan, Donna Karan, Ellie Saab, and—"

"All right already, I feel you!" Rico laughed. "I know one damn thang: y'all better be worth every fucking penny y'all are making me spend today."

Special ran her small hand on the side of his cheek. "Don't worry, young'un, we're going to make you feel real good. And I do mean real good."

"That's right, daddy; when we're finished with you you're going to want us out here on a regular," added Keli.

"Good, 'cause I swear I'm going to have a fucking ball enjoying you two fine-ass broads. Let's do this!" Rico started his SUV.

Just as Special relaxed in her seat her cell phone started ringing. She pulled her phone out of her purse and frowned when she saw Jolly's number on the caller ID. "Damn, it's Jolly."

"Aww fuck that shit, Special, don't answer that!" pleaded Rico.

"Don't worry, young'un, I won't let him fuck off our thang. Be easy." She flipped open her phone. "Talk to me, Jolly."

"Where y'all at?"

"Why?"

"I'm meeting Dena in thirty minutes at the Cafe restaurant inside of the Cherry Creek mall, and I want y'all to meet her so when y'all get together at the party Friday everything will have a natural feel to it."

With a reassuring smile aimed at Rico, Special told Jolly, "All right, we'll meet you there in thirty. We're on our way there now."

"Good, I'll see you then." Jolly hung up the phone.

"What did that fat fuck want?" Keli asked.

"He wants us to meet him at a restaurant inside of the Cherry Creek mall called the Cafe. We need to meet old girl. Talking about he wants us to get that part of the game out of the way so we can have the natural feel when everything pops off at the party."

"That fool don't miss shit huh?"

"Not much, that's why I don't really mind fucking with his fat, grimy ass. He be on some bullshit at times but when it's time for the serious paper he's going to be on point." Special noticed the smile on Rico's face and shook her head from side to side. "Stop ear hustling, young'un. Mind ya business and stay out of ours, hear?"

"I don't give a damn about y'all's BI, Special. As long as I can get mines the way y'all promised, I'm good right here."

Special reached over and unzipped his pants and pulled out his limp organ and began to stroke him slowly and watched with amusement as he gradually grew harder and harder. She smacked her lips loudly and said, "Mmmmmm, look at all of this, Keli; our young'un is packing!"

Keli sat up and leaned over from the back seat so she could get a look at Rico's dick. When she saw how big it was inside of Special's hand she said, "Yeah, we gone have some fun with that. Girl, give him some of your head game so he can know for sure what the business is."

Special bent forward and put his dick inside of her mouth and began to suck him very slowly. He moaned and felt as if he was about to come at that very moment, because the combination of Special sucking his dick and Keli sucking and nibbling on his right ear had him right at that point. *Thank you, God! Thank you!* he said to himself as he tried to keep his concentration on his driving.

Special pulled away from his manhood and smiled. "See, young'un, your money will be well spent."

Rico's face was flushed as he took a few deep breaths. "I know that's right. Damn, you two got game for real!" They laughed as they finished their short trek to the Cherry Creek mall.

Special and Keli went into the Cafe restaurant to meet with Jolly and Dena while Rico remained outside in his truck and made some business calls. Jolly and Dena were sitting in the back of the restaurant, sipping drinks. After they were seated Jolly made the introductions. "Special and Keli, this is Dena. Dena, these two lovely ladies are the women who are going to make everything we've planned go down."

Dena was a caramel-colored sister with what looked like a very expensive, long weave job in her hair. Her style of clothing was extremely expensive and Special was immediately impressed. Her voluptuous breasts looked divine to Special. Dena, who was accustomed to stares at her assets, took Special's actions as a compliment and smiled. "So, you guys are going to get me out of this horrible mess of a marriage I'm in?"

"If taking your hubby for all of those high-end bills will free you, *mami,* then yeah, we're your girls," Keli stated confidently as she, too, stared at Dena's bosom.

"Good. And yes, taking all of my dear husband's high-denomination bills will definitely free me. That bastard has it so I can only spend so much money per month and there's been no way I could get me some to stash for a great escape. With the money earned from this I can be rid of that sick bastard once and for all."

"Understood. Don't worry, we got you. But I have a few questions so I can peep how this will go down Friday," said Special.

Sensing that Special was the one who was in charge of this operation Dena smiled at her. "Please, ask away."

"Understand that I'm not prying into your relationship because, for real, I couldn't care less about you and your husband's personal get down. What are we going to need to do to ensure we get that invite for this freak show the day after the party? I mean will we have to do anything in particular to guarantee we'll be able to make it to the second phase of this move?"

"All you two gorgeous women have to do is show up at the party looking your best. And from what I see now I don't think that will be a problem for either of you."

The ladies took the compliment. "Your husband likes to watch you with men as well as women, which turns him on more?" asked Special.

"To be honest that freaky bastard gets off the same with both. I never understood this sick fascination with him because we've never had a problem with him performing superbly in bed with just me. But there's something inside of his sick head that drives him crazy to see me have sex with others. I don't want to sound like a prude because, believe me, that's not me at all. I've enjoyed several of our moments with the men and, honestly, some of the ones with women as well. I've tried to convince myself that it's just sex, so enjoy it. But over the years it's begun to weigh heavily on me. I'm starting to feel disgusted with myself."

"And now you're ready to be out?" asked Keli.

Slightly embarrassed, Dena dropped her eyes. "Definitely."

Special and Keli both gave Jolly a cold glare, as if saying, "You cold, fat bastard!"

Jolly returned their glares with one of his own, as if saying, "Fuck this bitch."

Dena shook off her embarrassment. "We enjoy ourselves. We drink, we dance, and get our party on. Kevin will have no problem figuring out that I am enjoying the company of you two and he then will pull me aside and ask me if we can have you guys over for some fun. I'll give him a little reluctance, as I always do whenever he wants me to have lesbian sex. As usual I'll concede and he'll smile and give me a kiss and tell me how much he loves me. After that everything will be a go."

"So before the night's over we'll know whether everything is good?"

"Definitely."

"What if he don't bite, then what?" asked Keli.

"Then we go to Plan B," said Jolly.

"Which is?" asked Special.

"You girls get to put your cat burglar skills to use and sneak to the safe and get what we need. Either way this shit goes we're going to get those fucking bills, ladies."

Special stared at Keli for a moment, then said, "You damn Skippy."

"Thank you, thank you, both, because I know this is going to go just right. It has to. I want this more than I've ever wanted anything in my life." Dena shyly added, "I also think I'm going to enjoy spending that little time with the both of you. I hope that doesn't offend either of you. I'm not a lesbian but you two turn me on in ways I can't even understand. I'm so wet right now that it's crazy!"

"Hey! Hold that shit, Dena, that's TMI for real! I'm trying to eat here," said Jolly.

Special and Keli laughed.

"Don't worry, baby, we'll get some fun out of this move. Ain't nothing wrong with enjoying yourself while making some money at the same time. It doubles the pleasure. As for labels, well, neither of us consider ourselves lesbians. Sex is for pleasure and we love to pleasure each other whenever we see fit. I think I can speak for my girl here and say that we will definitely enjoy giving you and those luscious titties of yours some pleasure," Special said with a smile.

"Hey!"

"Shut up, Jolly! Stop hating, your fat ass just salty because you won't be able to get none," Keli said and the three ladies all laughed.

Special saw Rico lingering in the front of the restaurant and said, "Since everything is everything we have to go now, there's more than one fish to fry in Colorado. We'll see you at the party, Dena."

"I can't wait, Special."

"Neither can I, honey, neither can I. See ya, Jolly." Special stood, followed by Keli.

"Yeah, see ya."

"Oh, Poppa Blue said give him a call."

"What does that old fart want?"

"Give him a call and find out." She shrugged.

Jolly turned in his seat and saw Rico waiting for the ladies and warned, "Be careful, Special."

"Always, fat man, always. Come on, Keli, let's go spend some more of our friend's money."

"I'm with that. Bye, Dena, see you Friday."

"I'll be waiting, sexy," Dena replied with a smile.

"I know you will with your fine ass. Byeeeeeeeee, Jolly," Keli said, laughing, and followed Special toward Rico.

Chapter 5

Brandy and Papio were enjoying a nice home-cooked meal of fried chicken, rice, and gravy with some mixed vegetables. She couldn't take her eyes off of him while they were eating. She loved his sexy ass and that was all there was to it. He could do no wrong in her eyes. She knew what type of man he was and none of that mattered. She knew he robbed and stole for a living, yet all of the wrong he did in life only turned her on more. She felt herself become wet as she stared at his six foot frame sitting at the table across from her. His long, silky hair was pulled back tightly in a ponytail as he always wore it, with the light taper on the sides, making him look totally divine to her. His bronze skin tone made him seem as if he had been born with a perfect tan. He looked at her with his light brown eyes and she clamped her legs closed to help control the sexual urges that were running through her kitty.

Papio stopped eating. "What up with you, Brandy? You horny huh?" he asked with a smirk on his face.

She blushed instantly. "Stop that. What makes you think I'm horny, daddy? I can't look at the man who owns my heart without wanting sex?"

"Check it, *mami:* we've been together long enough now for me to know when you're wet and ready to do the damn thang."

"Is that so? Please, do tell."

"For one, it's a dead giveaway when you look at me with those pretty brown eyes all slanted low and shit. That means you're either getting wet or already wet and ready to do me something."

"You are terrible. Continue please, I'm really enjoying this." She twirled her hair in her fingers.

"Next, you keep finger combing your hair."

"So?" She folded her hands on the table.

"That tells me you want this dick. You only do that around me when you want to get started."

"You are so bad! Go on." Brandy was fully enjoying this little game.

"And last, it's when you look at me and lick your lips like you're doing right now. That tells me that you're thinking about giving me some of that bad-ass head you give. But on the real, the combination of all of that plus the fact that you just got off your cycle is a dead giveaway. Brandy wants to get fucked real good tonight!" He laughed as he set his fork on his plate. "So, was I on point or what?"

Her answer to his question was her rising out of her seat and stepping to him and sitting on his lap. She gave him a tender kiss and whispered in his ear, "As always, my daddy is always right. I want you to fuck me, daddy. I need that dick bad. Come break this pussy off please?"

Hearing those words caused him to gain a monster erection. "Go on upstairs and get naked while I grab a bottle of some good wine. We're going to be awhile so prepare yourself for a long night, *mami.*"

She licked her lips seductively. "Mmmmmmm, that's what I was hoping you'd say, daddy. Hurry up!"

She jumped off of his lap and ran up the stairs to- ward the bedroom with a smile on her face. Papio shook his head from side to side as he got up and went into the kitchen to get a bottle of wine for their sexcapade. When he heard his cell phone he moaned because he knew for sure if someone was calling him at this time of the night it couldn't be something he wanted to hear, especially with him about to go give it to Brandy. *Damn,* he thought as he went and grabbed his cell. When he saw the 305 area code he groaned be- cause he knew for sure he didn't want to talk to anyone in Florida right then. He also knew that he couldn't not take that call. It was the Cubans calling, and when it came to Mr. Suarez and his millions, Papio had no other choice but to answer the call. With a sigh he an- swered the phone. "Talk to me."

"Mr. Suarez requests your presence as soon as pos- sible, Papio. I have been instructed to tell you that it would be in your best interest to get to Miami within forty-eight hours."

Papio knew how much Castro, Mr. Suarez's number one flunky, hated his guts. With the feeling being mu- tual Papio always went out of his way to piss Castro off as much as he could every chance he could.

"So, the boss has demoted you to making phone calls for him? How you do out there in sunny Florida, Cas- tro? You good, *papi?*" Papio said sarcastically.

"Fuck you, you slimy, scum motherfucker. Get here by Friday evening. Or better yet, don't come. I'd love for Mr. Suarez to have me come and get your black ass."

"What! Ever! Check it, can you tell me what this meet- ing is about? I have a lot on my plate at the moment and I need to know what the business is. Especially if I gots to drop everything and fly out to the MIA."

"Money has been taken from Mr. Suarez indirectly and he wants you to help him find the person who had something to do with it. That's all I know, so don't ask me another question, Papio."

"Come on with that shit, Castro. I can't just up and leave what I got on the table right now for some weak shit like that. He don't got no one else who can do this? Let me speak to Mr. Suarez."

"His exact words to me were to tell you to get out here and why. I've done that, Papio. Get here or, like I said, I'll enjoy being ordered to come and get your ass, slime ball."

"Yeah, we know your fat ass just loves following orders, you fucking flunky motherfucker! See you Friday, bitch!" Papio hung up the phone before he could get a response from Castro. He picked up the bottle of wine and headed upstairs. *Time to give Brandy some of my feel-good tool.* When he saw Brandy lying on the bed naked with her legs spread wide open he stared at her for a moment and thanked God for blessing him with one bad-ass woman. *Time to get busy!*

Papio's flight to Miami went quickly. It had been a little over a year since he was last in Florida. Just thinking about that trip pissed him off because it reminded him about the time he spent with Special out there. The time they shared in Miami once meant a lot to him but now that memory did nothing but make him feel like a true chump. He thought he was impressing Special, but all he was really doing was falling for her fucking trap. What made it worse was he actually gave that bitch a million dollars on that trip. *Ooh, I can't wait 'til the day when I can get my hands on that bitch. I'm not going to shoot her ass; I'm going to strangle her with my bare hands,* he thought as he walked through the airport toward the exit. Since he didn't plan on being out there for any longer than a day all he had with him was a carry-on bag.

He jumped into a cab and gave the driver the address to the Suarez estate. He could tell by the brief pause by the cab driver that he knew about the infamous Cuban drug lord. Mr. Suarez ran shit from Florida to California. He had his fat hands on everything from weed, cocaine, and X pills to heroin. At one time Papio was one of his most important dope boys.

Papio moved so much cocaine for the Suarez organization that he was considered one of the organization's top men, even though he was not of the Cuban descent. His mixture of black and Puerto Rican made several of Mr. Suarez's top people disgruntled, but Mr. Suarez didn't care because, when it came to making money, Papio was the best at it. All of that came to a screeching halt when Papio was arrested for conspiracy to distribute thirty kilograms of cocaine. He had been set up by another employee of Mr. Suarez's and consequently ended up receiving a thirty-year sentence in federal prison. Papio, being the man he was, always prepared for everything, made one of the boldest moves ever made against the Suarez organization. He had an associate of his barter a deal for his freedom from prison. In exchange for his freedom he had his associate give the assistant US attorney the location to a warehouse in Oklahoma City that had 2,500 kilograms of cocaine, 5,000 pounds of the potent marijuana called Purp on the streets, and $4.5 million in cash. The Feds wanted names but Papio and his associate never gave up the Suarez organization. In the end the enormous amount of drugs and money was too much for the assistant US attorney to turn down, so after three years in federal prison Papio was a free man. With bold moves made on his part, Papio was able to give Mr. Suarez the money back that was lost in exchange for his freedom with another half million. This maneuver earned him favor with Mr. Suarez only because he had always remained loyal to the Suarez organization. Even while facing a thirty-year sentence, he never took the coward's way out by ratting on the Suarezes. Mr. Suarez gave Papio the opportunity to pay him back for what was taken from him in Oklahoma City. No rush was set upon Papio because Mr. Suarez wanted to use his debt to be able to have some control over Papio. Papio had full intention of clearing that debt but things went left for him after the incident with Special out in Texas. Now that he was about to get back to the grind he wondered again what exactly Mr. Suarez wanted with him.

If it was money he wanted he could have requested that over the phone. For him to have Castro get at him and summon him to Florida meant it was something serious. Something serious meant good things for Papio. He would either be able to clear some of his debt or make some money for himself. Knowing how Mr. Suarez got down it could mean both, and that thought put a smile on Papio's face.

He pulled out his cell and made a call. When his main man Twirl answered the phone Papio said, "What it do, my nigga, you good?"

"Am I? I've been holding it down being the X man out here while my hero gets his mind right. I'm still sitting pretty because my hero left me good, but the question is, is my hero ready to come back and be the man he once was?"

"Back and better than ever, dog. I won't lie. I'm still fucked up behind what that bitch did to me, but I got to get my shit in order. Sitting my ass in Oklahoma for damn near a year sulking ain't gone keep me living the way I'm accustomed to, ya dig? So yeah, it's time to get some more motherfucking money. I need about seventy million to reach that goal and I'm about to be dead serious about getting that number, my nigga, you with me?"

Twirl laughed. "Seventy million? You fucking right I'm with you, my nigga. You're still my motherfucking hero, dog! You keep a nigga living good, there's no way in hell I will never not roll with your ass. But on the up and up, G, are you ready to do this the Papio way?"

"I know no other way, my nigga. If I thought I wasn't ready to do me we wouldn't be having this convo, my nigga. I'm back and I'm colder than ever. Fuck the world; it's all about me and this fucking money. I play to win and you know better than anyone else I don't play fair."

"Yeah, my hero is definitely back! I love it! Where you at, fool? You got a nigga straight on amp status ready to get this cake."

Papio laughed. "I'm in Miami about to meet up with some people. I'll be flying out of here later on tonight headed your way. I'll hit you when I get to my spot."

"The Westin by the airport?"

"You know it. Do me a favor and have my ride there for me when I touch. We'll go get at Q and see what he has for us and then we can chop it about some other shit I gots on my mind."

"Special, huh?" asked Twirl with a serious tone in his voice.

"Yeah. I gots to get that bitch, dog. Don't get it twisted, I'm serious about this money, but I'm equally serious about getting that bitch back for what she did to me."

"That's what's up. We'll find that broad, my nigga. I've had some of my peeps on the prowl but it's like she's vanished from the scene like a puff of smoke. I know for a fact she ain't making any moves out this way. So maybe she took her game OT."

"Either that or she took that punk-ass eight million she came up and retired from the life all together. It don't matter to me, dog, if she's out of town or retired. Sooner or later a motherfucka always gets homesick, and when that bitch gets homesick and decides to come get a little taste of the West again I'll be right there to greet her scandalous ass."

"Until then, it's time to get that money right?"

"Exactly. Let me bounce. I'll hit you before I catch that bird west."

"Holla at ya, my hero!" Twirl hung up the phone.

When the cab driver pulled in front of the huge wrought-iron gate of the Suarez estate he turned and gave Papio a quizzical look. Papio smiled. "Don't panic, *papi*, it's all good." The big iron gate began to automatically open. "See? Now take me to the front of the mansion," Papio instructed the cab driver.

Papio was surprised to see Mr. Suarez himself standing in the doorway talking to Castro. This normally didn't happen; in fact, it might have been the first time that Mr. Suarez greeted Papio at the front door. *This shit must be important,* thought Papio as he paid the cab driver and got out of the cab with his carry-on in his hand.

"Good afternoon, Mr. Suarez? How are you?"

Mr. Suarez smiled at Papio and gave him a firm handshake. "I'm well, *Señor* Papio, just fine. Thank you for coming to see me. You will soon learn that this meeting will be worth your valuable time. Come, let's get right to business, yes?"

"*Sí*, let's." Papio followed Mr. Suarez into the mansion.

Castro had his normal scowl on his dark Cuban features as they entered the mansion. Always wanting to get under Castro's skin, Papio greeted him sarcastically. "Hey, Castro, what's up?"

Castro's response to Papio's greeting was the middle finger.

"You can go get the chief now, Castro," Mr. Suarez instructed as he motioned for Papio to sit on the comfortable leather sofa in the library.

"*Sí*, Mr. Suarez," Castro said and quickly left the room.

The chief? thought Papio as he sat down next to Mr. Suarez. "So, how have you been Mr. S?" asked Papio.

"Living well, *Señor* Papio. And you?"

"Things have been kind of slow for me lately so I've been patiently waiting for the right time to make some moves. Hopefully things will pick up for me in the next few weeks, that way I'll be able to give you something on my debt."

"After we finish here today you'll definitely be in a better position *Señor* Papio, especially with the debt you have to me." Mr. Suarez reassuringly put his hand on Papio's shoulder.

Papio was about to ask him what he meant when Castro reentered the library followed by an extremely tall Indian. Papio's heartbeat increased considerably as he stared at the old Indian, who looked like a cross between Paul and Jon, the two Seneca Indians who came to take his life in Texas. Papio's palms became sweaty as he tried to figure out what the fuck was going on. *Calm down, baby boy, put that poker face on and peep game. Never let 'em see you sweat. You're in no danger; if you were Mr. Suarez would have given some sort of sign by now. Or was this fat fuck playing me the whole time?* Papio said to himself as he watched the elderly Indian shake hands with Mr. Suarez.

"*Señor* Papio, this is Chief Hightower, chief of the Seneca Indian Tribe. Chief, this is *Señor* Papio. This is the man I think will be able to bring you some justice."

Papio stood confidently and reached out his hand toward the chief. "Pleased to meet you, sir."

While gripping Papio's hand firmly, the chief said, "It is a pleasure to meet you also, Papio. I have heard good things about you from Mr. Suarez here and I do hope that you will be able to assist me."

Papio gave them both a confused expression. Mr. Suarez said, "I know you're confused, Papio; sit and let me explain exactly what is going on." After they were seated Mr. Suarez continued. "As you already know my, ummm, business ventures are far and wide. The chief here has been a long-time associate of mines out in Niagara Falls, New York. We've made quite a substantial amount of money over the years. Twenty-five years to be exact. I consider him family, Papio."

Keep that poker face on, Papio; never let 'em see you sweat, Papio kept telling himself over and over as he stared directly at Mr. Suarez. "I understand, Mr. Suarez, but what I don't get is what do you need from me?"

"You and I have done some very serious business over the years as well and you know firsthand how I deal with people who cross me or cause any harm to those I consider family."

"True."

"Like I said I consider this honorable man here my family. A terrible tragedy has happened to the chief here and I think you may be able to assist in making this right. I'll let the chief further explain. Chief?"

Chief Hightower cleared his throat. "Like Mr. Suarez has explained we have done business with one another for quite a long time. Over the years my part in running the operations of my business in New York has diminished considerably. I gave the responsibilities to my two sons, Paul and Jon. Fifteen months ago some very brazen young men robbed a souvenir shop owned by my tribe. In the back of this particular shop was a very large amount of drugs and money. My sons were duped by a female from Harlem, she gave the location of the money and drugs to a man who called himself Harlem Nick."

"Whoa. Excuse me, Chief, I know for a fact that Harlem Nick was found dead last year in a car wash or something like that. My mans out of the Bronx who was on lock with me in the Feds got at me right after that went down," lied Papio.

"This is true. Harlem Nick was found dead in a Quick-Wash right outside of the New York City limits. My sons felt that he was put in a double cross by his partner who helped him rob our shop."

"Oh. Okay, I see."

"My oldest boy, Paul, was involved with the woman who gave the location of the shop to Harlem Nick and his accomplice. Jon, my youngest, was able to get some vital information from her: he learned the name of the accomplice. Jon was involved with a female who knew the whereabouts of this man."

Papio's heart felt as if it were about to burst. *Do they know the business or are they asking me what I think they're about to ask me?* he said to himself as he stared directly at the chief.

"This woman made a deal with my sons to set up this man for them for the sum of four million dollars."

"Wow, that's a lot of change just to get a nigga back."

"Yes, it was. But my sons were ashamed of their actions and felt that by getting this accomplice they could save face to me and Mr. Suarez here for the large sum of money that was taken from that souvenir shop."

Damn, what kind of luck do I really have? Papio asked himself.

"Please let me interrupt you for a moment, Chief," Mr. Suarez interjected. "Before I let the chief go any further, Papio, I have to ask you a question."

"Sir?"

"You were on the East Coast around this time when this travesty was committed against the chief's sons, were you not?"

Papio wanted to smile because finally Mr. Suarez had tipped his hand as he knew he would. *Gotcha, fat man,* he said to himself. "I was in New York about a week before Harlem Nick was killed. As a matter a fact I met with him and spent some time with him shopping and clubbing. After I finished handling my business I was out of there like pronto. You know how I get down, Mr. S, once my moves are made I'm a ghost."

"*Sí,* this is true. Do you mind telling us what exactly the move was that you made while you were out there? You see, I do not believe in coincidence *Señor* Papio, and it seems rather strange to me how you just happen to be in the same state where money and drugs have been stolen from *me,* not once but twice. You do remember what happened to Lee, correct?"

"Yeah, I remember what happened to that fool. I also remember that I was in New York when he was killed. I don't really care for this type of questioning, Mr. S, but I understand this is some serious business and since I have absolutely nothing to hide I will tell you my business, only because I know it's safe in your hands. Fifteen months ago when I was out in the NY I hooked up with my old cell mate's little brother, Kango. I hooked up with his crew and we hit a Bank One in the Bronx. I came up a little over a million dollars off of that lick and then I hit another move on some dope boys out of Dallas. That's how I was able to give you that money I gave you when we last saw one another."

"I see. Please don't be insulted, *Señor* Papio; you know I try to dot all of my I's and cross all of my T's. I had to make sure that you had nothing to do with this, we need your help in making this right." Mr. Suarez remained stony-faced.

"My help? How can I help you with this Mr. S?"

"I'll let the chief finish now."

The tall Indian nodded. "I do remember reading in the *New York Times* about that bank robbery being committed at that time so I too believe you, Papio."

"Thanks," Papio said sarcastically. He was cool as could be on the outside but inside he was a bundle of fucking nerves.

"As I was saying, that money that was taken belonged to Mr. Suarez and that made my sons determined to get it back or at least get the accomplice for what he did to them. So they agreed to pay the four million to this woman."

"I see where this is going now: this broad crossed your sons too and now you want me to help your sons find the bitch." Papio couldn't believe his luck.

The chief shook his head sadly. "No, Mr. Papio, that's not it. I do need you to help me locate this woman, but you won't be assisting my sons because they are no longer alive."

"Damn. I'm sorry, Chief, I didn't mean any—"

The chief raised his hands to stop Papio and continued. "My sons were led into a double cross by this woman. She gave them the information they needed to get this man and when they went to go handle the situation somehow they were murdered. My sons were found dead in a Dumpster in back of a high-end furniture store called Cantoni in Dallas, Texas. The accomplice who helped Harlem Nick rob my sons is a very lucky man now because I no longer want his life. All I'm concerned with now is avenging the deaths of my two children. The only way I can do this is by finding the woman who double-crossed my boys."

"And you want me to try to find this woman?"

"I not only want you to find this woman, I want you to take her life. She killed my sons or helped have them killed, for this she has to die, Papio. I've repaid my debt to Mr. Suarez and he feels that you're the man who can handle this for me."

Before Papio could speak Mr. Suarez said, "Nothing is for free in this life, *Señor* Papio. For your time and efforts on this matter I am willing to squash your debt to me. You do this justice for the chief and you owe me nothing from our past issues."

Papio was doing back flips on the inside he was so happy, but he still needed to play the game like this was all news to him. "Let me get this straight. You want me to locate this female and take her and for that you will dead my bill? That's a whole lot of money, Mr. S, are you serious?"

"Have I ever played any games with you, Papio? When I put my stamp on something it is what it is. You do this for me and the chief and you owe me no more. *Sí?*"

"*Sí*. I have a lot on my plate, Mr. S. I don't really have the time to just drop everything I'm doing so I can play seek and destroy. I gotta eat, too." Papio was going to kill Special for free but with this turn of events he was going to try to get some cash out of the deal.

"I understand this, and as an added incentive I'm willing to give you one million in cash now for your services, Papio," the chief said seriously. "As you can see I'm an old man, I'm afraid I don't have too much time left on this earth, so it's imperative that I know for a fact that the woman who's responsible for my only two sons' deaths meets her fate before I leave this world."

One million! Thank you, Father, thank you! thought Papio. "One million plus my bill is squashed with you Mr. S? Am I really hearing this correctly?"

"Yes, you are, *Señor* Papio. So what is your answer?" asked Mr. Suarez.

Papio stared at both of the old men sitting next to him. He remained silent like he was thinking things over. Meanwhile he knew damn well that he was going to say yes but at this point he knew he had them by the balls. "Deal."

"By taking this responsibility we expect results, Papio."

"Come on, Mr. S, unless you know exactly where this broad is you know I can't promise you that."

"True," conceded Mr. Suarez. "But I expect for you to make this a top priority. Nothing comes before this mission."

"I won't promise you that either, sir. I mean if you want me to handle this you gats to let me handle it my way. I'm playing seek and destroy here, sir; it's going to take time and money to find this broad."

"It shouldn't take you too long to find her, she plays in your playground."

"What, she fucks around in Oklahoma City? If that's the case then no shit I'll have her ass before the month is over." Papio was acting like he didn't know the woman they were speaking about.

Mr. Suarez shook his head no and said, "No, she plays in California. Southern California to be exact."

"That helps but Southern Cali is a big-ass spot, it's going to take me some time. I can do this, sir, and for a million plus what I owe you I will do this. Just don't put that kind of pressure on me, because I already have things in the works that will bring me way more than just a million dollars."

"I have always given you leeway when you've needed it, Papio, and you have never let me down, for that I will again extend that leeway you ask of me." He turned toward the chief and said, "Like I told you, Chief, I have full confidence that Papio is the man who will bring you the justice you desire."

"Then he also has my full confidence, Mr. Suarez," the chief said solemnly.

"Then it is agreed. Papio, you will find this woman and take her life as painfully as possible. You will then take a few snapshots of her dead body to confirm the kill. Agreed?"

"Agreed. I have one question."

"Yes."

"What's this broad's name?" Papio asked even though he already knew the answer to his question.

Chief Hightower pulled a surveillance photo out of his pocket. It was a shot of Special walking inside of his casino/hotel with his two sons. He passed the photo to Papio and said, "Her name is Special."

Chapter 6

Special arranged for a limousine to take her and Keli to the party at the Regency Hotel ballroom. She made a few changes after their time spent with Rico; not only had they changed hotels from the DoubleTree to the Hilton in downtown Denver, but she made sure that neither Rico nor Jolly knew where they were resting their heads. This was a crucial maneuver because when everything was everything it was imperative that they had a nice head start on both Jolly and Rico.

Earlier in the day Rico kicked in lovely. He gave both of the ladies $10,000 apiece for a full night of straight freaking and fucking. By the time he dropped them off at their rental car he was so gone Special knew that she could get anything she wanted from him. And that was exactly what Special intended on doing.

Rico made the crucial mistake of inviting two snakes into his home. *Never take strangers to your house; big mistake, Rico, gigantic!* Not only did he show them where he lived, but he was so cocky with it that he actually explained all of his business to them. By being so flossy he didn't realize he was giving them vital information about all of his moves. He showed them several bundles of X pills and invited them to pop a few. Special declined but Keli was into that so she popped a few with him. It seemed the higher Rico got the more he talked. He told them about how he was connected to the North Side Mafia (NSM) of North Denver. He explained how he controlled most of the major drug dealings in the city of Denver. What really tripped Special out was when he showed them over a million dollars in cash. *Now how in the fuck does a dope boy keep that kind of money where he sleeps? This clown is just begging to get got. And got he will get,* Special thought as she watched Rico in amazement. The next morning when she made all of the necessary changes with where they were residing she felt good about the moves they were going to make.

Now as the limousine driver pulled in front of the Regency Hotel, Special and Keli were about to get the next phase of this mission started. *Colorado is about to be real sweet for us,* Special thought as she stepped out of the limousine looking like she was about to walk down the red carpet of the Academy Awards. Givenchy on her feet, a form-fitting cocktail dress by Angel Sanchez hugging every edible curve on her body, and a million-dollar smile on her face, she paused for Keli to exit the limousine. Keli was dressed equally as sexy as her lover/friend but with just a tad bit more zeal.

A Donna Karan micro skirt with a pair of Jimmy Choo exclusive ankle boots gave her that Rihanna rock star look. The outfit was topped off with a blond shoulder-length wig that gave her an extra little bit of exoticness.

As soon as the women stepped into the ballroom of the hotel all eyes were on them, including those of Mr. Kevin Ross, the man of honor for the evening. He was having a conversation with a professor from Colorado State University when he noticed the ladies enter the ballroom.

My God, who the hell are those two? he asked himself as he was no longer paying any attention to what the professor was saying.

Dena was standing at the bar when Special and Keli entered, and smiled when she saw her husband, along with every other male inside of the ballroom, checking them out. *This is going to be easier than I thought,* Dena thought as she sipped some of her apple martini and slowly stepped toward Special and Keli.

"Ladies, I'm so glad you could make it," Dena said as she gave them both an air kiss on each cheek.

Special smiled and played along. "We wouldn't have missed this for anything in the world, Dena. I mean what else were we going to do out here? It's not like we had anything else planned."

"You saved us from a dreadfully boring evening, girl-friend," added Keli as she checked out what Dena was wearing. The earth-tone evening gown Dena was wearing matched her light complexion perfectly. Her shoe game impressed Keli as she noticed the pair of open-toe Louboutin pumps she was wearing. What struck Keli as the most impressive thing was Dena's jazzy, short haircut. It was so Halle Berry that Keli wished she had the nerve to sport a cut like that.

"So, are you ready to meet the man of honor?" Dena asked, then she whispered, "Or should I say the scum of honor." They all laughed as Dena led the ladies toward her husband.

When Kevin saw his wife headed his way he smiled and excused himself from the conversation he was having. When he was in front of Dena he kissed her on the cheek. "You didn't tell me you invited some of the most beautiful women in all of Colorado, darling."

Dena gave him a fake smile. "It was a surprise, dear. I didn't know that my friends were going to be in town until just yesterday. Since they didn't have any plans I decided to invite them to your party. I figured you'd like. You do like, don't you, dear?"

"Mmmmm, definitely, darling. Now please introduce me to these lovely ladies."

"This is Special and this is Keli," Dena said as she pointed toward each of the women. "They're from Atlanta; we used to work together when I lived in Georgia."

Kevin smiled because he understood exactly what his wife meant. She subtly told him that Special and Keli used to strip with her when she worked at the infamous Magic City strip club in Atlanta. That turned him on even more than looking at Keli in that sexy but classy short micro skirt she was wearing. He wanted these women and he knew that his lovely wife had made this happen for a reason. She was trying her best to make sure that he did have a very happy birthday indeed.

With his smile still in place he said, "It's definitely an honor to meet the both of you. Thank you for coming to help celebrate my birthday. I do hope you're able to enjoy yourselves this evening."

With a flirtatious smile on her face Special said, "Oh, I think we're going to have a great time." Her brown eyes were firmly planted on Dena's cleavage. When she saw out of the corner of her eye Kevin's eyes bulge slightly she knew that her point had been made.

The live band that had been rented for the evening started playing Luther Vandross's "Never Too Much." Kevin grabbed his wife's hand and said, "Come, dear, let's go out there and help get this party started."

Dena smiled at her husband. "Excuse me, ladies."

Special and Keli watched as the couple went onto the dance floor and started dancing as if they were the happiest couple in the world.

Special shook her head. "Looks damn sure are deceiving huh?"

"You got that right. Looks like we're in with this trick."

"Definitely in. We might as well enjoy ourselves. Come on, I want to see what's good over there on that long-ass buffet table. Keep your eyes open. I got a feeling we might be able to come up on some future moves in this piece."

"You are always on the prowl, girl."

"You better believe it, K. I'm in it to win and I damn sure don't play fair. Come on, let's eat!"

Special and Keli enjoyed themselves tremendously; they ate, drank, and danced until they were tired. As they were getting ready to leave Dena approached them with a huge smile on her gorgeous face. She gave Special a hug and whispered in her ear, "We got him. He wants you two to come over tomorrow evening for dinner. He's asked me to approach you and Keli and offer you guys a nice sum for spending the evening with us."

"Is that right? How much is dear Kevin talking about?"

Dena raised her eyebrows. "Name your price. I've been told to agree to whatever it is. He wants all of us to do the nasty real bad."

"Tell your husband that we'll see him tomorrow at your home and to make sure to have twenty thousand dollars cash waiting for us; we don't do checks."

"Done. Okay, let me get back to him, we have to finish saying good-bye to the other guests. I'll give Jolly a call and let him know that everything is on for tomorrow."

"You do that," Special said as she gave Dena a hug and then led Keli outside and into their limousine.

"This is going to be easier than we thought, plus we're about to get an extra ten stacks each. Not bad at all."

Keli smiled at her. "Yeah, that's the business. You like her huh?"

"She seems like good peeps. For real she got a raw deal fucking with that freaked-out husband of hers. She doesn't deserve to be fucked over like that."

"What you got in mind for her after everything is everything?"

"I'm not sure yet. I do know I'm not letting Jolly's fat ass fuck her over, she's got enough of that shit from Kevin. What you think we should do?"

With a shrug Keli said, "I'm down with whatever you want to do, it's your call."

"Let's see what we get from this move as far as the bills are concerned and then I'll decide how we'll look out for old girl."

"That's what's up."

Special stared at Keli with a sultry look on her face as she relaxed into the comfortable seats of the limousine and slightly parted her legs. Keli didn't need any further hints; she licked her glossed lips and dipped her head between Special's thighs. "Mmmmmmmm, now, that's what's up!"

***

The next day was spent priming Rico for the big move Special came up with for his stupid ass. They had lunch at a Mexican restaurant in North Denver and continued to be amazed at how Rico kept slipping up around them. *How in the hell has this clown made it this long in the dope game out here slipping like this?* thought Special as she listened to Rico continue to brag about how much money he had and all of the trap spots he had around Denver. After they finished their lunch Rico escorted them outside of the restaurant and said, "What up, y'all trying to go back to my spot and make it happen for a few hours?"

Keli looked at Special and smiled when she told Rico, "Nah, young'un, we got some other moves to make. Tell you what though, since time is getting short we'll get with you later after we handle our business, cool?"

"How much later are we talking about, Special? It ain't like I ain't got shit lined up. I can't just be waiting on y'all all day and end up getting shook again. That shit ain't cool at all."

"We're out of here tomorrow evening, baby, and since you've been so good to us there's no way I'm going to leave your town without breaking you off one last time. And believe me what we've given you already isn't even our best. We've saved the best for last, daddy. So fall back and let us handle what we came to Denver to take care of and then we'll get back to the freaky shit. It shouldn't be no longer than eleven, twelve at the latest."

"All right, I'm feeling that. Now give Rico some love."

"You are too silly with your fine ass," Special said as she gave him a kiss on his cheek.

He frowned. "Come on with that weak shit, Special, that ain't no love! Give me some love, Keli, and show your homegirl how it's really done."

Keli smiled and stepped to him and gave him some mean tongue action.

After a full minute had passed she pulled away from him. "Is that how you like it, baby?"

Rico laughed. "Hell yeah! Damn, I'm going to miss y'all. What a nutty gotta do to get y'all fine asses back out here?"

"You already know the answer to that question, young'un: as long as you got those ends right we'll be back whenever you send for us. Now let us go so we can get things taken care of."

"I'll be waiting on your call Special, don't shake me."

"See ya, young'un," she said as she followed Keli to their rental car. Once they were in traffic Special told Keli, "Okay, this is how it goes down: tonight after we finish the business with Kevin and Dena we'll get back to the room, get fresh, and pack all our stuff, then we'll hit Rico and let him know we're on our way to his spot."

"We're going to go on and freak that fool one more time?"

"Nah, fuck that, he's been blessed enough with all of this good pussy we done gave his ass. We're going to take some of his knockout shit that Dena has and slip it on his ass. Then we're robbing that stupid nigga blind. When he wakes up everything he has that's worth something is leaving with us. That's why we're about to go get us another rental. We'll keep this one to go to his spot but we're going to need an SUV for our road trip."

"Road trip?"

"Yeah, we're rolling back to Cali because there's no way we'll be able to fly all of the dope and money and shit we're going to take off of the young'un."

"I see. Damn, girl, when did you make up your mind to make this move?"

"When I saw how flossy that young fool is. He's a jack waiting to happen, we might as well be the ones to make it happen to his stupid ass."

"You're not worried about him being connected to those North Side Mafia Mexicans?"

"Fuck nah! Why should I be? Those are some local-ass Denver Mexican, they don't have no real weight behind them outside of the state of Colorado. When we make it back home we're good. See, I made a few calls, and guess who their main enemies are?"

"Who?"

"The Surenos."

"Are you serious? Wow, that's like perfect. There's no way in hell he'll ever try to come get at us then. Those L.A. Mexicans ain't no joke when it comes to their enemies."

"Exactly. So don't worry about a thang, it's all good, K. Now all we got to do is make everything do what it do with Dena and hope that her husband has plenty of those high-end bills."

"I know that's right. We are going to get our freak on with Dena right?" Keli asked with a mischievous grin on her face.

"You just want to suck on those big, firm titties she's got."

Keli laughed. "You damn right!"

Joining Keli's laughter with her own Special said, "Me too!"

After renting a Lincoln Navigator for their trip back to California Special and Keli went back to their hotel and got some rest. Special had so much on her mind that she couldn't sleep. Even though they had re-mained quite busy during their stay in Denver she was still unable to rid herself of those damn thoughts of

Papio. Here she was way out here in Colorado about to make two nice licks for a decent amount of money and she had to still be wondering about him. *Damn.* A part of her wanted to call him just to see how he was doing—shit, who was she fooling—a large part of her wanted to do nothing but call his fine ass and beg for his forgiveness. She couldn't fake it; she loved him more than she ever thought possible. *Ugh! I gats to get that nigga out of my head because if I don't shit will never be right. I could go on and . . . Nah, fuck that nigga; if I got at him all he'd do is try to set me up like he wants to hook back up and then smash my ass for crossing him. Ain't no way am I going to fall for the fifty-two fake out; that shit just ain't happening,* she said to herself as she drifted off to sleep.

The ladies were dressed casually as they pulled into the driveway of a low-key-looking home. Special thought Kevin would have had them living in a mansion or something more of that nature. *I guess he really doesn't have it like that,* she thought as Keli stopped and put the car in park. Just as they got out of the car Kevin came outside of his home dressed in a pair of Dockers with a matching shirt. *So low-key,* again thought Special as she flashed her famous smile.

"How are you lovely ladies doing this evening?" Kevin stiffly asked as he escorted them into his home. Dena was sitting in the living room when they entered.

"Would you like something to drink? Dinner's just about ready," said Dena.

"Some wine would be nice," said Keli as she sat down next to Dena.

"Yes, wine would be nice," added Special as she sat down on the sofa right next to Kevin, who seemed to be pleased by that maneuver.

"I don't want to seem rude or anything like that, Special, so I truly hope you won't take my straightforwardness as being so, because that is not my intention. I just prefer to handle my business in an efficient yet direct manner."

"I don't see anything wrong with handling business in the proper fashion. I mean after all business is business and pleasure is pleasure."

"My sentiments exactly. So here you are, as agreed upon, ten thousand dollars cash."

Special accepted the money from him and put it inside of her small Gucci purse. She met Kevin's eyes. "I want you to know that after we're finished eating you will see that we are here to earn every penny of this money, Kevin."

He laughed. "Oh, I have no doubts about that, Special. Normally I'd sit back and watch my lovely wife as she is being made love to but with you two beautiful women here I have to be a part of this. I mean just looking at either of you turns me on in ways I haven't felt in years. Dena will forever excite me but you two do something to me that I can't even put into words."

Special patted his leg softly. "That's good, Kevin, because we're going to do things to you that I'm sure you've never had done before."

Dena returned and gave the ladies their drinks. "Dinner is ready. I thought it would be more relaxing if we ate outside in the backyard with the weather being so nice out."

"Splendid idea, dear," Kevin said as he stood and followed the three beautiful women outside to the backyard.

Once they were all seated at a long glass patio table positioned a few yards from an Olympic-sized swimming pool, Dena began serving the food. "I hope you like shrimp, ladies. I had Kevin prepare his specialty, Malaysian shrimp. They're so succulent I'm sure you will enjoy them. Also I fried some Omaha tenderloins for a perfect combination."

"Mmmm, all of this looks delicious," Keli said as she began to nibble on some of the shrimp. "This is good!"

Everyone laughed as they too began to eat their meal. After they were finished eating they sat back and sipped some more wine and enjoyed some light banter between one another. Dena knew that it was time to kick this thing off so she stood and boldly started to undress. Once she was naked she asked Keli, "Do you want to join me for a swim, Keli? The pool is heated and I'm sure we can make it heat up some more."

Without waiting for an answer she took a few quick steps and then jumped into the warm water of their swimming pool. Keli smiled at Special and Kevin as she quickly pulled off her clothes and followed Dena inside of the pool. She swam to the shallow end and grabbed Dena around her waist and pulled her close to her. The kiss they shared was electric; it felt as if their mouths were made for one another. Keli put both of her hands on Dena's firm breasts and sighed. She had counted the minutes waiting for this opportunity. She pulled away from Dena's mouth and dipped her head and began to suck first the right breast then the left. Dena's nipples responded to this attention and immediately became rock hard. "Ooooooooo, that feels so damn good, Keli. Yes, yes, baby, suck 'em just like that. I love that, baby."

Upon hearing his wife's moans of passion Kevin asked, "Do you want to join them, Special?"

Special shook her head no and said, "Uh-uh. Let them make their own magic in that water; we can make our own magic right here." She slid from her seat and began to unbuckle his belt. When she had his pants pulled down around his ankles she dropped to her knees and began to suck his dick like the pro she was. She knew she had him with her extraordinary head game by the moans and groans coming from his lips.

"Yes! Dammit, Special! Yes! Suck that dick, baby! Suck it good!" he screamed as he watched his wife and Keli in the pool kissing and rubbing their hands all over each other's body. Before he felt himself start to come he pulled out of Special's mouth and said, "Whoa, hold up, baby, let's pause and take this inside. I have some goodies that will help this party continue deep into the night."

With a naughty glimpse in Keli and Dena's direction Special asked, "What you got for me, daddy?"

"Let's go inside and you'll see for yourself. You do indulge don't you?"

"If you mean do I get down with a little feel-good boost every now and then, then the answer is yes. A little toot will put me in a even freakier mood."

"Exactly." He turned toward the pool and said, "Dena, bring Keli inside so we can enjoy one another more thoroughly."

Dena was so caught up with Keli's tongue on her clitoris that she almost wanted to ignore her husband's request. *Fuck, this woman knows how to eat some pussy! I've never had my pussy sucked like this before,* she said to herself as she reluctantly pushed Keli's head from between her legs. "Come on, baby, time to get this money."

Keli smiled at her. "You know this. But I want you to know that I am going to finish what I started before we leave."

"I had no intention of letting you leave without finishing anyway, girl!" They both started laughing as they climbed out of the pool and followed Kevin and Special inside of the house.

Kevin led them to the master bedroom and Special was impressed. There was nothing low-key or modest about this room, that was for sure. A huge California king-sized bed was placed right in the middle of the room, mirrors were everywhere you looked, the entire room was mirrored, and Special knew that Kevin was definitely into watching himself freak and get freaked. She shook her head and smiled at him as he told Dena, "Go get the goodies, dear, while I have the pleasure of these two beautiful women."

Special had a smile on her face as she took off her clothes so Kevin could see her goodies. When she was naked she stepped to Keli and began kissing her and rubbing her hands all over her thickness. Kevin became rock hard watching the ladies as they did their thing.

Dena returned carrying a silver tray with several lines of cocaine placed on it along with several pills. *Cocaine and ecstasy are going to help us last all night long,* thought Kevin as he smiled when Dena held the tray up so he could be the one to have the first snort. He bent his head and began to snort the first two lines of the cocaine. Dena smiled as she watched him inhale the knockout cocaine she had placed on the tray. She then took the tray toward Special and Keli and held it up to them. They each took a few quick snorts of the real cocaine and instantly felt as if they were flying. Keli popped an X pill and grabbed Dena and laid her onto their bed and began to eat her pussy as if she would be the last pussy she ever would eat. Dena screamed over and over as Keli devoured her pussy with her tongue. She was in heaven as she came harder and harder. "My God! Don't you stop! Don't you stop eating this pussy, Keli!"

Kevin was feeling the effects of the cocaine mixed with the knockout drug and was ready to feel how good Special's pussy was.

He grabbed her waist. "I have to take you from behind, baby, bend over and let me hit that firm-ass doggie."

Special had a smile on her face as she ripped open a condom she had in her hand and put it inside of her mouth. She then dropped to her knees and began to place the condom on his dick with her mouth. When she saw that the condom was firmly in place she turned around and slapped her backside and said, "Come and fuck this pussy, daddy. You want it, it's all yours."

Kevin had a smile on his face as he grabbed her by her hips and eased himself inside of her. Special backed that thang up and made sure he was as deep as his medium-sized dick could go. She then began to work hard matching his every stroke. She wanted him to hurry up and come because she knew the effect from him coming and the knockout drug would speed up the process and lay him down for the night. She was trying to be out of there as soon as she could. She was surprised when after ten minutes Kevin still felt hard and strong and showed no signs of coming yet. So she began to put that ass in overdrive and throw it at him with all that she had. The longer it took the more turned on she became. *Mmmmm this shit is feeling good,* she said to herself as Kevin was steady pounding away in that pussy. Special came for the fourth time and was starting to get tired when she felt Kevin begin to twitch inside of her. *Finally,* she thought as she watched Keli and Dena slip into the sixty-nine position and begin to eat each other out. She smiled and thought about how good that must feel. *I got to get me some of that before I leave,* she said to herself as she watched Dena's huge bosom bounce all around as Keli ate her pussy.

"Ugh! Oh yeah! Oh yeah, I'm coming, bitch! I'm coming!" screamed Kevin as he filled the condom with his nut.

Bitch? That's funny. Nigga, this bitch is about to get your ass, she said to herself as she stood and stretched. She stared at Kevin and could tell he was about to be out any minute. "Sit down, daddy, and watch as I help my girl please your wifey."

She stepped to the bed where Keli and Dena were getting their freak on and began to suck on Dena's titties. The ladies slipped into a triangle daisy train without being told to do so. Keli's face was stuck between Special's legs, sucking her pussy feverishly while Special had her tongue as deep as it could get inside of Dena's pussy, all at the same time Dena was sucking Keli's pussy, thoroughly enjoying herself. This went on for over twenty minutes before any of the women realized that Kevin was knocked out cold on the floor next to the bed. Special noticed first and pulled her face from Dena's pussy and started to laugh. "Okay, ladies, I do think it's time for us to get this money. Our boy here is out for the count."

Keli and Dena both came up for air and laughed also. "Damn, I was so caught up with this good-ass pussy I almost forgot what we really came here for," said Keli as she sat up and smiled at Dena. "Girl, we need to take your ass with us when we leave. I can see me having a ball with your sexy ass."

"After we do this don't worry about a thing, baby, we will remain in touch," said Dena.

"That's what's up. Now, come on and show us this safe so we can see what we got."

Dena smiled as she stood and led the ladies into the study downstairs. She went to a huge portrait of Kevin's father and mother and moved it aside. "Damn, that's just like some movie shit. I never knew people really had shit like that," Special said as she stood right next to Dena as she opened the safe. When the safe was opened Dena stepped aside and let Special look inside. Special gasped when she saw all of the high-denomination bills each encased in plastic. She pulled the stack of bills out of the safe and set them onto the desk.

"Okay, let's check this shit so we can see how we're going to do this."

"What do you mean how you're going to do this? I thought the plan was to get with Jolly and let him sell these to his people," Dena said with a confused look on her face.

Special put a finger to Dena's lips and said, "Shhh, be quiet and listen, Dena." She then grabbed each bill and began to inspect them thoroughly. She thought about what Jolly had told them and gasped when she saw that the last six bills out of the twenty-five bills were orange. Not only were they orange but they had President Woodrow Wilson on them! That meant that these were the $100,000 bills Jolly had told them about. *My God! There's six of them! That's twelve million fucking dollars!* Special thought as she turned and faced Keli with one of the $100,000 bills in her hand.

Keli knew instantly what Special was showing them and asked, "How many?"

"Six," whispered Special.

"Six? Well I'll be a mothafuck! We hit the mothafucking jackpot for real!" screamed Keli.

"You damn right. This is how it goes down. Pay attention, Dena, and pay attention closely. Jolly has no intention of giving you your share of this move."

"What? Uh-uh, Jolly wouldn't do me like that, Special, you're tripping."

Special sighed heavily. "All right, I know you don't know us from jack and you do have some history with that fat fuck. But believe me when I tell you this, that nigga is going to cross you out and leave you to fend for yourself after everything is everything. Now if you play this shit like I tell you to then you will win by fucking with us."

"What are you talking about?"

Special turned to the table and grabbed the bills. "We expected fifteen bills at the most but we have twenty-five here. We expected maybe one of these $100,000 bills but instead we have six. So the figures have changed like dramatically, baby girl. We're going to play Jolly's fat ass like this. We're going to give him the fifteen bills. One will be one of these $100,000 bills. That will make his greedy ass sit comfortable and everything will be good. He knows we're not trying to sit and wait out here for him to make the deal so he's going to pay us out of his pocket. That's when you'll learn that he's crossed you out. Don't panic though because we're going to take these other bills to L.A. with us and I'll have my money man get us the same prices Jolly gets and then we'll split these other bills evenly. Do you feel me now, Dena?"

"You damn right I feel you. I swear I'm going to get that fucker back for this shit!"

"Don't waste your time, baby, we're going to get his ass back by doing exactly what we're doing." Special placed each of the bills on top of the desk and made a count of what they had. She set five of the $100,000 bills aside with three of the $10,000 bills and two $5,000 bills, and said, "This is how we're going to do this. I'm going to give Jolly the fifteen bills he expects and we'll keep these other ten."

Doing the math quickly in her head she came up with the exact figures and continued. "With these ten bills we'll have $10,000,520."

"Wow! But how are you going to get the money for them? Jolly won't set you up with his buyer when he finds out you have more bills than you said you did," said Dena.

"I told you to listen and pay attention, Dena. I see you haven't been paying attention. I already told you that I got my money man in L.A. who will take care of all of this for us. So don't trip, we're in the good. Me and Keli will take these bills to Jolly and get our split, which should be around $800,000 apiece."

"Huh?" asked Keli. "I thought we'd clear way more than that from those fifteen bills, Special."

"Nah. See with three five-hundred-dollar bills, six one-thousand-dollar bills, two five-thousand-dollar bills, three ten-thousand-dollar bills and one $100,000 bill they all add up to $2,000,640. Divided by three comes to $880,000 apiece. Which is damn good for real. Jolly's fat ass will be happy and we'll be good too."

"Shit, we'll be really good after we get the ends for the other ten bills," Keli said with a smile on her face.

"Fucking right because $10.5 million split four ways brings us $2.6 million each."

"Four ways? You've lost me again here, Special. Why is the split four ways?" asked Dena.

"We have to split it four ways because my money man, Poppa Blue, will get an even split. That's how I get down with my man because we've been together for years. It's all good, baby, and believe me this way you're getting way more than you would have gotten from Jolly, even if he would have kept it real with you. We win this way, baby, and we win big."

"I love it!" Dena exclaimed.

Special checked her watch and saw that it was a little after 10:00 P.M. *Good, ahead of schedule,* she thought. "All right, ladies, let's get things together so we can be out of here in the next fifteen minutes."

"Why can't I just leave with you two? Fuck Kevin. I'm ready to be gone," Dena said as she began to get dressed.

"Nah, we got to stick to the script because Jolly will then know the business and then I might have to end up killing that fat bastard."

"Do you really think he's not going to figure it out anyway? I mean once Kevin reports what's been stolen to his insurance people it's going to become public knowledge."

"True. But I'll be able to play that off as Kevin being smart enough to turn his loss into a major gain by lying to his insurance folks. Jolly will know its bullshit but he won't be able to move against me because it would be too weak of an excuse. And he knows my mans and his folks would come looking for his scary fat ass. So sticking to the script is the best way."

"I agree with Special," added Keli.

"By sticking to the script we got to tie you and your hubby up, so you should go on and take your clothes back off. We gats to keep this as authentic as we can."

Dena hesitated for a moment and said, "Okay. Can you two answer a question for me honestly?"

"What's up?" both of the ladies asked in unison.

"What's going to stop you two from keeping all of that money to yourselves? I mean you could just say fuck me too when you leave here."

Special smiled at Dena. "Baby, I don't play fair and I play this game to win, but you got to be true sometimes, being grimy don't always equal a win in my book. Most times but not all of the damn time."

"That's right. Plus, you're good peoples and you been fucked over long enough by that joke-ass husband of yours. It's time for you to get your blessings, Dena, and we're going to give them to you. Trust us because we got you on this. We made our decision to look out for you the first day we met because that's when we figured out Jolly was going to do you dirty. You're good, baby, once we get that money you will get yours, real talk," said Keli.

With tears in her eyes Dena gave them both a kiss and said, "Thank you, thank you both so much."

"It's all good. Now come on, we gats to get you tied up before we bounce."

"How will I be able to get in contact with you?"

"You won't. We'll get at you once everything is everything. Either by text or e-mail. We got the numbers already from Jolly so don't trip. Just play your husband to the left and be patient because in no time you will have more than two and a half million to do whatever you want to."

That put a huge smile on Dena's face. "Will we be able to get together when everything is right?"

Special looked at Keli and answered for the both of them. "Baby, we'd love to get together and do the wild thang for a weekend. We will go somewhere nice and make it happen real big. Now, come on, let's get shit together," Special said.

Chapter 7

Thirty minutes after leaving Dena and Kevin's home Special and Keli arrived at Rico's condominium in North Denver. Their plan was to be quick with their business. Get in and get right to freaking Rico's ass just as they did with Kevin. Instead of slipping him some of the knockout cocaine they were going to slip him a mickey in his drink. That way once he was out everything would be just as easy as it was with Kevin. By the time Rico woke up they would be at least a couple of hours outside of Denver headed toward California.

Everything went according to plan, thought Special as she got out of the car followed by Keli. She had a smile on her face as she thought about how happy Jolly's fat ass was when they gave him the fifteen high-denomination bills. He happily gave them their share of the money and couldn't wait to get them out of his space so he could get at his peoples. That alone told her that he had a better deal waiting for him than he let on. Which was cool because after everything was everything they would be the ones who would come out on top. As long as he was happy Special was happier. *Now it is time to get some more money,* Special thought as they stepped inside of Rico's home.

Rico had on a silk robe and slippers as he let them inside and led them toward the bedroom. Special could tell that he was high on something because he was sweating and couldn't stop waving his hands around. "I'm sure glad y'all ain't shake me. I've been waiting for this all damn day. Come on, take them clothes off so I can lick and fuck both y'all all damn night," he said as he chucked off his robe.

"Damn, daddy, we can't get a drink? Why you in such a rush? Like you said we got all night," said Special.

"I'm hot and horny as fuck. I popped a couple of X pills and they got me thizzin like a mothafuck. Go on and get yourselves comfortable. I'll get you something to drink."

"Nah, lay your thizzin-ass down and let me get you relaxed while Special go get the drinks, baby," Keli said as she took off her clothes quickly and lay next to him on his bed and began to lick on his chest and stomach, working her way down toward his dick. By the time she had his dick inside of her mouth Rico's eyes were closed and loud moans were coming from his lips. Special smiled and thought, *that's my girl.*

She then went into the living room where the bar was located and grabbed a bottle of Belvedere and made each of them a drink. After the drinks were ready she took a sip of two of them and then pulled out the pill that was going to knock Rico's ass out and crushed it into the third glass: the one glass that didn't have her peach-colored lipstick around the rim. That way she would know which glass to give him when she went back into the bedroom.

She almost dropped the drinks she was holding when she saw Rico on his knees with Keli behind him with damn near all of her right hand inside of Rico's asshole. *What the fuck does this young fool have Keli doing to his ass?* she wondered as she continued to watch as Keli basically fist fucked him. Keli saw that

Special had returned and gave her a shrug of her shoulders as if to say, "This is what he wanted." Special shook her head from side to side as she listened to Rico moan and groan.

"Ooooh yeah, *mami,* just like that! Just like that, put all of that hand in Rico's ass, baby! Yes! Harder! Harder, *mami!* Please do me harder!" screamed Rico.

Special couldn't believe this shit. Even though she had heard about niggas who liked to get fist fucked she really thought that was for gay dudes; she never thought a young dope boy thug like Rico would ever be into some shit like that. *Damn freak,* she thought as she stepped in front of him and put the drink to his lips. "Here, drink this, daddy." She watched as he emptied the glass quickly.

She smiled as she set the glass down and then crawled under him and began to suck his extra-hard dick. The feelings Rico was experiencing intensified as Special gave him some of her best head while Keli was fisting him. Special had only had him inside of her mouth for a minute or so before he exploded with a monster orgasm. He came so long Special had to spit him out of her mouth in fear of choking from all of his sperm he was releasing.

Keli got up and went into the bathroom to wash her hands. By the time she returned Rico was knocked out and Special was already looking around the bedroom for whatever she wanted to take. "Go check in the other rooms and see what you find while I go through here."

"Gotcha," Keli said as she hurried out of the bedroom.

Forty-five minutes later the ladies left Rico's condominium with over ten bundles of X pills, seven kilograms of cocaine, some expensive platinum chains and watches, as well as diamond earrings and diamond bracelets. They were definitely excited about all of this loot but the cherry on top of the cake was the money. They took over a million dollars in cash from Rico. *That man has to be the most stupid drug dealer in criminal history,* thought Special as they finished loading all of their ill-gotten gains inside of their rented SUV. Not until they were on their way out of Colorado did Special sit back in her seat and relax. *A job well done on all accounts. I love this life,* she thought as she closed her eyes.

Special and Keli had been back in Los Angeles for only a day and it was already time for more work to be done. Special was meeting her money man, Poppa Blue, so she could give him the ten high-denomination bills so he could get the money for her. She was also going to get the particulars for the jewelry store jobs Poppa Blue told her about. She couldn't hide her smile as she pulled into Poppa Blue's driveway and saw his wife Bernadine walking out of their home with a small child in a stroller. Her smile quickly faded when she saw Poppa Blue come out of his house arguing with someone on his cell phone. When he looked up and saw her he gave her a signal with his hands to stay inside of her car, said something to his wife, then marched toward Special while still fussing with someone on the phone.

He got into Special's new BMW, covered up the cell with his right hand, and said, "Drive, head toward Bakersfield." He then got back on his cell and started back arguing. "Listen to me, you fat fuck, I don't give a damn what you've heard or what you think. Special is a vet at this shit and if she said that's all she got then that's all she got. She wouldn't screw up her rep by beating you out of a few crumbs, Jolly."

"Come on with that shit, Poppa Blue, no way in hell is ten-plus million some fucking crumbs! You and I both know that shit! That bitch fucked me over and on top of that shit she had the fucking nerve to hit one of the major dope boys out here. That crazy-ass Mexican is trying to get a line on her ass now so he can have her and Keli's asses strung the fuck up. I don't even have to tell you how close I am to giving him as much assistance as he needs."

"You do that shit and as God is my witness I'll call in every favor owed to me and have your fat ass put down! Do you hear me, Jolly? Don't fuck with me; you'll lose."

"So I'm supposed to just fall back and accept getting beat out of my end of a move that I put together? That's what you're telling me, Poppa Blue?"

Blue gave Special his evil eye look as he sighed. "For one, Jolly, what makes you so sure that Special beat you out of anything? What proof do you have?"

"The move was set up too sweet, Poppa Blue. It's all over the news out here. The fool is hollering how he lost twenty-five bills worth more than several million dollars. The key word here is twenty-five! That sneaky bitch gave me fifteen bills, Poppa Blue! Fifteen! Not only that, but the fool also told his insurance people that six of those bills were $100,000 bills. That bitch gave me one of those bills, Poppa Blue, just fucking one! So if there were six of them that means that bitch got five of them. That alone is worth ten million. So don't play me like this because I know for real if she did get me you're in on it. Cut me in is all I'm asking; don't fuck me like this, Poppa Blue, not when it was my move, all mine! And all I got out of it is a punk-ass $880,000. That's some real cold shit and you know it."

Poppa Blue sighed. "Now you're insulting me, too. I should hang this phone up on your fat ass! Can't you see what the fuck I'm telling you, Jolly? Special didn't do you, fool! That clown on your end is playing the insurance people, trying to make a come up on his losses. You been in the game too long now not to be able to see that weak shit."

"I don't know, Poppa Blue, this is a straight, square-type nigga. He don't have that type of nuts for real."

"Look at your ass sounding like a square-ass lame your damn self. Fool, if Special did have something to do with more bills being took, you're right, I would be in on it, because she doesn't have a way to get rid of any shit like that. That's why I'm telling you on my name she didn't have shit to do with it because she would have put me up on it from the be-gin. Maybe that clown's wife got him, you ever think about that, Jolly?" Poppa Blue asked with a smile on his face.

Jolly paused as he gave some thought to what Poppa Blue had just said. "Come to think of it, that bitch hasn't even been sweating me about the ends she's supposed to get from the move. That's some strange shit right there. She was supposed to be using this move to get on with her life and shake that wack-ass fool."

Poppa Blue's smile widened as he rubbed his fine, all-white beard and told Jolly in his deep, baritone voice, "See, Jolly, you need to think about everything before you go flying off the handle on some weak shit. Special wouldn't beat you for nothing because she's not built like that. I put her in the game when she was just a pup; she's now one of the best females in the life. And that is all my work, so you can see how I take it personally when someone accuses her of some bullshit."

Not really buying Poppa Blue's words but admitting to himself that maybe, just maybe, he could be right on this one, Jolly said, "I feel you, Poppa Blue. Let me check some traps and see what's up with that bitch Dena."

"Do that and keep me informed on what's what."

"Say, Poppa Blue, don't tell Special what we talked about huh?"

Poppa Blue smiled as Special turned her BMW on to the 405 Freeway north headed toward Bakersfield. "Don't worry, Jolly, I'll keep this conversation between me and you." After he closed his phone Poppa Blue faced Special and shook his head. "Girl, you are a mess. See how you got me lying and playing these fucked-up games? You know I don't get down like that, Special."

Special started laughing. "You need to quit, Poppa Blue. You're getting 2.5 milly plus for my move out there. Who gives a fuck what Jolly's fat ass thinks? Fuck him. Now, what's up on those ends?"

"Let me see those bills." Special reached inside of her purse, a rather large Dooney & Bourke bag and pulled out the plastic-encased high-denomination bills and passed them to Poppa Blue.

"Damn, girl, you did good for real. These are exactly how my man Jimbo described them to me. Yeah, this is real nice."

"Thanks for the praise and shit, but what about that fetti?"

"Patience. I'll get with Jimbo when we get back from checking everything out with this business in Bakersfield. I should have your ends no later than a couple of days. Do you need any cash now? You seem like you do with all of this damn sweating me you're doing."

"Nah, I'm good personally, but I want to be able to look out for Dena so she can put some distance between her and that freaky, perverted husband of hers."

"Ahh, I see. It's good to see that you've developed some kind of compassion. For a while there I thought you were made of ice. I guess it's true."

"What?"

"Love makes people change."

"Love? You need to kill that shit. You know who and what I love, Poppa Blue, and don't you even try to throw Papio into that equation. Ugh!"

Poppa Blue laughed but didn't respond because he knew it would only anger Special. He also knew that she was madly in love with Papio but was just too afraid to admit it to him or herself.

He shook his head sadly and then told her in a tone that was all business, "This is how it goes down out here in Bakersfield. Tomorrow you drive down here and get a room at the Travel Lodge, a small bucket motel on the outskirts of town. Hit me after you get the room and I'll have a partner of mines come by and drop you off what you will need for this nice and easy lick."

"Weapons?"

"Yeah, a pistol and the magic wand."

"The magic wand? Stop playing with me, Poppa Blue."

"I'm serious. It's a magic wand of sorts because it's going to make your moves be so easy that this could change the robbery game completely. It's a device created by an associate of mine and it's going to be put to use for the very first time tomorrow evening when you hit two jewelry stores back to back."

"You're talking but you ain't really told me shit yet. Explain."

"My man will drop you off what will look like a regular garage opener remote. But this will be far from that; it's going to be the tool you use to kill all the electronic surveillance inside of the jewelry stores. When you pull up in front of the store you aim the device directly at the front door. You will then hear several beeps. Once you see the red light on the device turn green the beeps will stop; that tells you that everything as far as the security cameras and alarms have all been deactivated. You will then proceed inside of the store and do you. You can get greedy if you want because you will definitely have time on your side with this. But I would prefer it if you went in and got the jewels that will be on the list my man will give you when he drops off the device, that choice will be yours. Everything you bring me other than what's on the list will be dealt with how we usually get down. I gots to get my ten percent."

She smiled at her mentor and said, "But of course."

"There will only be one person inside and you'll be able to handle that with ease: a little Iranian lady. After you've handled your business get right to the next store, which will be four blocks away. Once there you repeat the same process with the device and make your moves. Only difference this time is timing is essential. Get in and make your move and grab what's on the list and get your ass back to the Travel Lodge, where my man will be waiting for you. Give him the loot, switch back to your car, and head on home."

"Since you didn't say anything about a vehicle being brought to me I can assume your man who's bringing the device is also bringing the vehicle as well."

"Damn, you're so smart, I didn't think I'd have to explain every little detail to your slick ass."

"I love you too, Poppa Blue."

"You better. Now, any questions?"

"You said these licks are worth 1.2 right?"

"Yeah."

"Any extra shit I take on the first move is me; that is, with your ten percent of course."

"Correct."

"And you're positive this device shit is on the up and up?"

"If I wasn't we wouldn't be having this discussion."

"I'm with it. What are we doing when we get down there?"

"A walk-through of sorts. We're going to go to the Travel Lodge so you'll know where that is as well as the routes you're going to take so you'll be comfortable when it goes down. After I'm comfortable that you got it down pat we'll head back home and you'll pay for a very expensive dinner because you do know Poppa Blue gots to get his eat on," Poppa Blue said and started laughing.

Special shook her head from side to side and started laughing also. "You are special, Poppa Blue, and I'm not talking about special like me, more like the yellow bus kind of special."

"Ahhh, she's young, beautiful, plus she has jokes." Special switched from the 405 Freeway north to the 5 Freeway fifteen minutes outside of the city of Bakersfield, California.

The next morning Special woke up after another rough night of dreaming about Papio. She loved that man and knew that nothing was going to come from her loving him and that thought hurt. *There are some places the mind shouldn't go, but goes there anyway,* she thought as she stood and stretched. *Time to get ready to go get that easy money.*

After showering and getting dressed she decided to go have some lunch with Keli and let her know that she would be getting their money later on that evening. She grabbed her purse and keys and left her home smiling as she thought about adding another chunk to her almost $9 million bank roll. *Shit, I could quit this shit and move somewhere fly and live the rest of my life content as ever,* she said to herself as she jumped into her car. *How can I be content without the man I want to be with in my life? Ugh! I love you, Papio, but I hate you too!* she thought as she pulled out of her driveway. She pulled out her cell phone and called Keli.

"Hey, girl, what's up?" asked Keli when she answered the phone.

"Nothing much. About to get ready to go handle some business in a little bit. You wanna go do lunch or are you busy?"

"Busy? I ain't doing shit but laying my fat ass down chilling. I was going to hit you up to see what was up on those ends and then see if you wanted to get into something."

"All right, meet me at the Red Lobster in Torrance. After we eat we can hit the Del Amo mall and do a little something until I bounce. As for the ends I'll put you up on that when we hook up."

"I hear you. I'll see you there in like thirty, cool?"

"All right, girl, bye." Special hung up the phone and began to think about Papio again. *I wonder what he's doing right now.* She smiled because she thought about the look on his face when she shot him. He was so shocked that all he could say was, "That's so fucked up, Special! You fucking shot me!" She turned and left without saying a word to him because she had to make him think she was really as cold as she was pretending to be. That thought hurt because, though she was a cold woman, she wasn't that damn cold. *Ugh! Stop thinking about him, Special! I am so missing the dark blue waters of the Caribbean right now! Ugh!*

Keli and Special enjoyed a nice seafood lunch at the Red Lobster and then went across the street to the Del Amo mall and did some lightweight shopping. Lightweight to them meant spending a couple of thousand dollars on boots and accessories instead of their norm: thirty or forty thousand on every top-notch designer out. A little after 2:00 P.M. Special told Keli that she had to make a move and that she would get with her later with her split from the move out in Denver.

"Let's hook up at my spot later and go out or something. Give Dena a call and let her know that we'll be getting with her tomorrow with her ends."

"Let's fly her out here so we can kick it and celebrate. You already know I'm trying to get with her fine ass again," Keli said with a wicked grin on her face.

"Damn, girl, don't you ever get tired of eating pussy?"

"Sex is sex to me, Special. I like to be satisfied. But for real there is one guy I am feeling. I just don't know if he's feeling me though."

"If he's seen you and not feeling you then he's a damn fool and ain't worth your time. So shake his ass if he don't step up to the plate like ASAP!"

"You are so crazy, girl, but thanks for saying that. So, what up; can we fly her out or what?"

Special shook her head from side to side and said, "You damn freak! Get at her and see if she can shake that fool. If she can this is what we'll do: we'll fly her out to Las Vegas and go spend the weekend out there devouring her fine ass together. You with that?"

"You already know, girl!" They gave each other a quick peck on the lips and headed toward their cars.

Two and a half hours later Special pulled her BMW into the parking lot of the Travel Lodge Motel and checked into a small, musty-smelling room. She called Poppa Blue and he told her that his man Lance was on his way to bring her what she needed. They also discussed the matter of the money split. As with every lick they pulled she'd keep a portion of the money she made and Poppa Blue would make sure that the rest would be deposited into her offshore account. This time she'd keep a couple hundred thousand from the $1.2 million she was about to bag. She couldn't wait to get with Poppa Blue and then go home to L.A. and relax.

No matter how much money she was about to make Special was tired of being alone. The thought of not being able to be with the man she wanted irked the hell out of her. She was staring at her cell trying to convince herself that calling Papio was the right thing to do when there was a soft knock on the door to her room. *Good, saved by the bell,* she said to herself as she went and opened the door for Lance. She smiled and let the small, bald man inside of the room. He wasted no time once he was inside. He went straight to the bed and pulled out a compact-sized Sig 9 mm pistol along with what looked exactly like a small garage door remote. After he set both onto the bed he turned toward her and spoke for the first time since entering the room.

"Here's everything you need. It shouldn't take no longer than a hour after you leave here to handle your business. I'll be here waiting for you. Outside is a brown Buick LaCrosse, it has a police scanner sitting on the passenger's seat already tuned into the local police station as well as the sheriff's, so just in case you will have ears and a nice heads-up. But I highly doubt any of that will be necessary. This Sig is loaded and ready to fire, hopefully that won't be needed either." He reached in his back pocket and pulled out a piece of paper and gave it to her. "Study this on your way to the first jewelry store so when you get there you will know what to swipe. Any questions?"

Special smiled at the little man. "Nope. See you in a hour or so." She grabbed the gun and the device off of the bed and left the motel room without a backward glance. She found the Buick LaCrosse parked next to her Beemer. The keys were already in the ignition and the scanner was crackling with the sounds of police reporting their movements. *Time to get this money,* she thought as she started the car and pulled out of the parking lot of the motel.

Fifteen minutes later Special pulled in front of the Hollier Jewels store. She sat there for a few minutes and got her bearings before she pulled out the device and aimed it at the front door of the jewelry store. Just like Poppa Blue told her she heard a few beeps and a moment later the red light on the device turned green. She inhaled deeply. "Here we go, Special. This shit better work, Poppa Blue!" She got out of the car and went inside of the jewelry store. The first thing she noticed once she was inside of the store was that the Iranian saleslady was alone just like Poppa Blue said she would be.

Good, this is going to be nice and smooth, she thought as she smiled at the saleslady. "Hi, how are you doing today?"

"Hello, I'm fine. How may I help you?"

Special took off her Prada shades so the saleslady could see her eyes and know that she was not playing any games with her. "I want you to remain calm and do as I say, that way I won't have to use this." Special pulled out the Sig and continued. "Now, I want you to open those cases right there and calmly place all of those black diamond rings inside one of your bags. Do it nice and slow and make sure your hands never leave my sight."

"Yes, ma'am, pl . . . please don't hurt me. I'll do whatever you tell me to."

"That's good. Now let's get started." Special watched the saleslady as she did what she was told. Once all of the black diamond rings were placed inside of the store bag Special said, "Now, let's see, place that bag on top of the counter here and grab another one and fill it up with those diamond bracelets, as well as those diamond necklaces over in that case right there."

The saleslady followed Special's orders and went to the next case and began to fill up another bag. While she was bagging the goods Special noticed a diamond-bezel Rolex and smiled. *A perfect gift for Poppa Blue's old ass,* she thought. "Okay, now give me that bag and grab that platinum and diamond Rolex right there in that case." She pointed to the watch. After the saleslady had passed the Rolex to Special she said, "Now, I want you to turn around and go into the back of the store. You have a job to do so I expect you to be calling the police as soon as you can. For your sake though it would be best if you gave me five minutes before you do that. Understand?"

"Yes, ma'am, I understand," the saleslady said as she turned and went directly into the back of the store. Special had a smile on her face as she grabbed all of the bags and left the store calm as can be.

Seven minutes after leaving the Hollier Jewels store Special pulled in front of Real Diamonds Inc. and repeated the process she did in front of the other jewelry store. Once she saw the green light shine on the device she went inside of Real Diamonds Inc. and robbed them without any problems whatsoever. As she pulled away from the store she heard that the police had been called and were on their way to the Hollier Jewels store. Her heartbeat picked up a few beats as she tried her best to remain calm during the drive back to the Travel Lodge. The route back to the motel was simple and easy to remember as she took the exact backstreets Poppa Blue had showed her the day before. Ten minutes after leaving Real Diamonds Inc. she pulled back next to her Beemer and smiled. She jumped out of the car, leaving two of the four bags of stolen jewels on the passenger's seat right next to the police scanner, Sig, and the device that made those two robberies the easiest moves she'd ever been a part of. She went to the room and knocked on the door twice and said, "See ya, Lance." She then turned and went to her car and got inside. By the time she had her key in the ignition she saw Lance come out of the motel room and get inside of the Buick and leave. *Mission complete,* she thought as she pulled out of the parking lot headed toward the 5 Freeway back to Los Angeles.

Special pulled into Poppa Blue's driveway a little after 8:00 P.M. and felt as if a big weight had been removed from her shoulders. On the outside she looked calm and strong but on the inside she was a nervous wreck. The entire ride back to Los Angeles had been a bundle of nerves for her and she was glad it was over. *Time to get my money and chill,* she said to herself as she got out of the car and went to Poppa Blue's door. Before she was able to knock on the door, Bernadine, Poppa Blue's wife, opened it and said, "Hey there, how are you doing?"

Special smiled and gave Bernadine a tight hug. "I'm just fine, B. How are you?"

"Living and enjoying this life. God has blessed me with a child. Come on in, old fathead is in his office waiting for you."

Special followed her inside of the house and asked, "Where's little man at?"

"That ball-of-energy child is sleeping for now, but I expect for him to wake up any minute wanting a bottle. I'm telling you, girl, that boy can eat!"

They started laughing. "Will it be okay if I took a peek at him before I leave?"

Bernadine frowned at Special. "Now you know better than to even ask me something like that, child. Of course you can."

Special smiled. "Thanks. Let me go deal with old grumpy bones."

"Mm-hmm, you better deal with his butt before I have to go upside his head with a bat!"

Special gave Bernadine another hug and a kiss on her cheek. "You are something else."

Without bothering to knock, Special entered the office of Poppa Blue. He was sitting behind a big cherry wood desk with several stacks of what looked like one-hundred-dollar bills piled in front of him.

"That's what I'm talking about, Poppa Blue."

"Yeah, it's a pretty sight, ain't it? Come on in, girl, we got some problems."

Special took a seat facing the desk. "Problems? What's up now?"

"First the business then the bullshit. Here's the ends for your girls: 2.6-plus apiece. As you requested, here's $130,000 for you. The other 2.5 has already been forwarded to your account in the islands. The ends from the Bakersfield move will be added to your account in a day or two. Cool?"

"You know it. Now what's wrong, Poppa Blue?"

He sighed. "Before I get into that I need to ask you something: have you made any moves against any Cubans?"

"Cubans? Not knowingly."

"Ahh, that's what I thought."

"Talk to me, Poppa Blue."

"There's been some people I know who's been inquiring on your whereabouts, Special. There's supposed to be a photo of you floating in certain circles. Word is that when your location has been determined to contact these Cubans out in Florida."

"What did they say the reason is behind them wanting to find me?"

Poppa Blue shrugged his shoulder. "They didn't say shit. All they want to know is a location on you. Got any ideas why?"

Special had no idea.

"Look at this, let's run the last few moves you made and let's see if we can find a link to this shit."

"Other than that lick with Papio and the Indians everything else has been relatively small for real."

Poppa Blue thought about what she said and then grabbed the phone and made a call. "Hey, Troy, tell me something about those Cubans who's looking for Special."

"What you wanna know, Poppa Blue?"

"Give me some knowledge on their get down."

"The Suarez organization has they hands in a lot of shit, but mostly dope. Shit, they got work on all coasts. Other than that there's really not much more I can tell you, Poppa Blue."

"Thanks, Troy, I'll holla at you." Poppa Blue hung up the phone. "You never heard of the Suarez organization, Special?"

"Nope."

"They're some majors in the dope game. They run work on damn near all coasts, does that help?"

"Nope. I mean unless they're connected to that clown Rico we just hit in Denver; that's the only move I've made against any dope boys, at least lately."

"What do you mean lately?"

"Remember last year when I told you Papio blessed me with that three million dollar lick on that Italian fool Nicoli I was stalking?"

"Yeah, and?"

"That's the last dope boy move I made until Rico."

"Let's check and see if those Cubans has a link to either of those two, the Italian, and the fool in Colorado."

"How are you going to do that?"

"Easy. I'm going to call Jolly first, then I'll hit Nicoli myself. He's out in New York doing his thing now."

"New York? Oh shit, hold up, Poppa Blue. Is there a way you can check and see if those Cubans are connected in any way to those Indians out of Niagara?"

"Yeah, I can do that. What, you think this may have something to do with those fools you laid down for your man?"

Special gave Poppa Blue the evil eye for that comment. "Check on that shit and see what you find out, Poppa Blue. If it is then, man, I gats to get the fuck!"

"Calm down, don't go off panicking on me. If this is the case then we'll find a way around this shit. No need to be spooking too early. Go lay low at your fly-ass pad and let me run a check on all of this. I'll give you a call in a few days."

Special stood. "All right. I'm going to fly out to Vegas and chill with Keli and a friend of mines for a few days. You know how to get at me." She stopped at the door. "Oh, I almost forgot, here." She tossed him the bag of the extra jewels. "The platinum Roley is yours. Call it a early birthday gift, you old fart. Now maybe you can get rid of that cheap-ass Timex you always wear."

"Ha. Ha. Watch your six, Special. This shit is serious."

"You don't have to tell me that. I'm the one who got some fucking Cubans looking for my ass," she said as she turned and left the office. As she was walking toward the front door she saw Bernadine sitting on the couch in the living room, feeding her little man. Special smiled and waved but didn't stop; she was in no mood now to be looking at any kids. Her life was in danger and she didn't even know why. She didn't know who these Cubans were but her gut was telling her it had something to do with those fucking Indians. And if she was right that meant it was on! *Ugh!*

Chapter 8

"Come on, Twirl, bless ya girl with some of that bomb I know you're holding," Keli asked with her pretty smile on full beam.

Twirl shook his head no and said, "You are too damn fine to be fuckin' with this shit, Keli. Why you get down like that?" He stared at how good she was looking. Twirl considered himself the X man but for some reason he couldn't sell any to Keli. He was really feeling her but he didn't want to fuck with a broad who was caught up like she obviously was with the X pills. He knew that there was no way in hell he was even supposed to care, but for some reason, other than Keli having a bad-ass body, he did care.

Pouting, Keli told him, "It's not like I'm hooked on that shit. I just have a better time when I'm chilling with my peeps when I'm thizzin'."

"Does your nigga go for you while you're thizzin' on that shit? That nigga needs his ass kicked if he does," Twirl said with more emotion in his voice then he intended.

Keli smiled at him. "No nigga will ever run this, Twirl. I'm a grown-ass woman and I will do me however I want to do me. And for your info, buddy, I don't have a nigga. I haven't been with a man in a minute."

Now it was Twirl's turn to smile. "So you saying you do the ladies?"

"Yep. I loves me some pussy, baby."

"Me too!" Twirl said and they both started laughing.

"Don't get it twisted, I do women but I loves me some dick. It's just been hard for me to find a man who's strong enough to deal with a woman like me. I'm getting my own paper, I'm living how I wanna live, and no one tells me what to do or when to do it."

"That's what's up, baby, but still fucking with this shit ain't a good look. If you was mines I'd keep you happy and keep your bad ass—"

Keli finished his sentence. "In check? See, that's exactly what I'm talking about right there."

"Not like that, boo, what I mean is I'd let you do you but I'd always look out for your best interest. If checking your ass from time to time calls for it then so be it. There's no need for you to be out there goofy while making your moves. And that's exactly how you be whenever you get down with those pills. Straight goofy! But look, I gots to roll, my mans just got in town and it's time for me to make some power moves."

"So, you're not going to let me spend my money, Twirl?"

"Only if you let me take you out when you get back from your Las Vegas trip."

"Oh, so you trying to hit this, Twirl?" she asked playfully.

With a serious look on his face he said, "I'm trying to do way more than just hit that, Keli. But before I go there I gots to make damn sure your mind is as tight as your fine-ass body. Feel me?"

"Yeah, I feel you. Thank you, Twirl."

"What you thanking me for, girl?"

She stepped up to him and gave him a kiss on his cheek. "For caring."

Twirl stood and said, "Hey, I thought you wanted to spend something with me."

"Nah, baby, you changed my mind. I'd rather be able to get with you when I get back from my trip than do that goofy shit," she said as she walked out of the coffee shop with an extra switch in her firm hips.

Twirl watched her leave and smiled. "Yes! I'm going to crack that bad-ass broad," he said aloud as he paid for his latte and left to go meet Papio.

Twenty minutes later Twirl met Papio at his suite at the Westin Hotel. Papio smiled when he opened the door for Twirl. "What's good, my nigga?"

Twirl entered the suite. "Dog, you don't know how glad I am to have your ass back in action. Shit has been super dry out here lately."

"I thought you've been eating good being the X man and shit."

"Don't get it twisted, I am eating, but thangs ain't like they was when I was getting down with you. You know you're my hero, fool."

Papio smiled. "That's right. Well, don't worry because you already know your hero has some moves ready for us. Let me get with Mama Mia for a minute and do some catching up and then we'll see what Q has for us. What's the word on them streets on that issue, dog?"

"Dog, shit has been real quiet, but the word has been circulating that some Cuban cats are looking for her, too."

"What? Aww hell nah! That's going to fuck up everything! If she gets word that she's hot she'll bounce and we'll never find that bitch. She gats a nice vault now, she can go anywhere she wants and lay it down without ever making another move. That's so fucked up."

"Too late now. Ain't nothing we can do about that."

"Bullshit." Papio grabbed his cell and called Miami. When Castro answered the phone Papio told him, "Put Mr. Suarez on the phone, Castro, and please don't give me any shit. This is real important."

Hearing the urgency in Papio's voice told Castro to kill any of the normal riffraff he would usually give. "It's Papio, sir; he says its important." He passed the phone to Mr. Suarez.

Mr. Suarez accepted the phone. "*Señor* Papio, is everything okay?"

"No, sir, it isn't. I just made it to L.A. and I've found out that the word on the streets out here is some high-powered Cubans are trying to locate Special."

"I figured I'd put the word out there and see if that would help speed up finding out where this Special woman is."

"No disrespect, sir, but that wasn't a good idea at all. If she gets word that someone as strong as you is looking for her she will get spooked and shake the spot. That will make things terribly hard for me to locate her, especially if she has a substantial amount of money to move on like the chief said she has."

"I see. So what would you have me do, Papio?"

"Send word to your people that Special isn't the person you thought was responsible for crimes made against you and yours. Hopefully that will let things fall back to normal, if not, then she's gone and it will take a whole lot of luck to find her ass."

"Done. I hope I haven't made this more difficult for you, Papio. I really want this put to bed rather quickly; that's why I made that call."

"I understand, sir. Time will tell whichever way it will fall. I'll be in touch."

"Adios, *Señor* Papio." Mr. Suarez hung up the phone.

"Okay, can you please explain to me that conversation you just had?" asked Twirl with a confused look on his face.

Papio smiled and then explained everything to Twirl. When he finished Twirl looked at him as if he were the smartest man in the world; either that or the luckiest.

"So, you're telling me you have the opportunity now to squash a bill that's close to ten tickets for killing Special. The same Special who set you up with the Indians and was about to leave you for dead? The same Special who shot your ass up in Texas and left two dead bodies for you to deal with? On top of all of that shit this Indian chief gave you a million dollars in advance because he trusts that you will handle the business all because this Cuban fool Mr. Suarez stamped you?"

Smiling, Papio said, "Yep, that's about it. Now you see why it's so important that I get that bitch?"

"You fucking right I see. Now we got to see what the streets will be talking about in a day or so to see if your man was able to make some damage control. If that works then we should be able to get a line on her ass sooner or later."

"Exactly. I'm banking on the sooner rather than the later though. Until then I'm going to chill for a week or so and get things together with Q and check some of my other peoples to see what we can get into. You remember that clown-ass nigga Grasshopper we the 1-2 on?"

"Yeah, what's up with his ass?"

"He still owes us from that move remember? It's been over a year so I might as well get some spending money from his wack ass."

Twirl started laughing. "Dog, you don't miss shit. Here it is you've been out of play for months, damn near a whole year, and yet you can get right back out here and start to make moves as if you've never been gone. You are the shit, my nigga; you're definitely my—"

Papio started laughing. "I know. I'm your hero! As long as you fuck with me you will get money, my nigga, remember I got a goal to get, so you need to be stacking this shit because once I get that one hundred mill I'm out the game for good."

"I've been stacking paper like a mothafucka, dog, and believe me when I tell your ass I'm trying to retire from the game right along with your ass. Real talk!"

"That's what's up. Now, did you bring my baby?"

"Yeah, it's parked downstairs in the valet parking. I sure hate that your ass is back for real, that Aston Martin has helped my bitch game tremendously!"

Papio laughed. "Yeah, it's definitely a bitch catcher. All sure you get at me ASAP. If shit comes out before a week you be ready because we will move as soon as I get word on any solid moves."

"You know me, G. I stay ready."

"This I do know," Papio said.

Keli and Special's short flight from Los Angeles to Las Vegas landed at seven that evening. They were meeting Dena at their hotel suite at the MGM Grand in a few hours. Until then they were going to go get checked into their hotel and relax before the fun began. They planned on gambling, sexing, shopping, and more gambling and sexing for the next three days. Special needed this break more than anything, especially with all of this Cuban foolishness that had come up.

Even though Poppa Blue hadn't been able to come up with anything new on the situation, she was still stuck believing that the Cubans were somehow connected to those Indians. If that was the case that meant her life was on the line, so it would be time to put her exit plan in motion. She had way more than enough money to disappear and live a good life somewhere like Aruba. *This move will be made earlier than I originally planned but I'd be better off making it earlier than not at all,* she thought as she followed Keli out of the airport and into the hot desert heat.

They caught a cab to the MGM and checked into a humongous suite. She smiled because she knew that no matter what happened later on she was going to enjoy the moment now and have a relaxing three days chilling with Keli's and Dena's sexy asses. Her mind was made up but she was still afraid; she didn't know what was going to pop off and that scared her. She wasn't used to being scared; this was totally a new feeling for her. Even though she knew Poppa Blue would watch her back she wondered if she should get at Papio and let him know what the business was. She shook that thought out of her head quickly, because there was no way Papio would give a damn about her and her problems. She fucked that off when she pulled the triggers of those guns out in Texas.

Stop! Stop it, Special. Deal with this shit how it comes, when it comes. You're in Las Vegas to chill so chill the fuck out and relax, she told herself as she stepped on to the balcony of their suite and stared out on to the famous Las Vegas strip. The bright lights up and down the strip were mesmerizing; Las Vegas was constantly growing with more and more outrageously huge casinos being built all the time. Though she had been to Las Vegas several times she seemed to always be shocked with how yet another huge hotel/casino had been erected on the strip.

She inhaled the desert air. *Everything will be all right,* she said to herself. She reentered the suite and saw Keli lying on the sofa in the living room of the suite, completely naked with her legs wide open. Keli seductively motioned with her forefinger for Special to come to her. Special began to undress as she slowly walked toward Keli, licking her lips in anticipation of what was about to happen next. Without saying a word Special stepped in front of Keli and pulled off her thong, climbed on top of her face and sighed as Keli began to eat her pussy slowly. *Mmmmm, yes, everything is going to be just fine,* she thought as she held on to the sides of the sofa as Keli continued to devour her pussy with her wicked tongue.

Mama Mia made the sign of the cross across her chest when she saw her only child pull into the driveway of their home in Riverside, California. *Thank you Father, thank you for bringing my* mijo *back to me safely,* she prayed silently as she wiped her hands on the apron that was around her waist and quickly stepped to the front door to meet her son.

Papio had a huge smile on his face when he saw his mother open the door to his home. "Hey, *Madre,* how ya doing?" He hugged her really tight for a minute.

"I've missed you so much, *mijo.* If it wasn't for your friends I would have lost my mind with worry. Please don't do that to me anymore okay?"

"I'm sorry, *Madre*, I didn't mean to cause you to worry, things got a little out of hand. You know if something ever happens to me you will be notified by Quentin and you will be taken care of, so don't ever think anything is wrong unless you hear it firsthand from him."

"Okay. Come, come inside so we can eat and talk some more." She led him inside of the house and Papio felt real good to be home. After Mama Mia had him seated in the dining room she began busying herself in the kitchen, preparing him a plate of her special enchiladas that Papio loved. He smiled as she set a steaming plate of enchiladas in front of him. "Now you eat because when you finish we have lot to talk about." Before he could say a word she returned to the kitchen. He shook his head and smiled as he dug into his food.

After Papio finished eating Mama Mia came into the dining room and he asked her, "Have you heard from Special since I've been gone, *Madre*?"

With a puzzled expression on her face she said, "No, I haven't, *mijo*. Tell me, what did you do to run that beautiful woman away?"

"I didn't do anything to her but try my very best to let her know how much I was in love with her."

"Was? You no longer in love with her, Preston?"

Papio didn't want to tell his mother what happened but he also refused to lie to her. He respected her too much for any of that. "I hate her, *Madre*. I can't stand her and whenever I see her I'm going to hurt her."

Before his mother could speak he raised his hands and continued. "She hurt me, *Madre,* she hurt me physically as well as emotionally." He stood and pulled down his Ed Hardy jeans so his mother could see the two bullet holes, one in each of his thighs. "She shot me, *Madre*."

"She did what? Why would she do something like that to you, *mijo*? This no sound right to me," Mama Mia said, shaking her head slowly.

Papio pulled his jeans back up, sat back down, and told his mother what happened in Texas. He hated putting her in his business but she needed to know exactly why Special wouldn't be coming around them ever again.

After he finished Mama Mia smiled at him and, "So, she saved your life from the men who came to hurt you and then she shoots you to stop you from coming after her. Now you want to hurt her for that, *sí?*"

"*Sí.* I'm going to make sure she pays for crossing me the way she did. I have never wanted to hurt a woman as much as I want to hurt her, *Madre.*"

With a wave of her small hands Mama Mia stood and said, "Bah! You can't hurt that woman, *mijo,* you still love her. I see it in your eyes. The eyes, they no lie."

Papio shook his head. "No, *Madre,* I don't. And, believe me, when I see her I'm going to do more than hurt her. I'm going to kill her. Now please change the subject okay?"

"Sure, *mijo.* Are you going to be home for a while this time?"

"I don't have any plans on leaving L.A. anytime soon, so yeah, I'm home for a little bit. Why, what you got up in that gorgeous head of yours?" he asked with a smile on his face.

"The movies! I hear there are some very good movies we can go watch, *sí?*"

He gave his mother a kiss. "*Madre,* we can go to the movies every day if you like. Right now I need to get showered and get some sleep. I'm kind of tired."

She smiled as she thought about what her child had just told her. She knew that there was no way in the world he would ever be able to harm Special. He was still in love with her; she knew it because he had the same look his father had whenever he denied his feelings. That brightened her smile as she went into the kitchen and began to clean up.

Dena had arrived at the MGM Grand a little after 10:00 P.M. She went straight to the suite and was met with hugs, kisses, and smiles from both Special and Keli. After taking a quick shower and getting dressed in some comfortable clothing, Dena came into the living room of the suite and smiled as she watched Special set stacks and stacks of what looked like hundred dollar bills onto the coffee table.

"Here you go, Dena, $2,630,000, a even four-way split between you, me, my connect, and Keli here."

Dena stepped to the sofa and sat down and stared at all of the money that was stacked in front of her. "Thank you. Thank you both so much. God, you don't know how good I am now knowing I can shake that miserable husband of mines."

"Do you think it's going to be that simple, Dena? I mean that joker may present trouble for you later in the game," said Keli seriously.

"That man is crazy and a freak but he ain't no fool. I'm headed back to Georgia and I wish his ass would try to come out that way messing with me. I didn't have a dime before and he used that to control me; now his ass can't touch me. I got enough money to live my life the way I want to. And you better believe I'm not even worried about Kevin's wack ass!" They all started laughing.

"Okay, then, with the business out of the way it's time for us to have some fun! Come on, girl, put all of that damn money inside of the safe so we can go hit the casino up and get our gamble on. After that we're getting fly so we can go clubbing," Keli said as she smiled at Dena with a lustful look in her eyes.

Returning that same lustful look Dena asked, "What are we doing after we finish getting our club on?"

Keli laughed. "Make each other come until the sun comes up!"

Special shook her head and was about to speak but was interrupted by her cell phone ringing. She saw that it was Poppa Blue on the caller ID and quickly answered. "What up, Poppa Blue?"

"Some strange shit has happened, but it looks all good though. The word is out that it was a mistake on the Cubans' part. They're no longer interested in finding you."

"That's the business. You don't know how relieved I am to hear that shit, Poppa Blue."

"Yeah, I felt the same way until I ran shit through my old head a few more times. Something doesn't feel right, baby girl, so until I can check into this more thoroughly I still want you to move as if shit is still hot, you got me?"

"Yeah, but—"

"No buts, Special! Let me do me and trust this old gut of mines. I've been in this shit long enough to feel when some shit just ain't good. You hear me?"

"Yeah, I hear you."

"Don't sound all down. Everything will be all right regardless of how we got to get down. I just have to be sure we ain't getting thrown for a loop. So do you, and have some fun out there. When you get back this way

I want you to lay it down at the house and relax. I may have some simple moves worth a nice chunk of change for you in a week or so."

"I hear you. Let me go. I'm about to go get my gamble on."

"All right. Make sure you keep your eyes open at all times, even while you're out that way."

"I always do, Poppa Blue, I always do," Special said as she closed her phone. She forced a smile on her face and told Keli and Dena, "All right, ladies, it's time to go see if we can win us some more money!" They gathered their things and left the suite, headed downstairs toward the casino area. Special was smiling on the outside but she was a nervous wreck on the inside. *I still can't shake this fucking feeling that all of this shit is going to end up leading me right back to Papio. Papio, damn,* she thought as she stepped into the elevator.

Chapter 9

Mama Mia was disappointed in Papio. She couldn't believe that after three very fast days he was already about to leave her again. "You promised me you would not be leaving again for a while, *mijo*," she said with a sad look on her face.

Her words sliced through him. "It's not like that, *Madre*. I'll be gone for a day or two. I have to go down to San Diego to meet some people for some serious business. Don't worry. I'll be back before you know it."

She sighed. "Be careful, *mijo*, and please make sure you give me a call to let me know you are okay, *sí?*"

"*Sí, Madre*, I will. Love you." He grabbed his carry-on bag and left the house before his mother became even more emotional. When he was inside of his car he grabbed his cell and called Twirl. "What's good, my nigga?"

"Just waiting on you, my hero, what's what with you?" asked Twirl.

"About to roll down to San Diego for a day or so to meet with some folks. Q hasn't got back at me yet so I decided to go check on some shit that way real quick like."

"You want me to roll with you?"

"Nah, I'm good. If shit looks good I'll hit you and you can roll down then."

"That's right. What up with that bitch nigga Grass-hopper?"

"The Feds knocked that nigga like a month ago. Plus, the word is that fool may have smoked his girlfriend last year, so he has a fork stuck in his ass because he's definitely done, game over."

"Oh well."

"My sentiments exactly. All right, I just wanted to touch base with you to let you know the business. Stay ready so you won't have to get ready."

"For sure," Twirl said.

Before Papio could close his phone it started ringing. He smiled when he saw that it was Brandy calling from Oklahoma City. "Hey, *mami,* what's good with you?"

"Missing you like crazy, daddy. What are you up to out there?"

"Doing what I do best, making a few moves and checking a few traps. I'm on my way to San Diego now to meet with Ringo's cousin from Negril."

"I sure will be glad when you fly me out to L.A. to spend some time in the sun with you."

"You know what? That sounds like a good idea. When can you take some time off?"

"If I put in for it now, in a week or so."

"Go on and put it in then. I'll fly you out here and we'll make it do what it do."

"For real, daddy?" she asked, excited.

"Have I ever been anything else but real with you, *mami?*"

"Nope, that's why I love you so much."

"All right then. Check it, I gots to go. I'll give you a call later on this evening."

"I love you, daddy."

He smiled into the receiver. "That's what's up, because daddy loves you too."

He knew she was loving that corny shit for real. He loved her in his own way but there was no way he could ever love a woman again, not seriously anyway. Special ruined that for him. *Special, damn I hate that bitch,* he thought as he turned on to the freeway headed toward San Diego, California.

Special pulled into the circular driveway of her luxurious home located in the Hancock Park area of Los Angeles. *Home.* Her home was her most prized possession and she loved being there. She felt totally safe here, not only because it was in a safe area but because of the security measures she and Poppa Blue set up when she bought the place five months back. She grabbed her bag and got out of her car and stared at her home from the outside. One of the largest homes in the area, her home exuded elegance and warmth.

She stepped through the front door, set down her bag in the foyer, and went directly up to her bedroom. After kicking off her Nike running shoes she fell on the bed and said, "Damn it feels good to be home." Though she was still worried about what Poppa Blue told her she refused to worry too much, because she knew she was safe as could be at her home. No one knew where she rested except for Poppa Blue and his wife. Even though Keli was a trusted comrade there was no way Special would ever let anyone know where her safe haven was located. She kept an apartment out in Marina del Rey for business and the extra shit, and that's where Keli thought she lived.

Now that Special was home she wanted to use this time to make some serious decisions. The first one that needed to be made was whether she was going to get in contact with Papio's ass. Not only did she miss him, but she had to admit she loved that man. On top of that it looked like she was going to need him, too, and that sucked, because she didn't know how to even approach him. *That nigga is most likely thinking about how he's going to murder my ass and here I am thinking about calling asking him for some damn help. Have I lost my damn mind?* she asked herself as she lay flat on her back and stared at the ceiling. The next decision that had to be made was if she was going to shut it down and leave the life.

All of that depended on if Poppa Blue found out something wasn't kosher with those Cubans. *Ugh, this shit is crazy. How can I go from being so damn good to being so damn confused and caught up? Ugh! This life is truly a fucking trip,* she thought. *Maybe I can still shake the spot and make moves from out the way. Come back and do me whenever Poppa Blue has something proper for me? Nah, fuck that, it's either I'm in or out. Later for that shit. Right now I'm about to go out back, get in the pool, and relax. When it's time to make it happen I'll make it happen,* she said to herself as she got off of the bed and pulled off her sweats. She stepped to her dresser and pulled out a string bikini swimsuit and slipped it on. She then grabbed the cordless phone and went outside to the backyard.

After getting comfortable in the shallow end of the pool she sighed and again wondered what Papio was doing at that very moment. Before she could change her mind she grabbed the cordless phone and called Mama Mia. She smiled when Mama Mia answered the phone. "Hello, you beautiful woman you. How have you been, *Madre?*"

"Special? Is this you?"

"*Sí*, it's me. How have you been?"

"Lonely, but fine I guess. You and my only child have chosen to desert me and I have missed you both terribly."

Hearing this made Special feel extremely guilty. "I'm sorry, *Madre,* but a whole lot has happened since the last time we saw each other."

"Bah, I know about all of that. What does that have to do with you picking up a telephone and giving me a call so we can talk?"

"You know about what? Did Papio tell you what happened between us, Mama Mia?"

"*Sí.* He told me everything, and I don't want to talk about that because I know you did what you did to save us both. He's stubborn of course and swears he hates you, but I see different."

"What do you mean?"

"I see the love he has for you in his eyes. The eyes, they no lie, Special. My son loves you bad. You hurt him, though, and for that reason he will be stubborn and try to fight the love he has for you. But you cannot fight real love. Do you understand me, *mija?*"

With tears sliding down her face Special said, "*Sí, Madre,* I understand. Tell me, what am I to do to help him get past what I did?"

"Time. Time heals all wounds, *mija,* be patient. But first you also must let him know how you feel about him. I know you love my son as well as myself because your actions say so. You would never have did what you did if you didn't. For that reason only is why I forgive you for hurting my child. He uses the scars to fuel his anger toward you, but I see them and think you did that to save your life, so I understand."

"You truly are a very special person you know that?"

"Bah, if I was so special then why haven't you called me before now?"

"I—"

"I don't want to hear excuses. I want to see you. I want to talk to you face to face. Preston is in the San Diego now taking care of business. He will be there for two days more. So when do I see you, *mija?*"

"Tomorrow. I'll come and get you and we'll go get a massage and spend the day together catching up. And, believe me, I have a lot to tell you, *Madre.*"

"I'll be waiting anxiously, *mija.* Now let me get back to my garden. I'll see you tomorrow, *sí?*"

"*Sí, Madre.*" Special hung up the phone feeling extremely giddy. "He still loves me! Yes! My Clyde still loves his Bonnie!" she screamed as she dipped her head into the pool and swam to the deeper end of the pool. After swimming back to the shallow end she thought about what Mama Mia had just told her. *He may still love me but right now he's trying to make himself hate me. I have to get at him. But first I'll spend the day with Mama Mia; that way I'll get a better feel on his fine ass. Damn, I am in love with that nigga.*

Papio made it to San Diego and went to the Hilton to relax until he got the call from Fay, Kingo's first cousin from Jamaica. Papio thought she sounded jazzy with her sultry Jamaican accent when he had spoken with her earlier. She told him that her other cousin Kango, Kingo's younger brother, was coming to town. Papio hoped they had a takeover planned because that was just what he needed right about now. *A takeover: a three-and-a-half minute bank robbery that gets you plenty of money.* Papio smiled as he thought about the takeover he participated in with Kango and his crew out in New York last year. That was one of the easiest moves he had ever been a part of. *Yeah, this San Diego trip may just come out lovely,* he thought as he grabbed his cell and sent a text to Fay letting her know he was at the Hilton.

He took a shower and just as he finished there was a knock at the door. He wrapped a towel around himself and went to see who was there. He smiled when he saw a dark-skinned older woman with a fly short Halle Berry–like haircut. From what he could see through the peephole she looked thick as Thelma from the show *Good Times* did back in the days. He opened the door. "Hello, you must be Fay. Come on in."

Fay stepped inside of the room and said, "Why you no dress, mon? I text you back to tell you mi on mi way to come and get yah. You no get mi text?"

"Nah, I was in the shower I didn't check my phone. My bad, give me a few minutes and I'll be ready. Have a seat."

Fay frowned as she sat down and watched as Papio went to his carry-on bag and pulled out a pair of jeans and a T-shirt. She openly checked him out and was nodding her head in appreciation of what she was staring at. "You look good, mon. I wonder if I should take you to the rompin shop real quick," she stated boldly.

Knowing from Kingo that the rompin shop meant having sex, Papio smiled at her. "Business first, *mami;* there's always time for playing later."

"T'is is true. So, you know my baby cousin Kango also?"

"Yeah, we did some things out his way last year. Has he made it out here yet?"

"Later tonight him and his men will be here."

His men. That means the crew is coming with him and that can only mean it is time for another take-over, Papio thought as he slipped on his fresh pair of Air Force 1's. He then stepped into the bathroom and made sure he was straight while adding a quick squirt of cologne to make sure Fay knew he not only looked good but smelled good as well. When he stepped back into the room he could tell she in fact liked how he was looking because she was eating him up with her eyes. *I hope my niggas Kingo and Kango won't be too salty at me for knocking this bad-ass broad off,* he thought. "All right, I'm ready. Where are we going anyway?"

"To eat. Afterward we go chill until time to get my baby cousin and his men. You do like to eat, don't you, mon?"

"You better believe it, baby."

Fay gave him a nod as she stood. "Good, mon, real good. Come, we go now."

Papio grabbed his cell and clipped it to his belt and followed Fay out of his hotel room, thinking about how he hoped she could fuck as good as she looked. *Wow!*

Special and Mama Mia spent the entire day getting pampered. By the time they made it back to Mama Mia's house they were both exhausted. Special was so relieved to have been able to talk to Mama Mia in depth. She felt as if a huge burden had been removed from her shoulders. Mama Mia made her feel that everything was going to be all right and that feeling was something she wanted desperately to keep a hold of. Papio still remained the wild card in everything though. Would he be able to accept Special after everything that had gone on between them? Mama Mia knew for certain he would but Special still had doubts. Time would tell.

Before saying good-bye Mama Mia told Special, "You know I have to see for myself in order to be positive."

"Believe me, when you see what I've told you, you will have no doubts whatsoever. Give me some time to make it happen, okay?"

"*Sí.* I have nothing but time. In the meantime I will be having a serious talk with Preston." She put her hand on top of Special's. "Don't worry, *mija,* everything will be fine. I knew when I first saw you that you were the right woman for my son and I still feel that way."

"Thank you for that, Mama Mia. I hope you're right." She gave Mama Mia a kiss and waited as she got out of the car and made it inside of the house safely. She headed back home feeling as if there was hope for her and Papio's future together.

Yes! she thought as she turned on the CD player and started jamming her favorite song, "Birthday Sex" by Jeremih. Even though it wasn't a top jam anymore it was still her favorite because whenever she heard it she thought about her Clyde. Papio was the man she wanted and it felt real good just thinking about them being together again. She knew she was on some square shit but it felt good and she wanted to be with Papio so bad it hurt. She was in love.

Her cell phone rang. When she saw it was Poppa Blue calling she hoped he was about to give her some much-needed good news. Her hopes were in vain.

"It's time to make preparations for the exit plan. Those Cubans are full of shit. You've made their list because you crossed out those Seneca Indians. Their father, chief of their tribe, is linked tightly to the Cubans. The Suarez organization is heavy and they've been working together for years."

"But how does he know about me? I never met no damn chief."

"I'm holding on to a copy of a surveillance photo that looks liked it was taken at a casino or somewhere like that. This is what was circulating for the last few days. My man tells me that the chief knows you set up his sons and beat them for a lot of money. The exact amount is unknown but you and I know what's what. It's time to shake the spot, Special; the game's over."

"Fuck! There's gotta be another way to deal with this shit, Poppa Blue. I'm not ready to bounce! Ugh!"

"There is no other way, Special. It's either bounce now or wait and see how long it takes for those Cubans to find you. From what my man tells me they already hired a gun to find you. That's why they tried to pull back the word on the streets to keep you in the dark so they could get at you easier. You really wanna play with those kind of niggas? Is it worth it? I say no, you got enough to vanish and live a normal life somewhere. This is the type of shit we prepared for years ago. I hate it but it's time to handle things like we planned."

"All right, get started. But don't sell my home. I'm keeping my house, Poppa Blue! Because whether you believe it or not I'm going to find a way out of this shit!" She hung up the phone and felt as if she was going to cry. *Nah, fuck the tears.* It was time to take the offense and see if she could salvage her crazy life. The only way she knew how to do that was to get in contact with the only man she knew who could bring the noise with her. The question was would he help her? *Damn. Papio, I saved your ass. It's time for you to return the favor, nigga. Fuck!*

Chapter 10

Fay took Papio out to eat at a local Jamaican restaurant she frequented. During the drive to the restaurant she explained to him some of her moves. She told him how she was considered the go-to man in San Diego; in her case she was the go-to woman. There wasn't much that went on out there illegally that Fay didn't have her hands on. She was a well-known supplier of everything from guns to drugs and she was also well known when it came down to some murder shit. Not only was she held in high regard for sending out her savages to murder up shit, she was wicked enough to put shit down on her own. She was known for her specialty: killing with her bare hands. *So that's why Kingo gave me her number when I thought I might need some help for those Cubans. His cousin is a straight gangsta for real,* Papio thought as he continued listening to her give him a description of her get down.

She finished just as she pulled into the parking lot of the restaurant. She smiled at him and said, "Hope I haven't scared you off, Papio. I would really like to get to know you intimately. You look like you could do some damage to mi bumpa."

Papio smiled at her and with a Jamaican accent of his own told her, "Fay, nuh she word, mon, everything kwel. Mi nah go no weh, and I can't wait to see how good that nookie be."

She smiled at him.

***

Forty minutes later, after enjoying a nice Jamaican meal of jerked chicken, rice, peas, and some kind of fish stew, Papio sat back in his seat and sighed. "That was good."

"Yeah, it was, mon. Now, tell me, Papio, how did you and mi older cousin Kingo get so close to one another when you were in the bing?"

Papio shrugged his shoulders. "We were cellmates for almost three years and we just clicked. Kingo is a good dude and I trust him with my life. I'm out here now making moves not only for myself but to ensure when he touches in the next three years he will be good, too."

"I see. No worry there, mon, my cousin will be just fine whenever they let him out the bing. He was doing quite well before he went in there and he will be fine when he returns."

"That's right. Check it, what's up with this move you got for me out here?"

Fay smiled brightly. "Something has came to me that will change the game completely, mon. The takeover game is about to be taken to an entirely higher level and the risks are going to be minimal."

"What are you talking about, Fay?"

She checked the time on her watch. "Later. We go now and get my cousin and his men, then we talk further." She stood from the table and left a hundred dollar bill on the table and strolled out of the restaurant with Papio in tow.

Fay parked the car at the curb in front of the arrival terminal of American Airlines. While they were waiting for Kango and his crew Papio asked, "If Kango is bringing his crew it's going to be rather crowded in here, don't you think?"

She smiled at him. "No worry, mon, all of that is handled already. Now tell me, after the business is over tonight will you be ready to give me a back shot? 'Cause I do plan to tek you to mi rompin shop and do you one."

"Hey, you're the boss of San Diego. Who am I to tell your sexy ass?"

"Good. I like that," she said with a smile on her face as she sat back in her seat and waited for her young cousin and his crew.

As soon as Keli made it back from Las Vegas she called Twirl to let him know she was back in town and that she wanted to hole up with him. He smiled as he listened to her tell him how much she had been thinking about him during her trip.

"So, you're saying you're feeling a nigga huh?" Twirl asked as he sat down in his living room.

"Boy, if I wasn't feeling you we wouldn't be talking right now, you better quit playing with me. And don't even try that weak-ass shit trying to play hard to get with me either. I know you're feeling me too, Twirl."

He laughed. "Yeah, how do you know that?"

"I see it in your eyes whenever I'm around your sexy ass."

"You may be confusing lust with me feeling you. I mean you are one bad-ass female, how do you know if all I want to do is fuck?"

"Stop playing with me, Twirl! Are we hooking up or what?"

"Are you going to slow it down with fucking with those pills and shit?"

"Will that make you happy?"

"On some real shit, yeah, it would. It's like this, baby: I'm feeling you, I mean really feeling you. But in order for me to let you be a part of my world I have to be able to trust you. Trust with me doesn't come all that easy. Knowing how you get down makes it even harder for me to trust you. Not saying you're on some grimy shit, but a nigga gots all types of shit going on and I don't have the energy nor extra time to be having to watch your fine ass all of the time."

"I respect that. Now check this one out, sexy: I'm a boss bitch and you know it. I play with the pills a little, yeah, but that's just when I want to play. When it comes to my business I am a million-dollar bitch and I play no games. Trust isn't easily given on my end neither, boo, but I've been watching your fine ass for a minute now and I like what I see, as well as what I've heard about you. Let's kill the wack shit and make it happen. I'm not asking to be wifey, Twirl; let's kick it and see where this goes. We're both in the life and we're both eating good; let's eat good together and see how this shit goes."

Damn, this broad is tighter than I thought, he said to himself before responding to her straightforwardness. "I'm with that, baby. So, what you getting into tonight?"

Keli pumped her small fists in the air and mouthed the word "yes!" She calmed herself quickly and said, "Hopefully I'll be getting into your fine ass later on."

"Nah, not gon' happen tonight, ma. I gots to handle some business out in Inglewood and after that I'll be at Kaboom making sure my business is being handled there."

"You gon' pull a all-nighter?"

"Nah, but it will be a late night for the kid."

"Why don't I meet you at Club Kaboom and we kick it while you handle your BI, then afterward we can go have some breakfast or whatever?"

"Or whatever huh?"

"Yeah, or whatever, nigga." They both laughed. "Seriously, Twirl, we can kick it and chop it up all while you do you."

"That's what's up. Meet me at Kaboom around midnight. I'll be posted in VIP."

"But, of course, I'd expect nothing less from your boss ass."

"You know it. And make sure you have on something real tasty, a nigga loves looking at your super fine ass."

She laughed and flirtatiously told him, "So all you like to do is look huh? What a shame."

"Believe me, ma, when I get a hold of your ass I'll be doing way more than just looking."

"Promise?"

"My word on my mother's life."

"Mmmmmm, that's what's up. See ya at midnight, baby." She hung up the phone with a gigantic smile on her face.

Papio and Fay were still chatting with one another when he saw Kango come out of the airport followed closely by his crew: Steven, Macho and his brother Brad. Papio was surprised when Fay started her car and pulled away from the curb without saying a word. "Hey, what are you doing leaving your people?"

"They will meet us at mi home. I had to make sure that they arrived safely with no tails. They good now, so now we go to mi home," she told him and continued driving.

Before he could say something his cell rang. Papio pushed the number five on his phone to accept the pre-paid call and said, "What's good, my dreaded friend?"

"Papio, you do good now I see. Finally outta ya funk, mon?"

"Was never in no damn funk, Kingo, just tripping a little bit. I'm good though, what about you?"

"You keep me straight so you know I'm well, mon. I can tell everything kriss with you out there because of what I see in here," Kingo said, referring to Brandy.

"You know how I do it."

Kingo laughed. "Yeah, mi know. Tell me, have you heard from that woman who stole your heart and then broke it in two?"

"Funny. Nah, that bitch Special knows to stay as far away from me as possible. It's curtains for her ass if I ever see that bitch again."

"Watch what you say, mon. You forget what kind of phone we on?"

"My bad. What's up with you though?"

"Not much, the same old thing, working out and staying good in this place. I go to team next month and my point may drop so it looks like I might get to go to the low."

Papio thought about what Kingo just told him and asked, "Why would you want to do that? I mean you're good there why go to a low?"

"I'm undecided because I want a change of scenery, you know, mon. Plus mi want to get closer to mi queen. But then again mi don't want go somewhere with no weights so I may decline it. No worry, though, every-thing kriss. What's with you? Have you gotten at mi people yet?"

Papio had a smile on his face as he looked at Fay as she drove toward her home. "As a matter of fact I have. I'm sitting right next to your fine-ass cousin Fay right now. Why didn't you tell me she was such a sexy older woman?"

"Mi older but I'm not your matter! I can do things to your young self that never been done!" Fay said, and started giggling.

"You be good with my cousin, Papio. I'm telling you, mon, she will eat you alive!" Kingo started laughing. "Let me speak to her a minute huh?"

Papio passed Fay his cell and smiled as he listened to the two cousins speak in their native tongue. He couldn't understand all of what they were saying because he wasn't fluent in patois but he did pick up a few phrases he knew, like bow, which means to perform oral sex; buddy, which means penis; boot, which means condom; and a few other select freaky words Fay used. He shook his head and smiled. *I am definitely going to enjoy knocking this freaky old female off*, he thought, and smiled again as Fay turned slightly and gave him his cell back.

"What it do, my man?"

"The phone's about to go so I'll get with you in a few days. Looks like all is good for you then huh?"

"Yeah, I told you I was straight."

"Stay focused and, remember, make every move the right move, mon."

"You better believe it. Later, dread," Papio said as he hung up the phone. He smiled at Fay and said, "Why were you telling him all of that freaky shit?"

She smiled shyly. "I hide nothing from my family. I just wanted him to know what my intentions are. He understands me better than anyone in this wicked life, mon."

"What did he say when you told him how you want to have your way with me?"

She laughed before saying, "He told me to go easy on you, you're still a child!"

Papio frowned. "Now ain't that a bitch. You're going to be in some trouble later, lady."

They pulled into the driveway of Fay's home, but before they were able to get out of the car a brown GMC Denali pulled in behind them. Fay smiled as she stepped to the truck and greeted Steven first. "Look at my baby brother. How you do, mon?" She gave him a hug and a kiss on his cheek.

Steven smiled at his sister and returned the greeting. He pulled from her embrace and stepped to Papio. "What's good, mon? You good?"

Papio shook his hand. "Always. And you?"

"Ready to make it happen, you know how we do," Steven said as everyone else greeted one another as they went inside of Fay's home.

Once they were inside and comfortable Fay wasted no time with preliminaries. "Okay, mon, I got good news for you. A friend of mines in Los Angeles has developed a device that can change the takeover game completely." She then went on to explain that her friend Lance invented a device that could disable the silent alarm inside of any bank, as well as their surveillance system before they entered the bank to rob it. After she finished the men stared at one another in total disbelief.

"Come now, cousin, please don't tell me you've had us fly all the way West on a humbug?" asked Kango. "You know something like that is damn near impossible."

Fay frowned at him. "Do you really tink I have the time to waste, cousin? Lance is vertical and he knows better to approach me with anything that would be a waste of mi time. He damn sure knows better than to try to play with mi money, mon. So, of course this is true and it damn sure is real."

"Has this Lance mon tested this device?" asked Brad as he lit up a blunt of the ganja weed Fay had given them upon entering her home.

"As a matter a fact he has. He had some of his people rob two jewelry stores back to back up in Bakersfield just last week and everything went perfect. The device he created deactivated all security cameras and disarmed all alarms before his people entered. I'm telling you, mon, this is exactly what we need to make more money than we've ever dreamed of having."

Kango saw the excitement in his cousin's eyes and knew that she was dead serious. "When do we put this device to use?"

Fay smiled. "Tomorrow afternoon. Lance will be here in the morning around eight or nine. I have already mapped out the routes I want you to take. You're going to hit two banks back to back. Wells Fargo off of Imperial, and Union Bank, that's about five blocks away."

"Vehicles?" asked Macho.

She smiled again. "Taken care of. You will use your primary vehicle to go to each bank. After the second takeover is complete you will then proceed to where your clean vehicle will be parked. Afterward you come back here and we count our money."

"If this goes without a problem what does this fellow Lance expect for letting us use his device?" asked Papio.

"Ten percent of each take."

"Why not just buy the damn thing if it's so perfect?" asked Steven.

"Lance doesn't want to sell. This is his ultimate come up and he wants to make sure no one gets a hold of it."

Papio smiled. "What's to stop us from taking it after we've finished our business with the banks?"

Fay shook her head. "Lance is no dummy. He knew that thought would cross our minds, that's why he informed me that he could disable the device at any given time and it would then become useless to us. We will remain on the up and up with him because this could make us more money than any other move we've ever made."

"Will he let us use the machine or device or whatever you call this thing on the East Coast?" asked Brad.

"He will. As long as we give him his agreed upon ten percent he will do business with us. There's also no worry of him dealing with too many others with this."

"How can you be so sure?" asked Kango.

"Because I know Lance. He's a scary man. If the word gets out that he's made this device every crooked man in Southern Cal will be looking to do him in for it. Let alone all of the heat that's going to come down once the Feds realize these robberies are going off so smoothly. No, we won't have to worry about Lance at all. So, is it agreed for tomorrow?"

With smiles on each of their faces the four Jamaican men and Papio all shook their heads yes.

"Good. Now relax and get some rest. When I return I'll take you and show the routes that will be used."

"Where are you going?" asked Steven.

Fay smiled mischievously and told her brother, "I have something to take care of."

Steven noticed how his older sister looked at Papio as she said this and shook his head. "Don't you ever stop, Fay?"

"Mind your business, baby brother!" They all started laughing.

Ten minutes after midnight Keli stepped into Club Kaboom looking divine in a sheer wrap-around skirt that left little for one's imagination. Her thick, firm legs were exposed by the split in the skirt to make every male head turn as she strutted into the club. When she made it to the VIP she saw Twirl talking to a couple of white men. She stepped up to the men and said, "Excuse me, gentlemen, but can I speak to my man for a sec?"

Each of the white men looked as if they were about to orgasm just by staring at the chocolate beauty who was standing before them. Twirl smiled. "I'll be right back, boys." He took Keli's hand and said, "Damn, girl, I told you to look tasty, not to come in this piece damn near naked!"

"You don't like?" she asked with a pout on her full, glossed lips.

He took inventory of her for a few seconds and said, "What's not to like? You damn right I like! But it's for me to enjoy, not the entire fucking club!"

"Stop hating, baby. They can look all they want, looking and touching are two totally different things. All of this ass belongs solely to you, baby. That is, if you want it."

Twirl smiled. "Oh, you're good. I mean really good."

"Uh-uh, *papi,* you got it twisted. I'm bad, very bad!"

"All right, bad ass, have a seat and order whatever you want to drink. I gots to finish speaking with my associates for a minute."

"Take your time. I'm good," she said as she sat down and finger waved to a few people she knew. Twirl shook his head as he went back and rejoined the white men and their conversation.

Keli felt her cell vibrating and smiled when she pulled it out and answered it. "What up, girl?"

"Damn, girl, you out clubbing already? You don't believe in the word 'rest' huh?" asked Special.

"I am resting. I'm chilling up here at Kaboom with the guy I told you about."

"Have you heard anything about somebody looking for me or asking about me in any way?"

"Uh-uh. You want me to get at my friend and see if he's heard anything?"

"Is that right? That's cool. Look, I'm thinking about shaking the spot for a minute and I was wondering if you wanna bounce with me?"

"For how long?"

"I don't know yet. For real I don't even know if I'm gonna bounce or not," Special said with obvious confusion in her voice.

Picking right up on that Keli asked, "What's wrong, Special?"

Special sighed. "Go on and enjoy your dude. Hit me in the morning and we'll do lunch and I'll put you up on everything."

"Are you sure? I mean I can shake this spot right now and meet you at your spot in under a hour."

That sentiment touched Special. "Nah, I'm good. We'll talk tomorrow though."

"All right."

"Tell me something though; he's in the life huh?"

"Yeah, he's straight though. Good dude for real."

"Get at him on some low shit, don't just throw my name out there. Hint about some shit and see what he says okay?"

"Cool. Girl, you know you got me curious as hell right about now. Fuck lunch, we're doing breakfast! You got me spooked, Special!"

"Believe me, K, I'm spooked my damn self. Breakfast it is. Be good, girl."

"Now you know damn well I'm too bad of a bitch to ever be good! Bye, girl." Keli hung up the phone, laughing.

Twirl came and joined her at the table and they began chatting about this and that while he watched as his runners made their moves inside of the club distributing X pills to whoever wanted to purchase any. "So, this is your get down? You do know that the owner of this club went to the Feds for some big X pill shit right?"

"Yeah, I know Siggy personally. Real solid dude. He's getting out in like a year or so I think."

"The fact that he got caught up doesn't spook you from getting down here?"

"Nah. It ain't like that. You know, damn near every club you hit out here has a bunch of niggas in there selling everything from weed, yayo, to the X. So what if I have a few people getting down like that? It's no biggie. The suits ain't trying to pop no runners with a few pills, they trying to knock the nigga with the major bundles and shit. It's all good, baby."

"I see. Other than pills what other shit you got popping, *papi*?"

"Whatever grooves makes the most, baby. That's why my ears are always to the streets. What about you, what's your major get down?"

"Different shit. Me and my girl, we hit a nice lick out in Colorado last week for a few tickets. Plus we took a chump nigga for his loot and jewels for some extra shit."

"I see you play to win. I like that."

"There's no other way to play the game, baby. Tell me, have you heard anything about anybody looking for a female to do her something?"

Twirl sipped his glass of Hennessy. "You have to be a little bit more specific, baby."

"A friend of mines is kinda spooked, she thinks someone out to get at her. I'm just trying to check a few traps to see if this shit is real or not."

"This friend, she's the one you put the lick down with in Colorado?"

"Yeah, we're jammed tight. She's a real one, too, baby."

"I haven't heard about anyone looking for no particular females to do something dirty to, but I'll keep my ears open for you though. What's your friend's name?"

"Special."

Twirl damn near spit a mouthful of his Hennessy in Keli's face. As calmly as he could he wiped his mouth and asked, "Special? What kind of name is that?"

Keli smiled and he could see the admiration she had for Special in her eyes as she told him, "That's my girl! She is special, *papi,* you best believe that."

Twirl shrugged. "If you say so, baby. I'll keep a ear out for you though and let you know if the streets are talking."

"Thanks. Now let me run to the ladies' room real quick. I'll be right back."

"Take your time, baby. I'm about to check a few things around the spot," Twirl said as he watched her leave the VIP. His mind was reeling now. *Here it is my main man is looking for this bitch Special and she damn near falls right into my lap. Damn. I got to get at Papio with the quickness,* thought Twirl as he stood. Then he glanced toward where Keli was walking and thought, *what about her? I'm not trying to fuck her off by looking out for Papio's ass. Fuck!* Stay true to his dick or stay true to the one nigga who kept his pockets right: that was a no-brainer as far as Twirl was concerned. He pulled out his cell and sent Papio a text message to get back with him as soon as possible. *Sorry, Keli,* Twirl said to himself as he went to check and see if his runners were getting his money right.

Chapter 11

Twirl watched as Keli climbed out of his bed and went into the bathroom to shower. He smiled as he thought about the incredible sex they had after they left the club. *Keli is truly one freaky, bad-ass broad,* he said to himself as he got off the bed and stretched. *Yeah, I'm definitely going to keep her ass around. But how in the hell am I going to do that shit after she finds out that I'm good with Papio? I'm sure she's going to shake me in a heartbeat after that. If she's that tight with Special she has to know the business with them and everything that went down in Texas. Fuck! That's some fucked-up shit for real,* he thought as he went into the bathroom to join Keli in the shower. *Might as well get as much of that good-ass pussy as I can before it's a wrap,* he said to himself. Keli smiled when he entered the shower stall and began kissing him.

They finished sexing each other in the shower and then went their separate ways, agreeing to meet later on in the day. As soon as Twirl was inside of his car he pulled out his cell and checked to see if Papio had returned his text. When he didn't see any messages from Papio he shrugged it off and decided that he'd get at him later with the business. *That nigga must be up to some serious business out there in San Diego,* he thought as he started his car and headed off to start his workday in the streets of sunny southern California.

***

Keli called Special as soon as she was inside of her car and on her way to Special's apartment in Marina del Rey. Special picked up and said, "Damn, girl, you weren't playing when you said breakfast, I see. It's barely eight o'clock in the morning."

"Even though I've had one hell of a morning I'm still worried about my girl. So, what are we doing, eating in or out?"

"I'm in the mood for some good waffles. Meet me at Tal's breakfast spot on Florence. I'll be there in thirty minutes."

"I'm on my way now. I'm out here in West Covina so it should take me about that to get there."

"Okay. Did you guy tell you anything?"

"Nah, he didn't know much, but he said he would keep his ears in the streets for me. But he did have one thing for me that was pretty right."

"What was that?"

"A big, thick, long dick!"

"You nasty. Bye, girl, I'll see you in thirty." Special hung up the phone, laughing.

An hour and a half later the women had finished eating their breakfast and a shocked Keli couldn't believe what she had been told. Special gave her the rundown on what was going on and how she had decided not to run. She just wasn't ready to leave her life, especially without a fight. But she knew that she would be putting Poppa Blue's and Bernadine's lives in danger by making this decision and that was not cool at all. In order for her to make this move be the right move she would have to get on the offense. And the best offense she could think of was to somehow convince Papio to help her. It sounded like a damn good plan; the only thing she was worried about was if she would be able to get him to help her. *Fuck!*

"How are you going to go about getting at that nigga?" Keli sipped her grape juice.

"I don't know, K. For real I just want to call that pretty nigga and beg for his help. But begging ain't in me and I know that arrogant fuck would love to throw that shit right back in my face."

"What about offering to give him some money? You did tell me that he was a fool for that paper right?"

Special smiled. "Yeah, that nigga is obsessed with money, he has to have it. That's the only thing that motivates his fine ass."

"That's it then, get at him with a nice offer and he should be willing to assist you. I mean with you guys' past that nigga wouldn't deny helping you out. If it's as serious as you said with him that nigga still loves you, Special. Shit, his own mother said it so odds are it's real."

"You think?"

"You damn right I think. Go on and call that nigga. What else do you have to lose? I'm telling you y'all made some nice moves last year. That nigga was feeling you then and he's still feeling you now."

Special sighed. "The past doesn't interest me, K, tomorrow does."

"The only way you can make it to tomorrow is to get through today. Make the call, Special."

"All right."

***

Papio wore a huge smile on his face as he got out of Fay's car and followed her inside of her home. He was amazed at the stamina Fay displayed the night before when she took him back to his hotel room. They fucked for over four hours! She freaked him every which way and the sex was off the meters! She left to go home around three in the morning and returned at 7:00 A.M. sharp. She came to his room and joined him in the shower and gave him one of the best blow jobs he'd ever had. After they finished they dressed quickly and were now at her home, waiting for Lance to prepare for the takeover of the two banks. When they walked inside of the house Kango smiled at the both of them but said nothing. It was Steven who spoke first.

"My mon, I'm glad you're able to join us this mornin'. I thought after my dear sister here was through with you, you might not be able to walk this mornin'." Everyone in the room laughed except for Fay.

"No need to speak on mi business, boy. It's time for real things, quiet yourself now." Fay was a totally different person today. Her cute features were now replaced with a determined and focused expression. Papio noticed that every man inside of the room became silent after she spoke. They obviously knew how she got down and knew that she was in a serious mood. *I'm liking this woman more and more,* he thought just as his phone started ringing.

Papio was stunned when he heard who was on the other end of the call but remained cool. "I know you heard me say hello, Clyde. What, you can't speak?" asked Special.

"I'm in the middle of something important right now, Special. What the fuck do you want?"

Upon hearing Papio say Special's name Fay turned and faced him with a concerned look on her face. Kango noticed and wondered what was going on but remained silent.

"We need to talk, Clyde. I need your help."

Papio smiled. "Oh, you do have nuts of steel, *mami.* You gots to know that there's nothing more important to me than hurting you something terrible right? But here you are asking me for some help. Check it, if your life was on the line I'd love to be there to watch you get fucked off, so, baby, believe that I am the last man you should be asking for some fucking help."

"My life is on the line Clyde. I know I fucked up and I know you hate me right now. Put all of those feelings aside, nigga, and listen to me. I have a business proposition for your ass. I'll pay you for your help on this shit."

"Pay me? What, you gone pay me with the ends I helped you get? You know the million I gave you plus the three million I split with your punk ass. Or better yet you're going to pay me with some of the four million those Indians paid you to cross me out with. Ain't that something. Bitch, eat a dick and die!" Papio hung up the phone. After he put his cell back into his pocket he noticed that all eyes were on him. He shrugged. "Excuse me for that shit, just a little domestic issue."

"We do understand, Papio. Believe me we do," Steven said with a smile on his face.

Fay had a frown on her face when she said, "How long have you known Special, mon?"

He stared at her for a moment, trying to see if she was upset with him for fucking with Special or if there was some other reason for this question. "We go back like a year or so, why?"

"I don't like coincidences and it's a big coincidence that Special happens to be the person who made the first move with the device we're going to use today."

"What?"

"You heard me, mon. Special is the person who hit those two jewelry stores in Bakersfield I told you about."

"All right. But what does that have to do with anything? I haven't spoken to that snake bitch in like eleven months or longer. She crossed me out and was about to leave me for dead. It ain't like I got love for her because I don't. Fuck her for real. She has nothing to do with me or my business out here."

Realizing that what he was saying was true Fay relaxed. There was no way that connection could have been made. The only reason Papio was here was because of Kingo and Kango. She smiled at her new lover. "Just making sure your lover wasn't trying to get into mi business, mon."

"Nah, no way can that happen. Like I said, fuck her."

Before Fay could respond there was a knock at her front door. She went and let Lance inside of her home. She returned to the study where they were all waiting. "Everyone, this here is Lance. Lance, this is the crew who is about to make you a massive amount of money."

"Hello," Lance said as he pulled out what looked like a garage door remote and sat down. "This is the device that will make everything go smoothly for the robberies. When you pull in front of each bank all you have to do is flip this switch and press this button here." He made sure everyone was able to see what he was showing them. "After the button has been pressed there will be a series of beeps until this light turns from red to green. Once this light is green then you will know that everything from the alarm system to the security cameras has been deactivated. You can then proceed inside of the bank and do what you do best."

Papio stared at the small, bald man for a few seconds. "How long will we have inside of the bank once the light has turned green?"

Lance shrugged. "Anywhere from thirty to forty minutes, tops. By the time everything is restored to normal you should be back here counting your money."

Kango looked at Fay and smiled. "Okay, let's get ready to do this. We know the routes and how we're going to move but this changes the game completely, men. We're going to empty the vault; we're emptying this place totally. We move as we normally move but we're taking everything inside of that place, a total takeover. We empty every drawer with the tellers as well as the vault."

"How long do you expect to be inside of the bank?" asked Lance.

"Eight, maybe ten minutes. That should give us enough time to get everything." Kango looked at Steven for confirmation. Steven gave a nod of his head yes.

"Then you'll proceed to the next bank and repeat the same process. Good, by the time you leave the second bank everything should still be deactivated."

"We need to get ready now. Have the weapons been secured yet?" Kango looked at his cousin Fay.

"Yeah, mon, they're in the garage inside of the vehicle. The other vehicle has been put in place also, everything is ready."

Kango stared at each man in his crew, including Papio. "Well, let's do this then."

***

Special stared at the phone after Papio hung up on her and shook her head from side to side. "That nigga is still an emotional fuck."

"What did he say, girl?" asked Keli.

Special gave her a replay of the conversation she had with Papio and told her, "Girl, I knew he was going to act like that. That nigga is super salty with me. I got an ace up my sleeve though, no way in hell am I giving up that easy. That nigga is my only shot for real."

"What's your ace in the hole?"

Special smiled. "Actually I have two. But right now I gots to get at Poppa Blue and see what he's up to. I'll give you a holla later, K."

"All right, but you make sure you watch your six, girl. It's time to remain strapped at all times. Any suspicious shit, start blasting first and ask questions later."

"You better fucking believe it." Special patted her Gucci purse on the seat next to her. "I got a nine in here and one in the small of my back. I'm not going out like a weak bitch."

Keli smiled. "'Cause ain't nothing weak about you, girl."

They stood and gave each other a hug and a kiss on the cheeks and left the restaurant.

Special pulled into Poppa Blue's driveway still thinking about what Papio told her when she called him. *Damn, that nigga sounded mad for real. I have to make him understand that every move I made was the best move to make. Fuck! I shouldn't have shot his ass. I could have left and everything would have been good. Ugh!* she thought as she got out of the car and went to Poppa Blue's front door. Before she was able to knock Poppa Blue opened the door, turned, and went into his office without saying a word to her. *Great, must be more bad news,* she thought as she followed him to his office.

After Poppa Blue was seated behind his desk he said, "I have received more information about this business, and it's ugly, Special. The Indians you knocked off was getting their work on consignment from the Suarez organization. When you made that smart decision to kill those two Indians for your man and his mother you basically signed a warrant for your demise."

Special began to say something but Poppa Blue held up his hand to stop her. "I'm not blaming you, just stating the facts. Now they don't have a clue as to where you are; they just know you move out West and they have that picture. That's the reason why they put the word out here to the people they deal with. I got a friend of mines who fucks with the Orumuttos and she told me that Danny Orumutto gave Mr. Suarez his personal assurances that if he got word of your where-abouts he would get right at him. So, you see, with all of these high-powered types on your ass it's a must that you shake the spot. There's no other way around this, Special. Take your ends, sell your home and take—"

"There is a way, Poppa Blue," Special cut him off. "Listen to me for a sec. I need you to go on and get ev-erything ready for me, all of the paperwork as far as IDs and passports and shit. I'm going to stick to the bailout plan for now, but I'm also trying to make some moves of my own. I'm not ready to just give up my life."

Poppa Blue stared at her for a moment with a sad look on his face before saying, "The only way you're go-ing to be able to end this is to take the Cubans out the game. You're not built for that kind of work. Those bastards are too strong, you ain't working with no power like that, Special. You can't win here!"

"Power goes to the one who instills the most fear, Poppa Blue. Fuck Mr. Suarez and his Cubans. You once told me that simplicity backed by authority is best in deception."

"I did. But what the fuck does that have to do with you being able to take out some strong motherfucking Cubans?"

She smiled at her mentor, a man she knew would die for her. "I need time, Poppa Blue. Get everything ready for me and I promise if I can't make the moves needed I'm out. Just give me a minute to at least try. Don't worry, I'd never do anything to put you or Bernadine in harm's way. I'm no fool. Give me a little time, that's all I ask."

"Always got to do it the hard way, just like your damn mama, God rest her soul."

"What fun is it doing shit the easy way?" Special asked with a smile on her face.

"Be careful, Special, please be careful."

"Always."

Papio was checking his messages as the final preparations for the takeover were being gone over by Kango. He saw that Twirl had told him to get back at him as soon as possible and quickly called him back. When Twirl answered the phone Papio said, "What's the business?"

"Dog! You won't believe the fucking luck I had last night."

"Check it, I'm about to make a real heavy move, so if this can wait let me get back at you a little later on?"

"I think I got a line on Special. Now if you want to get back at me you can do that. I just figured you'd want to hear that shit."

"You figured right. What you got?"

Twirl quickly explained how he met Keli and how she told him about Special and her problems. When he finished he said, "I won't fake it with you my nigga, I am really feeling Keli, but my money comes before any bitch. I have to remain loyal to the nigga who has kept my pockets right."

"I feel that, good looking out, G. It looks like we may be able to use this to my advantage and still keep you and old girl together."

"How's that?"

"Let me handle this business and I'll get back at you when I'm done. Don't panic though, it's all gravy, baby." Papio hung up the phone just as Kango was telling everyone it was time to mount up. It was ten minutes after 10:00 A.M. when they loaded into a hunter-green GMC Yukon. Each man began to check and re-check their weapons as Brad pulled out of Fay's garage. They then began to make sure that the earpieces they were wearing were working properly. They each ran a quick sound check and agreed that everything was good. They were all dressed identically in black army fatigues. Since all of them had long hair they each had on skull caps to cover their long dreads. Papio had his long ponytail tucked under his skull cap.

Brad pulled in front of the Wells Fargo bank and cut off the engine while Kango turned on the device and pressed the necessary buttons. After a few beeps the green light came on. "Let's do this," Kango said.

He opened his door and climbed out of the SUV and hurried inside of the bank, followed closely by Steven,

Papio, and Macho with their silenced weapons held down by their sides as they entered the bank. Once they were inside Macho stepped to the first guard and aimed his weapon at his head and whispered, "Don't move or you die."

Papio went to the middle of the bank and was busying making sure that everyone was on the floor like Kango had ordered them upon entering the bank. Without hesitation Kango and Steven were over the counter, getting busy emptying each drawer by the bank tellers, filling each of the duffel bags that they had over their necks. As each bag was filled they were tossed toward Papio, who was standing in the center of the bank keeping everyone under watch while Macho watched the door. Steven and Kango proceeded to the vault and filled four more duffel bags. They quickly jumped back over the counter and grabbed the other bags that had been tossed by Papio's feet. Papio backed out of the bank slowly as Macho watched his back. Once they were out of the bank they casually stepped to the SUV and Brad pulled away from the curb calmly. They were laughing as they headed toward the next bank. The total takeover had taken all of eight minutes and twenty-seven seconds. *Damn!*

Fay smiled as she watched as Kango and the crew left the bank without incident. She got into her car and proceeded to drive to the next bank and continue to be the crew's extra eyes. *This is like taking candy from a baby,* she thought as she pulled into traffic.

Papio pulled off his ski mask and asked, "Why do we have to wear these fucking masks if the cameras are off?"

"Better to stay prepared just in case, mon," Steven said as he hurried and emptied the last of the duffel bags into a large Gucci suitcase.

"Okay, here we are, time for take two of this shit, mon," said Brad as he came to a stop in front of the Union bank.

Kango pulled out the device and repeated everything he did at the Wells Fargo bank. Once he got the green light on the device they were out of the SUV and into the bank just as before. Everything went just as smooth inside of the Union bank as the first takeover, all the way up until the exit. As Papio was stepping past Macho to leave the bank, one of the customers of the bank got to his feet and pulled a weapon and screamed, "Freeze! Police!"

Macho didn't hesitate. He fired his weapon four times and the undercover police officer went down. Macho followed Papio outside and into the SUV.

As they sped away from the bank Kango asked, "What the fuck happened?"

"A fucking cop drew on us. I had no choice I had to put him down, mon."

"Fuck! Are you good?"

"Yeah, I'm good," Macho said in a shaky voice.

"All right, Brad, this changes shit a touch, mon. Get us to that fucking vehicle like now!"

Brad put his foot down harder on the accelerator and the Yukon picked up speed quickly. Six minutes later they pulled next to a brown Lincoln Navigator, switched vehicles, and were on their way back to Fay's home. No words were said because each man understood that this would be the most crucial part of the entire job. A cop had been shot so shit was thick and they were all very nervous.

Kango was on the phone with Fay, and sighed with relief when she told him that the cops had just arrived in front of the bank. "Good. We're ten, maybe twelve minutes from your house now."

"Keep it at speed limit, mon, and you'll be just fine," she assured him and hung up the phone.

Kango smiled for the first time since leaving the bank. "We are good." Papio let his head rest on the back of his seat and sighed with relief.

Chapter 12

Special was lounging in her media room watching television when she heard the news anchor on CNN start to report about two bank robberies that happened one after the other in San Diego. Everything about the two bank jobs seemed so similar to the two jewelry stores that she robbed in Bakersfield that she sat up in her seat and continued to listen to the news report. When the news ended she grabbed the phone and called Poppa Blue. As soon as Poppa Blue answered the phone she asked him, "Have you heard about those two banks that got hit out in Diego?"

"Yep, as a matter of fact I just got off of the phone with Lance's ass. He swears he had nothing to do with them but I can tell he's lying his ass off."

"Mmmmm, what do you think it would cost us to get that device off of Lance?"

"I was thinking about that shit too, especially since it's so hot down there with that police officer getting shot. Lance may just want to come up off that thing. I got at him after the jewelry jobs about selling and he told me no way, maybe he'll have a change of heart when he hears how the Feds are all over this shit now. He's so damn scary I'm sure he'll want to deal. The thing is if he did have a part in those banks we're going to have to make a move quick. I'm sure the others he's put in this mix are thinking the same thing we are."

"True. Get at his ass, Poppa Blue, and set up a meeting at your spot ASAP! Get back at me when you have it set up. I need this, Poppa Blue. I need this bad."

"What are you trying to do, Special?"

"Make some moves so my position of power can become stronger. I told you I'm not trying to lose the life I've worked so hard for without a fight."

He sighed. "Okay, I'll get back at you in a little while."

"Thanks," Special said as she hung up the phone.

If I can get that damn device maybe I can use that shit to get at Papio. This could be the tool I need to get that greedy nigga back on my side. How could he ever refuse me with something so sweet as Lance's device? He'd be able to get that $100 million in no time. She sat back in her seat with a smile on her face, then sat back up and snapped her fingers. "Fay! Nobody robs two banks back to back in San Diego without Fay knowing something about it. Ain't that a bitch." Special grabbed the phone again and called Poppa Blue back.

"What now?" Poppa Blue asked as soon as he answered the phone.

"You're slipping with your old age, old man."

"What are you talking about?"

"Think about it: who's the one person who would definitely know about two back to back bank jobs in San Diego?"

Without any hesitation Poppa Blue answered, "Damn, Fay."

"Exactly. If Fay knows the business then she's the one Lance is fucking with."

"If not then it's like you said, she knows something about it. I'll call you back in a minute." Poppa Blue hung up the phone.

Special hoped Fay would be willing to help them. Her life depended on that shit. *Come on, Fay, look out for ya girl,* she said to herself as she sat back in her seat and stared at the television.

"Harder, mon! I say harder! Fuck mi good! Fuck mi," Fay screamed at the top of her lungs as Papio had her bent over the end of the bed inside of his hotel room. They had been having sex for over an hour and Papio was thoroughly enjoying himself. Fay's sex game was vicious and it turned him on in a major way.

But still every man had his limits and she was pushing him real close to his as he came for what felt like the sixth time. Actually it was just his third orgasm. He pulled himself out of her still soaking wet pussy and sighed. "Damn, baby, let's take a break for a minute, you killing a nigga," Papio said as he went and lay down on the bed.

Fay stood and stepped to the side of the bed and looked down on him and shook her head. "How can such a Shotta like you be so tired, mon? We just get started not too long ago. Look at these, you haven't paid much attention to them yet, mon," she said as she grabbed her nice, large breasts and gave her big, erect nipples a squeeze. She rolled her eyes in her head and smiled. She then climbed on top of him and bent forward so her dark nipples were inches away from Papio's lips.

He smiled as he began to suck and nibble on her nipples. "Mmmmmmm, yes, now you see what mi talking about, Top Rankin! You do me all night, baby! We got the money, now you give me the buddy! Give mi all this buddy all damn night, mon!" she screamed as Papio eased himself back inside of her. She rode him for twenty minutes before they both came hard together. She slid off of his sweaty body and smiled as she went into the bathroom to relieve herself. She returned to see Papio knocked out cold. She shook her head from side to side and said, "Americans, humph. Always talk the talk but can barely walk the walk." She had a smile on her face though as she got back in bed and cuddled beside Papio.

She was in a perfect mood. Even though her city was smoking hot she was good because they made a huge amount of money from those two takeovers: $62 million combined from both banks. After giving Lance his agreed upon 10 percent they split the remaining $55.8 million six ways, and came away with a stunning $9.3 million apiece.

What a glorious day! But this successful day came with a heavy price to pay. The heat was on and Fay knew without a doubt that she would be receiving a visit from the authorities soon. That's why she decided to come to Papio's room and chill, so she could get her mind right before the local or federal authorities came and got at her. Her brother and the rest of Kango's crew had already driven to Los Angeles, where they would lay low for a few days before returning to the East Coast. Papio told them of an ingenious way for them to get their money back to the East without any problems: simply take it to the post office and mail it. It was so simple that they all had to laugh when he told them exactly how to box it up and mail it off. So by the time they made it back to the East, their money would already be waiting for them.

She smiled at Papio's sleeping form and thought, *this mon is good, he really good. I wonder what other business we can do together.* She put her hand on his limp penis and began to rub him slowly, trying to see if she could revive him for one more round before she went to sleep. After a few more minutes she sighed and gave up and started thinking about her plans to deal with the authorities when they came to get at her about those bank robberies. She wanted to laugh because it was going to be so damn easy. She would lie her ass off and let them try all of the little games they liked to play with her to try to get her to slip up and give them some information. Those two takeovers were so damn smooth that they were baffled and them looking so stupid would only make them go at her harder.

With this thought in mind she realized that she was in no damn mood for any of that shit. "Ahhh, I think it's time for mi to go on a little vacation." She stared at Papio again and wondered how he'd feel about them taking a little trip to her home in Negril. She was just about to cuddle up next to him when her big butt touched the large wet spot on the sheets. *Ugh! How did he miss the wet spot?* she thought as she got out of the bed and went into the bathroom and grabbed a towel. As she returned to the bed her cell phone rang. She checked the number and smiled when she saw Poppa Blue's number up in L.A. She picked up the phone and returned to the bathroom before answering. "Say, old mon, how you?"

"I would be just fine if you would have put me up on that shit you got off with Lance's scary ass," Poppa Blue said seriously. "But since you kept that to yourself I'll just say I'm all right."

Fay laughed. "I should feel the same way. I heard about the jewelry stores, Poppa Blue."

"Lance talks too fucking much." They both laughed.

"That he does. Now tell me wah you want, old man?"

Not willing to discuss that kind of business on the telephone, Poppa Blue told her, "Two nights of chilling up here in L.A. Dinner and some serious talk about some serious money. You with that?"

"Right now that would be very welcome, it's rather hot down mi way, mon."

Poppa Blue laughed. "Now that's an understatement if I've ever heard one."

"Still, you no tell me what this is about?"

"Lance and his invention, Fay."

"You want?"

"I need."

She sighed. "I'll be up there in the morning, mon. This will cost you more than dinner, old man."

Poppa Blue laughed. "Come on, Fay. I'm too old to be trying to hang with your freaky ass!"

"Mi don't do old mon anyway. I would give your old ass a heart attack if I put this Glamity on ya, mon."

"I know that pussy is good, Fay; don't forget I've been there and done that. Now, what time will you be here exactly?"

"No later than nine A.M. Where do we meet?"

"Call me when you hit the city and I'll tell you then."

"Everything kriss, mon." She hung up the phone and returned to the bed where Papio was sleeping soundly. She climbed in and cuddled next to her lover and thought about what Poppa Blue had just told her. *Interesting*. Could Poppa Blue be able to talk Lance into selling the device? If he could then there would be way more money coming for them. The 9.3 they just took would be nothing compared to what they would get with that device in their hands. She wore a satisfied smile as she went to sleep with that thought on her mind.

Back in Los Angeles Poppa Blue called Special back and told her, "I'm having Fay come down this way in the morning. We're going to meet here at my place, so be here around nine-thirty in the morning."

"Did you tell her what the meeting was about?"

"Yep."

"Do you think she'll be interested?"

"This is Fay we're talking about, of course she'll be interested. The big question is will we be able to scare the hell outta Lance so he'll sell us that damn device. In the morning, Special, don't be late." He hung up the phone.

Poppa Blue picked the phone right back up and called Lance. When Lance answered the phone Poppa Blue told him, "Listen to me, you highly intelligent, super stupid fuck. Have your ass at my house at ten A.M. sharp. Do you hear me, Lance? Because I'm not fucking with your goofy ass."

"Come on, P . . . Poppa B . . . Blue, what did I . . . I do?" stammered Lance.

"You already know what the fuck you did so don't fuck with me with this, Lance. Have your ass here at ten A.M. Not one minute before or after ten A.M. sharp!"

"I'll be there, Poppa Blue," Lance said dejectedly,

"You better." Poppa Blue hung up the phone with a satisfied smile on his face. He hated doing poor Lance this way but he had to scare the living hell out of him in order to get him to sell that device. Whatever it took to get it out of him, Poppa Blue was willing to do. He made a promise to a lovely woman years ago that if something ever happened to her he would always take care of her only child. That child was Special. He would go to his grave keeping his word on that promise he made over twenty years ago.

The next morning Fay had Papio drop her off at her place and told him that she would be spending a few days in L.A. before flying to Negril for a much-needed vacation. She invited him to join her and he told her he'd think about it. Even though he knew he wouldn't be going out there the thought was a good one.

"Gimme a call before you bounce so we can get together at the rompin shop a few more times," Papio said with a smile.

Fay smiled as she gave him a soft kiss on his lips. "You already know mi had that thought in mi mind, mon. Let's hook up later this evening."

"Call me," Papio said as he turned and got into his car and left.

Fay stood there and watched as he pulled out of her driveway. "You know damn well I'll be calling, rude boy!" She turned and hurried inside of her home to get dressed so she could make the short trek up to Los Angeles for her meeting with Poppa Blue.

Forty minutes later she was showered, packed, and dressed. She grabbed her purse and was walking into her garage when her cell phone rang. She answered the phone as she got inside of her brand new 2011 Jaguar XJ. She was easing the $87,000 vehicle out of her garage when she heard the federal operator inform her to push the number five to accept a call from a federal inmate. She pressed five just as she turned into the street. "Wah you know, mon?"

With concern in his voice Kingo asked, "Are you good, mon? Me see things that disturb me so."

"Everything kriss, man. You know how things go at times, everything and everyone good."

Kingo sighed with relief. "Papio?"

"He's especially good, man. Just left me a little while ago and headed back home."

"You need to go home and see your motha," Kingo said in code, meaning that she needed to get out of San Diego for a while because of the heat that would come from the bank robberies.

Understanding his meaning she said, "Don't I know it, man. I'm on my way to L.A. now to meet with some people and then I'll fly home for a nice rest."

"Good. I love you, man."

"Mi love you too. Now go do whatever it is you do in the bing."

Kingo laughed. "Mi cousin Fay, still crazy as eva, mon".

"Bye!" She closed her phone and concentrated on driving and watching her back for any tails at the same time. Never one to be caught slipping, Fay was definitely a gangster in this wicked street game.

Special arrived at Poppa Blue's home at exactly 9:30 A.M. and smiled when she saw Bernadine strapping that beautiful baby inside of his car seat. She got out of her car and waved at Bernadine as she stepped quickly to the front door. Poppa Blue opened the door and growled some form of greeting as he turned and led her toward his office. Once he was seated he sighed. "All right, I got everything in order as far as the papers are concerned. The ends are straight and you shouldn't have any problems getting situated; the question now is where do you wanna live?"

After sitting down across from him on the other side of the desk, Special smacked her lips loudly and said, "Right here in my beautiful home in sunny California." She held up her hand before Poppa Blue could speak, and continued, "Got to put forth an effort to make this shit go my way, Poppa Blue. I'm not trying to let those fucking Cubans run me away from my home. I know how you feel, but let's see how this goes here; then I can see if I got a real chance with this shit. I know if I can get Papio on my team we can make some shit happen."

"Why do you have so much confidence in that young man? What makes you think he has the juice to fade those Cubans? Mr. Suarez has been in the game a minute now and there's not too much he hasn't seen. Papio, from what you've told me, is a money-getting man. How does getting money equate to giving you the power to bring it to the Cubans?"

She smiled. "It's not about bringing it to the Cubans, it's about outthinking they ass and staying one step ahead of them."

Poppa Blue nodded his head. "That's exactly what I'm trying to do here by putting the exit plan in play. We move now, we're one step ahead and we should remain that way."

"Running is never a good plan unless that's the only option, Poppa Blue. If I bounce and make one misstep along the way all of this would be for shit. I have to see if there's a better way first. And I feel in my gut that Papio can give me a better way to deal with this shit."

"I hear you, but you still gots to get that fool on your side again. You can't forget that he's really not trying to fuck with you, Special."

"That's where you come in, my OG. Make this happen with Lance and Fay, Poppa Blue. I need this. And if by chance this shit don't pop off like I want then I have another move that I will be putting in motion also."

"And what is that?"

"Gangstas only respect gangsta shit. If need be I can bring it to the Cubans in a way they will never expect because I got the edge in this war for real."

"How in the hell do you think you have an edge over them? You're really tripping the fuck out here, Special."

"Am I? Think about it, Poppa Blue, they don't know that I know they're looking for me. They're sitting back thinking they're in the driver's seat of this shit. I can counter all of that shit by taking the offense on they ass and make some serious moves against them."

"Come on, Special, don't go and get suicidal on me here, baby girl. You got responsibilities to take—"

"I know what I got, Poppa Blue! And I know what I got to do, too! Why do you think I'm trying my damnedest to make this shit go in my favor? I'm no fool, you already know that, but I'm no punk bitch either. I will utilize every single option before I make a final move. If I have to take it to those bitch-ass Cubans I want you to know that I am prepared to do just that. But only if I feel it's the right move to make. Until then I'm trying to see what comes from this meeting."

Before she could speak again the doorbell rang and Poppa Blue stood to go let Fay inside. As he was leaving the office he told Special, "Be cool and let me handle all of this shit. That means don't say shit, Special; do you hear me?"

With a smile on her face she gave a nod of her head. "Whatever you say, Poppa Blue."

Poppa Blue returned with Fay behind him and made the introductions. Even though they both had heard plenty about one another over the years neither of the

women had actually met the other. Once Poppa Blue
was seated he wasted no time and asked Fay, "Tell me
what's what down your way with that bank shit, Fay.
You good or is the heat on your ass?"

She shrugged. "I'm good for now because I'm no
there, mon. I know when they sit back and look at tings
good they will come a-looking for Fay. But Fay will be
in the islands relaxing in the sun on the beach with a
nice ganja blowing in the wind."

"You say that shit like you're not ever coming back to
San Diego."

"You know mi will be back, mon, just need time to let
tings cool off some."

Poppa Blue shook his head slowly. "Not wise. You
should go back and face whatever they bring at you.
That will keep the suits shook left. If you bounce that
will make them more suspicious and then they won't
back off your ass anytime soon. If we're going to be successful in getting that device off of Lance's ass we don't
need no heat on you because we're going to make shit
do what it do big fucking time. We might as well get
as much as we can and then fall back and leave those
bastards clueless."

"That makes plenty sense, mon. I wasn't tinking like
that before. You know just didn't wanna go through the
bullshit, mon."

"I understand but we got to look at the big picture
with this."

"I agree, mon. Now tell me all of the business, Poppa
Blue." Before Poppa Blue could speak Fay shook her
head. "Tell me everything about her and what she has
to do with all of this, Poppa Blue, or I'm not in." Fay
pointed toward Special.

"My life is on the line, Fay. I got some heavy beef, and the only way I'm going to get out of it is to get that device so I can use it to get the assistance I need to help me make some good moves against those who's out to get at me," Special said.

"Mmmm, okay, I see. Does that brother Papio have something to do with this, mon?" Fay watched Special closely before she could answer her question.

Fay knew something or she wouldn't have used Papio's name. Special knew not to play any games with her, so without hesitation she said, "Papio is the one man who can help me. I need him but the only way I can get him to even think about helping me is with that damn device."

Respecting her honesty Fay gave a nod of her head and said, "Okay, wa yu de pan, mon?"

Poppa Blue laughed. "She doesn't understand patois, Fay. The plan is simple though, first, we get Lance to sell that device. After that, we get at Papio and see if we can entice him to help Special here."

"From what I can tell Papio won't be too eager to help her. He seem real mad the other day when he talk to her."

"You've seen Papio?" asked Special.

Fay smiled devilishly. "Nuff respect, Special, because I can tell you and that fine brotter have a history, but Papio has taken me to the rompin shop and did wicked tings to mi pum pum."

She may not have been able to understand patois but she could tell by the gleam on Fay's face that she was talking about having had sex with Papio. And that thought pissed her off big time. But she refused to show anger. She shrugged and said, "Your business is your business, Fay. I need Papio because I know he can help me out of this jam I'm in. . . ."

"Good, then I don't see why we won't be able to work together, mon. Papio, he good mon though, he helped me out on the banks the other day. Real cool customer he is, mon."

"What?" both Poppa Blue and Special asked in unison.

Since she knew Poppa Blue was an old-school head that could be trusted totally she felt comfortable telling him as well as Special what happened at the two banks in San Diego. After giving them a play-by-play of the events in San Diego, both Special and Poppa Blue sat back in their seats with a new kind of admiration for Papio.

"So that fool is real with his, huh, Fay?" asked Poppa Blue.

"Yeh, mon, he the real deal. That's not the first time he met with mi cousin's crew, they make moves back East, too. That's why I give him a call when I get word from Lance. Mi cousin asked me to get in contact with him for this job; they like his work."

Damn, that fine-ass nigga is serious when it comes to getting money. But what the fuck does he see in this old-ass Jamaican lady? Okay, her body is still tight and she is pretty; never thought he'd go for someone like her though, Special thought as she subtly surveyed what Fay was working with.

"Papio is the ace in this game and we're going to need him if Special is going to be able to make the right moves. Even though he's salty at my girl here I think we'll be able to get him to come around."

"Right you are, Poppa Blue; when it comes to the money I'm pretty sure that everything bless, mon. If you want I will give him a call and see if I can get him to help."

"Nah, I have to do that on my own, Fay, thanks though," Special said seriously.

Fay shrugged but said nothing. The doorbell rang and Poppa Blue went to answer the door. He returned a few minutes later, followed by Lance. When Lance saw Fay and Special he knew instantly that he was going to give up his precious device. And to be honest with it he was going to be glad to get rid of that damned thing. He was terrified with what he had been hearing on the news. They had already figured out that there had to be some way that the alarms and the security cameras had been tripped. So far the Feds felt that it was an inside job; it wouldn't be too long before they started looking at other angles. Yes, it was definitely time to part ways with the device and move somewhere nice and sunny other than California. Hawaii, maybe. *Yes, Hawaii would be nice,* he thought as he sat down next to Fay.

Before anyone could speak the calm, bald man spoke confidently. "Ten million and not a penny less, Poppa Blue. Ten million dollars for my device, plus all of the equipment to properly maintain it."

Poppa Blue smiled. "But what if it trips out on us? Does that ten million guarantee you to come fix it?"

If you can find my ass it does, thought Lance, but to them he said, "But of course. Do we have a deal?"

Poppa Blue looked at Fay, who gave a slight nod of her head; then he looked at Special, who did the same.

"Yeah, Lance, we got a deal."

"Good. Here's the account numbers you will need to transfer the money. Once that's done I'll bring over the rest of what you will need. Until then here's the device." Lance reached inside his baggy trousers and pulled out the device and passed it to Poppa Blue.

Poppa Blue accepted the device. "That's doing good business, Lance. I appreciate this."

"No problem. Take it easy, Poppa Blue, and please keep my name away from any of this business."

"That goes without saying, Lance. Have a nice day and we'll be in touch in a few days." Poppa Blue stood and showed Lance out of his home. When he returned he stared at Special for a moment and asked, "You good?"

She smiled at him. "I will be when I return from Miami."

"Miami? What the fuck are you going out there for, Special?" Before she could answer his question he said, "Wait, never mind. I really don't want to know do I?"

Special smiled at him and Fay. "Nah, you really don't."

Chapter 13

Special's flight to Miami arrived a little after 2:00 P.M. She quickly deplaned and by two forty-five she was inside of her rented convertible BMW, leaving Miami International Airport, headed toward one of the most notorious neighborhoods in Miami's Dade County.

She took Palmetto Expressway north to 826 East and got off on Twenty-seventh Avenue, entering the city of Opa-locka. As she was driving through the neighborhood full of drugs and thugs she couldn't believe how one side of this sunny city could be so fly and beautiful and one side could be so gloomy and grimy. *Just the way life is,* she said to herself as she turned the car onto 161st Street and Thirtieth Avenue: the neighborhood that basically belonged to the ruthless gang called Behind the P-Boys.

She parked in front of a small house and blew the horn twice, letting Scrape know that she was outside waiting for him, because there was no way in hell she was getting out of her car. She hated that she didn't have a pistol on her, because the way some of the thick-headed dreads were eyeing her had her spooked to the highest order as she continued to wait for Scrape to come outside. She was about to blow the horn again when the front door of the house opened and Scrape came outside with a wide, toothless smile on his face. She shook her head from side to side as she watched him stroll confidently toward her. *Look at this damn fool; got more money than any of these thugs around here and looking like a two-bit petty hustler dressed in khaki shorts and a tee. Damn shame,* she thought and smiled at her long-time friend as he approached her car.

"Damn, girl, why you out here blowing that damn horn like that? You scared to get out the car or some shit? You know you could have came to the door. You're safe around my way. I know you know that right?"

"Boy, why in hell don't you have your teeth in your damn mouth? That is some nasty-looking shit, Scrape. Get your ass in so we can go for a ride and talk some serious business."

Scrape got into the car and lit up a Newport cigarette. "When you called and said you had some real serious shit to holla about that got me wondering, so here we are, go on and holla."

Special eased the Beemer away from the curb. "I need you, Scrape. I need you to give me as much information as you can get on some Cubans out this way."

"Out this way as in Opa-locka?"

"Uh-uh, Miami."

"There's like what, a couple million fucking Cubans out there, Special. You're going to have to be a little more specific."

"Have you ever heard of the Suarez organization?"

That question seemed to have grabbed Scrape's attention because he flipped his cigarette out the window and asked, "You gotta be fucking with me right? Anybody who gets down out here or in the MIA knows about those Cubans. What do you want to know about them? No, better yet, why in the fuck are you even inquiring about them?"

"It's a long story. I need to know as much as I can about them, Scrape. And if need be I may need you to make a move for me against them," she said seriously as she turned the car onto the freeway headed toward South Beach.

Scrape stared at her as if she'd lost her mind for a few minutes before asking, "Do you know how hard it will be to touch them? Those fools are on some Scarface time for real, Special. If you got beef with them you should relocate somewhere and lay it down, 'cause those fools don't play."

"I got two million dollars for all of the information you can get me on them, Scrape. I want you to sit back and watch them and find their weakness. They have one, you just got to be patient enough and look for it. Two million cash up front. If I need you later in the game I'll call on you so we can then put the information you find into use. If I don't call you then you still win two tickets."

"Two milly, huh?"

"That's what I said."

"And there's a chance you might not even have to put what I find to use?"

"A strong chance, but that don't mean you can try to fuck me, Scrape. If I call on you I expect for you to have something for me, so do your work and find out how I can get at them if I need to take the offense."

"What if there isn't a way to get at them, Special?"

Special shrugged her shoulders. "Then you're going to give me back every penny of my motherfucking money."

Scrape sat back in his seat and let what she told him run through his ever-calculating mind. After a few minutes of thinking he asked, "When will I get that two milly?"

Special smiled as she pulled in front of the Ritz-Carlton in South Beach. "Sit tight, I'll be right back." She jumped out of the car and strolled inside of the luxurious hotel. She stepped to the front desk and gave the clerk her name. After her reservations were confirmed she asked, "Has a package arrived for me yet?"

The clerk hit a few keys on the computer and then said, "Yes, ma'am, it has. Give me a moment and I'll get it for you."

Special pulled out her cell and checked her text messages while she waited for the clerk to return with the $2 million she had mailed there before she left Los Angeles. She smiled because that was Papio's move for transporting large sums of money back and forth. She couldn't help but think about him as she waited inside of this particular hotel because this was where he had shown her one of the best times of her life. Just thinking about the incredible sex they had there for the seven days they spent in Miami was actually getting her moist.

The clerk returned carrying a medium-sized package and gave it to Special. "If you'd like I can have this sent up to your suite, ma'am."

"No, thank you. I have to drop it off to a friend. Could you make sure that a bottle of rosé on ice will be in my suite before I return? I should be back in a couple of hours."

"No problem, ma'am," the clerk said as he passed Special her suite key card.

"Thanks," said Special as she spun on her Jimmy Choos and strolled back outside to her car. When she stepped outside of the hotel she shook her head at the sight before her. Scrape's thug ass was hanging outside of the rented BMW, hawking at every woman who passed by.

"What's what, *mami?* Hey, you, you ain't trying to holla at a nigga? That's cold, *mami!* Your loss! Bitch!" Scrape yelled and started laughing, totally enjoying himself.

Embarrassed to the max by his actions Special got inside of the car and said, "Nigga, if you don't sit your no-teeth-having ass down I'm going to take this money back inside and let those rental cops who was aching to kick your ass come and kick your ass! Sit down, Scrape!"

"You need to kill that fake stuck-up talk, Special. You must've forgot I know how you get down and ain't nothing stuck-up about your fine ass."

She smiled. "Whatever, nigga. Here." She tossed the package on his lap. "Two million, Scrape. Get me what I need, boo. I need you on this, serious shit."

"I know you do, *mami.* Don't trip, I got you. I don't know what or if I'll find anything for you but if it's something to find you best believe I'll find it. If you need me to put that work in you know I got that too. Just know this: those Cubans are not playing; if we move we can't miss. We got to have a direct fucking hit because we won't get another chance at they ass."

"If we have to move I'm planning on making damn sure it's a direct hit. I can't afford to miss," she said sadly.

"Damn, girl, what you done got yourself into?"

"Trust me, you don't wanna know, Scrape."

"You know what, you're right. I don't wanna know! Take me back to my hood, being around all these fake fuckers has given me a headache! I'm a Dade County Opa-locka nigga!" They both started laughing as Special got back onto the freeway, headed back to the gloomier side of sunny Miami.

***

Papio couldn't believe what he had just been told. Fay was lying next to him in his suite at the Westin, telling him everything that was discussed at the meeting with Poppa Blue and Special. She told him about the purchase of the device from Lance as well as about Special hoping to be able to get him to help her with her problem.

So that bitch thinks she can get me to help her out of that shit with the Cubans huh? That's fucking funny for real. The stupid bitch doesn't even know I'm the one looking to do her ass for the Cubans. Yeah, this is going to be even easier than I thought, Papio thought as he gently rubbed Fay's shoulders.

"Wah you tink about dere, mon? You real quiet now," said Fay.

Not trying to expose too much to Fay he asked her, "Did that crazy bitch say what she needs me for?"

"No, mon, she say only she needs you to help her. Are you going to do that? She seems willing to offer you a lot of money. Never good to turn down good money, Papio."

"I'm no fool, Fay; if the ends are that good you know I'll take it. But there's some shit in the game and before I up and bite for whatever she offers I have to look into this. Kingo always told me to make sure I check every trap before walking through any door."

"That's some good advice, mon. But listen here and pay me some good attention. That dere lady loves you, mi see it in her eyes. She not only needs you, she wants you in her life, mon."

Hearing Fay say that hit Papio in a place he wasn't expecting: his heart. His defense mechanism kicked in immediately. "I'm not trying to hear any of that, Fay.

That bitched crossed me; she can't be trusted." Before Fay could say anything he changed the subject. "So, now that you are part owner of that device when you gon' let a nigga make a move or two with it?"

Ahhhh, so you love this woman back huh, mon? That's sweet, she thought before answering his question. "Too hot right now to be making any moves down my way. I'll have a few people look into some things and be in touch."

"You're not going to Jamaica now?"

"No, mi going to go back home and see if they come and talk to me. Better that way, go on and get that madness done. They will watch Fay for a minute and see that everything is same old same and back up off me. When everything is fine we will get wicked again." She started laughing. "Now come and let's get wicked right here, mon, before I have to go back dere."

Papio smiled at her. "Spread your legs then. I'm ready to eat that sweet pussy some more."

"Good! Mi want ya to eat!"

Special was relaxing in the Jacuzzi bathtub, sipping some rosé champagne, thinking about Papio. Wondering what he was doing at that very moment. Wondering if he still had feelings for her like Mama Mia said he did. She sighed and realized that sitting in the bathtub thinking about him was depressing. Here she was in Miami, Florida and no way in hell was she going to spend the entire night sitting in her suite sulking like some weak bitch. She was going to get dressed and go make it do what it do. *Never know what I might come up on,* she thought as she got out of the bathtub and picked out something to wear for the evening.

After getting dressed in a white tube dress with some dangerously high-heeled shoes by Prada, Special was ready to hit up the MIA and have some fun. She didn't know where she was going when she got into her rental so she just drove around, listening to the radio with the top down, enjoying the evening air of South Beach. It was close to midnight when she heard the local DJ say something about the hot new rapper Nicki Minaj performing at Club Cinema. Special smiled as she entered Club Cinema into the GPS system of the Beemer.

Twenty-five minutes later she was pulling into the parking lot of the club. She checked her makeup and once she was ready she got out of the car and headed toward the front door of the club, totally ignoring the long line that was damn near around the block. She had already palmed two hundred-dollar bills inside of her right hand as she stepped toward the bouncer. When the huge bouncer focused on her he smiled and wondered what she was going to offer him to get inside of the club. *If she offers some pussy she might just get lucky because she is one bad-ass female,* the bouncer thought as he openly admired all of that cleavage Special had poking out at him. Without saying a word she got on to her tiptoes and gave him a soft kiss on his lips and reached out her right hand. The bouncer shook it and accepted the two bills from her. He then lifted the rope and let Special enter the club. Once she was inside Special didn't look back as she let her hips sway from side to side to give the bouncer a good look at all of that ass she was packing. He realized that he had been played but he was loving what he saw. He then opened his hand and saw the $200 and felt even better about his decision. *If I'm lucky I might be able to get at her later when the club lets out,* he hoped as he turned around and went back to mean mugging the crowd.

Special went to the bar and ordered a flute of rosé and then began to survey the club to see what was cracking. She spotted several famous people floating around the club or standing in the VIP, looking as if they owned the place. The same old shit no matter what state it was, always the same at clubs like this, the athletes walking around all toned and muscled, acting like they're the cream of the crop; the actors, actresses, singers, and rappers walking around craving attention from anyone who wanted to give it to them; and then there was the ballers, the street niggas who made it big who had it to floss but really wanted to be as low-key as possible even though they were blinged out just waiting to catch a Fed case.

Special laughed at it all as she sipped her drink and walked around trying to enjoy herself. Nicki Minaj was the latest female rap sensation and she had been locking the airwaves up for a minute now. Special actually liked some of her music, even if it was somewhat childish to her. She admired Nicki Minaj more for that firm ass she had than anything else. The DJ announced that Nicki Minaj was in the building and was getting ready to hit the stage within the hour.

Special checked the time on her diamond Cartier and saw that it was a little after 1:00 A.M. She may not have been having a total blast but at least she was out her suite and doing something instead of thinking about Papio's ass or stressing about those fucking Cubans. *Fuck that wack shit. I'm going to either get me some dick or a hard clit to lick tonight,* she thought as she turned and started walking back toward the bar to get a refill on her drink. Suddenly she stopped and smiled at who she saw out on the dance floor shaking her sexy ass with some overdressed wannabe. At first Special wasn't sure but when the strobe lights hit that gorgeous Dominican woman with the flaming red hair she knew for sure it was Inga she was staring at. The waitress that she and Papio freaked the last time they were in Miami. Yep, that flaming red hair was what she spotted first but when she saw that divine ass that confirmed it for her. Special stood there for another minute, staring at her while reliving that amazing night they spent in the suite at the Ritz. Thinking about that got her juices flowing so damn strong she felt as if her pussy juice was sliding down her leg. She started squirming where she was standing, watching Inga as she shook her ass all around the dance floor.

"Uh-uh, no fucking way!" Special said as she set her flute onto the bar and stepped quickly out onto the dance floor. When she made it in front of Inga she whispered into her ear, "remember me Ingy?"

Upon hearing her nickname the redheaded woman turned and faced Special and smiled. "Special!" She grabbed Special around the waist and gave her a kiss on the lips. The dude Inga was dancing with stepped back and smiled as he watched the two women, thinking that he was going to get real lucky and end up with both of these lovely creatures in his bed by the end of the night. Wrong! Special and Inga began dancing with one another, totally forgetting him. When the song ended Special took hold of Inga's hand and led her toward the bathroom without saying a word. Once they were inside of a stall Special dropped to her knees and lifted up Inga's micro skirt and pulled her thong to the side and began licking her wet pussy. "Mmmmmmm, Special, I've missed you sooooo much," Inga moaned as Special brought her to an orgasm quickly. They switched places and Inga returned the favor.

Twenty minutes later the ladies were standing in front of the mirror in the bathroom, fixing their makeup, preparing to reenter the club. "Where is Papio, Special? He did come with you didn't he?" Inga asked as she applied some gloss to her luscious lips.

Special stared at Inga's firm double D-cups and shook her head no. "Not this time, *mami*, he's busy back on the West Coast. I'm only in town for one night. My flight leaves tomorrow at two."

"So I only have the rest of the night with you?" Inga asked with a devilish smile on her face.

"Tonight and the morning. I did say I leave at two in the afternoon. You want to leave now or shall we at least catch the show?"

"Why not, Nicki Minaj is so hot! We might even get her to sign our boobies if we're lucky!"

They both started laughing as they went back into the club to watch the hottest female rapper in the game do her thing. They had a great time but both of them knew that that was just the prelude to the time they were going to have once they made it to Special's suite at the Ritz. It. Was. About. To. Go. Down!

The next morning when Papio woke up, Fay was getting ready to make the drive back to San Diego. He smiled at her. "You are something else, baby. I love your energy for real. But check it, why did you put me up on all of your BI with Special and those niggas Poppa Blue and Lance?"

Fay fastened her bra. "I respect Special; her name has good things behind it down my way, mon. Poppa Blue and I go back and the respect and love is mutual; he a good mon, too. But I like you more than I like the both of them, mon. You do good work, plus you can be trusted to the point that you impressed mi family. So you get special treatment from Fay. You have that right to know what I know."

"Thanks, Fay, that means a lot to me."

"No big. Okay, baby, let Fay go now. I'll give you a holla when it is time to make some money. You most likely will hear from your girl and Poppa Blue before me though. Do the right thing, mon, and don't let your feelings interfere with the business." She gave him a quick kiss and left without letting him say a word.

After the door closed to his hotel room Papio wondered if he should even listen to them when they got at him. Of course he should listen, he had to! This was how he was going to get at that bitch to handle his business and settle his debt with Mr. Suarez. *What the fuck are you thinking nigga?* he asked himself as he grabbed his phone and called Mr. Suarez out in Miami.

After going through the usual insults and banter with Castro, Mr. Suarez came on to the line and Papio told him, "Sir, it looks like things will happen sooner than expected. I have a line on Special, so you can be expecting my next call to inform you that everything is everything."

"Good. This is what I like to hear, *Señor* Papio. I'll inform the chief, we'll be waiting for your call."

"*Sí*, sir." Papio hung up the phone. Since he knew they would be getting in contact with him soon. He decided to go home and chill with Mama Mia until Brandy came out to L.A. next week. He was excited about introducing her to his mother. He knew if Mama Mia loved Special she was going to go crazy over Brandy. He didn't know how wrong he was.

***

Oh my God this feels so damn good! Special thought as she woke up to Inga sucking her pussy so damn right she felt as if she'd died and gone to heaven. That girl had a mean pussy-eating game. It felt as if she couldn't stop cumming last night and now it felt even stronger.

"Yes! Yes! Suck that pussy, Ingy! Suck it, girl! Yes!" Special screamed as she came again. She sighed and smiled as Inga rose from between her legs with a satisfied smile of her own on her face. "Damn, you're good, girl. I mean really good."

"I've missed you so much, Special. I think about that night with you and Papio all of the time."

"I can't tell, why haven't you called me then? We could have set something up. You know it's nothing to have your sexy ass flown out to Cali."

"With school and work I didn't have any extra time. I was seriously thinking about giving you guys a call this summer though. Now that we've bumped into each other I know I'm going to give you a call soon!"

"I like that. You make sure you do because I got some plans for you that's going to blow your mind," Special said with a smile on her face as she thought about Keli. *Damn, that chocolate thang is going to love this sexy red for real.*

"How is Papio? Still looking divine I hope?"

Special shrugged. "Yeah, he's good."

Sensing something was amiss Inga asked, "Is everything okay between you two, Special?"

"Not really, but everything will be good soon. We've had a few bumps in the road but we'll be all right," she said hopefully. Special needed to change the subject or she might start getting depressed. "Come on, baby, let's get dressed and go have a nice brunch on me before I bounce. You got me hungry as I don't know what right about now."

Inga smiled. "Before we go eat let me eat you some more okay?"

"Why don't we eat each other?" Special asked with a wicked grin on her face.

"Mmmmmmmmm," was Inga's reply as she climbed on top of Special's face so she could have full access to her sweet, hot pussy, and the eating began.

Chapter 14

Papio had a huge smile on his face when he saw Brandy step out of the gate from her flight from Oklahoma City. She was looking casually sexy in a pair of jeans and a baby tee, with some bright pink flip-flops on her feet. Though she was pushing forty Brandy could pass for twenty-five easily. Her light brown skin seemed to be glowing as she smiled at the man who captured her heart a year ago. She walked up to him and gave him a tender kiss. "Wow! I can't believe I'm finally on your home court, daddy."

"I known it's been way overdue, *mami*. It's all good. Come on, let's go get your stuff so we can get to the room and make it do what it do. You know I've been missing your sexy self like crazy." He led her toward the baggage claim area.

"Room? I thought we would be staying at your house so I could finally meet Mama Mia."

"We are. Whenever I'm in L.A. I keep a suite at the Westin to make my moves, that's like my office. Since the Lakers are playing game five tonight against the Thunder I thought it would be cool if we went to the game. You know, so we can watch my boys beat up your home team," he said with a smile.

"Now you know you're down bad for that hating you're doing, daddy. My Thunder is going to shock the world by upsetting those fakers!"

"We shall see. I made a few calls and got us some pretty good seats at the Staples Center tonight. We might not have Jack seats but we're on the fourth row center court so we're good."

"Fourth row center court? You never cease to amaze me, daddy. You're already making this trip just perfect for me."

"You ain't seen shit yet, *mami*. I got you for seven days and I'm going to make this one a trip to remember for real."

She squeezed his hand tightly. "I'm going to make sure I give you some extra good loving so you will remember what you got out in Oklahoma City."

"I know that's right. Come on, let's hurry up so I can get you to the room so you can give me all of that extra long!" They were both laughing as they left the airport.

Keli and Twirl had been spending all of their spare time with each other and it was a no-brainer that they were now exclusive. Twirl was feeling her in ways he never thought possible. Keli became giddy whenever she even thought about being with Twirl. Was this love? *It has to be,* she thought as she smiled at her man as he entered her apartment.

"Give me a minute, baby, and I'll be ready," she said as she returned to the bedroom to finish applying her makeup.

"Come on, Kee, you gots to hurry up. You know the traffic heading downtown is going to be crazy. I'm not trying to miss any of the game. Tonight we gots to smash Oklahoma City and take they heart before we fuck around and get upset by Kevin Durant and them young studs."

"Don't panic, baby!" she yelled from the bedroom. "We got this in the bag, the Lakers don't lose at home! We're going to blow those fools out tonight, watch!"

"That's what I want to do is watch but you're in there taking your sweet damn time; we're going to be late," he mumbled.

Keli said, "I heard that, slick."

With a sheepish look on his face Twirl said, "You weren't supposed to. Come on, baby, let's go."

She shook her head from side to side. "I'm coming, but you will be repaid for your slippery tongue, boy." She stepped past him with some extra switching in her thick hips. "I know exactly how I'm gonna repay your horny ass, too. You won't be getting any of this big old ass tonight, buddy." She slapped her firm behind for added effect.

Twirl smiled. "Come on, Kee, you know I was playing!" They both started laughing as he opened the door of his Escalade for her to enter.

Special was relaxing in her media room watching the pre-game talk show before the Lakers game started. She was sipping a glass of wine when Poppa Blue called her. "What's good, Poppa Blue?"

"Just sitting here, getting ready to watch the game. Got a call from my man and he has something nice for us."

"Yeah, how nice?"

"Some real tricky niggas out of Seattle are in town to watch the game tonight and they want some company."

"They on some freaky shit or what?"

"Probably. Their ends are long and they're ready to spend. You can go that route if you want but I was thinking more of a straight jack move. Hit your girl up and meet them after the game, then take them for everything they got."

"Now you know I'm with that; not really in the mood to get all freaky with it anyway. How much you think they got with 'em?"

"My man tells me they're here to score some work so they pockets are thick, he just couldn't be exact with it. Either way it should be a nice come up. The jewels they rocking should be worth a few tickets combined."

"How many of them is there?"

"Two."

"Where are they staying?"

"The Westin down the street from LAX on Century."

"Weapons?"

"None. Straight slipping."

Special liked what she was hearing. "Where do we hook up with them?"

"After the game my mans said they will hook up with you at the Guys & Dolls Lounge in West Hollywood. You know where that's at right?"

"Yeah, over there on Beverly and San Vicente. All right, after everything is everything do we do them or what?"

"Nah, everything is good because my mans said they on some chump time; they won't make any noise at all. Take them for the ends and jewels and step. Get with me tomorrow and I'll set up the sell of the loot and we'll split up then."

"Cool. Tell your man to be looking for two of the baddest bitches inside of the spot around eleven-thirty and everything will go from there. Any other news for me?"

"Nah, everything is quiet right now."

Special stared at the two 9 mm pistols that were within arm's reach. "Don't worry about me, Poppa Blue, I got this. I'll get with you tomorrow."

"Nah, you get with me after everything is everything to let me know that you and your girl are good."

"Gotcha." She finished the call with Poppa Blue then immediately dialed Keli's number.

"Got a nice move set up for us, K."

Keli gave Twirl a quick glance and asked, "When?"

"Tonight. I need you to meet me at my spot in a couple of hours so we can get everything ready. We're to meet some suckers at the Guys & Dolls Lounge in West Hollywood."

"Damn."

"What's up?"

"I'm on my way to the Lakers game with my boo."

Special sighed and thought about that for a minute and then asked, "What are you rocking?"

"You know how I do, girl, I'm good. A pair of jeans, cute blouse, plus some Manolos on the feet."

"That's what's up then. How about this: you meet me at the Guys & Dolls Lounge after the game. We'll hook up in the parking lot and take it from there."

"I can do that."

"Are you sure? If not just let me know and I'll make this move solo."

"It must really be nice you talking about some solo shit huh?"

"You know how I do it when it comes to this paper, any free money is always nice money, K."

"I know that's right, girl. I'll hit you when I'm on my way."

"That's cool, see you in a little bit then." Special stood to go pick out what she was going to wear to the Guys &

Dolls Lounge. *Has to be sexy right in order to rock those Seattle chumps' minds. Game on!*

Keli closed her cell and turned to face Twirl while he drove. "Babe, after the game I got me some business to take care of, so I'm going to need you to drop me off out in West Hollywood, 'kay?"

Not really feeling her words but refusing to sound like a sucker, he said, "Cool. Do you need me to hang with you?"

"Me and my girl Special will be good. I'll get with you after I'm done."

"Yeah, whatever," he said, trying not to sound upset with what she told him but knowing he sounded upset anyway. *Damn, look at me acting like a simp nigga for a broad. Not cool, Twirl, not cool at all,* he thought as he pulled into the parking lot of the Staples Center.

Keli tried her best to hide her smile. She knew it bothered him that she had some moves to make and that made her feel real good about the direction their relationship was headed. If it didn't bother him what she was about to go do with her girl then he really didn't give a fuck about her. Since it did, that told her that he was feeling her just as much as she was feeling him. *Good!* As they walked toward the entrance of the Staples Center she had an extra bounce in her step. She was in love with a man for the very first time and it felt great!

Papio was just opening the car door for Brandy when he got a call on his cell from Q. After closing the door he flipped open his phone and asked, "What's up, my favorite white boy?"

"Some last-minute shit just hit me and I thought you might be interested."

"It depends on if it's worth me interrupting my evening."

"I can't give you an exact figure on the ends but there's enough jewelry that should be worth over a ticket, maybe two. The ends should be nice because these fools are some dope boys out of Seattle. They're out here to score some Purp and a whole bunch of X, from what my people have told me."

"Why not wait until they score and then knock them off for the work?"

"Then you wouldn't get as much. This way you can get the ends for the work and I can keep the jewels, or we can just do our normal split, your call."

"Right now I'm on my way to the Lakers game so it's going to be kinda hard for me to make any last-minute moves, Q."

"Actually it won't be that hard at all."

"Please explain."

"Tell me that you still got your suite at the Westin."

"You already know I do so why do I have to confirm that?"

"Because these fools from Seattle just happen to be staying at that very same hotel."

Papio laughed. "You're bullshitting me?"

"I bullshit you not. And what makes it even sweeter they don't have any weapons. This should go down real smooth, dude. You want in or what?"

Papio turned and stared at Brandy as he waited for the light to turn green. "Yeah, I'm in."

"Good. They're on their way to the game as well so you'll have plenty of time to get set up for their return to the room. The suite number is 8556."

"All right, let me get at Twirl and see what he has up for the night."

"Will it be a problem if he can't get down with you?"

Papio smiled at Brandy. "Nope, I got somebody else on deck if he's busy. I'll get at you after everything is a wrap."

"I see that devious smile I haven't seen in a long time, daddy. What's going on in that head of yours?" Brandy asked, grinning.

Papio held up a finger, signaling her to wait as he hit the speed dial on his cell and called Twirl. "You in the mood to bust a nice move tonight, dog?" Papio asked Twirl.

"You know I'm always ready to make some money, my nigga, what's the business?"

Papio quickly ran everything down to him and finished with, "It should be nice and easy, dog: we strong arm in and get the ends and get right back out down to my suite and chill for the evening. They're boys so they won't bring any attention to them by calling for the peoples."

"That's right. Plus you said they don't got heat. Damn, they slipping like that?"

"That's what Q said, but you know we'll play it as if they have heavy artillery and be safe with it until we have the room secured. No slipping on our end."

"That's what's up."

"Check it, I'm on my way to the Lakers game now. From what Q told me they're already at the game, so when the game is almost over I'll bounce and hit you up, and we'll meet back at my suite at the Westin."

"I'm at the Staples Center now, dog. I'm walking in as we speak."

Papio laughed. "Damn, everybody is watching the Lake Show do they thang tonight huh?"

"You fucking right!"

"All right then let me bounce."

"I'll hit you when the game is almost over. I gots to leave a little earlier anyway to drop my breezy off in West Hollywood."

"For sure. Get at me as soon as you drop her off."

"Bet. I'll holla." Twirl hung up the phone.

Papio turned to Brandy. "After the game I'm going to make a few moves and you may be needed, *mami*. You good?"

"Just like I was needed in New York. Will we ever have a vacation without having to get gangsta with it, daddy?" She smiled, letting him know that she would do whatever he asked of her.

He returned her smile. "You know how I do it, *mami,* so ain't no telling. This one will be easier than the New York move was. All I'm going to need you to do is go to a room for me and knock on the door. Once it's opened me and my mans will handle the rest. You will then go back to our room and chill until I come back."

"That sounds simple enough. I swear you're something else, daddy."

"You know how I do it when it comes to this money." He turned onto the 110 northbound toward downtown Los Angeles and the Staples Center.

Special was all smiles as she watched the Lakers blow out the Oklahoma City Thunder. She slipped into a pair of Dereon jeans, laced up her Jimmy Choo open-toe boots, and went to the bathroom to make sure she was looking right. She applied some light makeup, checked her hair, and decided to let it hang loosely down past her shoulders. "Time to get that money, you bad-ass bitch you," she said aloud and smiled at her reflection in the mirror. She left the bathroom and grabbed her purse, keys, cell phone, and pistols and went downstairs to the garage. Once she was inside of her BMW she called Keli to see if she was on her way to the Guys & Dolls Lounge yet.

"Heading there now. Be there in like twenty." Keli told her.

Special then called Poppa Blue to let him know that the move was in progress.

"Be careful, Special, and make damn sure that you get at me right after you've handled this business."

"All right, I got you. Stop worrying, you know how I do it."

"You damn right I know how you do it, that's why I want to hear from your ass when you're finished!"

"What! Ever! Breakfast on you in the morning, old man," she joked and hung up the phone.

Twirl pulled into the parking lot of the Guys & Dolls Lounge. "All right, baby, you make sure you get at me after you've handled your BI. I got some moves to make with my mans so if you hit me and I don't pick up I'll get back as soon as I'm good."

"All right, babe, you be safe." Keli gave him a nice lengthy kiss before getting out of his SUV.

Chapter 15

Twirl watched as she entered the Lounge and was mesmerized again by all that she was packing. He couldn't control the jealous feelings that overtook him at that very moment so he tried his best to shake it off and get his mind on the upcoming move he was about to go make with Papio. *Stay focused on the money, nigga; that broad ain't going nowhere,* he said to himself as he pulled out of the parking lot and headed toward the Westin.

He pulled out his cell and called Papio. Papio told him that he was on his way to the suite and he would meet him there. They were going to chill and wait for the Seattle dope boys to come back to their suite, and then go get them for all of their money and jewels. Twirl had to smile as he drove. He couldn't help thinking about how Papio always seemed to make getting this money seem so damn easy. "As long as I keep fucking with this nigga my ends is going to get longer and longer. I love that shit!" he said aloud as he turned onto the freeway.

Special entered the club and made a beeline straight toward the bar where Keli was seated, sipping on a Corona beer. She waved at the bartender and pointed toward the bottle of beer Keli had in her hand. "Have you been here long, K?"

"About fifteen minutes or so."

"Poppa Blue just hit me back and told me that those fools are on their way here now. They're with his man Pat Pat."

"Pat Pat? That fool from Mississippi? I remember him from when he first got out here. He used to fuck with my cousins from Nutty Block Crip outta Compton."

"Yeah, he just got out the Feds a few months ago and he's been making some strong moves with Poppa Blue so you know he's correct."

"That's what's up. Is he going to be there when we move on these fools?"

"Uh-uh. He's going to shake once we hook up with them. I don't know the arrangement he has with Poppa Blue and I really don't give a damn, all I'm trying to do is get this money and get the fuck, feel me?"

"You know it. Run the play to me. How are we going to put this down?"

"We're going to let those suckers drive the car and lead us right to the riches. Since they're super slipping it should be nothing for them to take us to the Westin so we can get they ass."

"What if they try some fifty-two fake out shit and don't take us to their suite at the hotel?"

"Then we get gangsta sooner than expected and make our move the strong way. You know how we do."

"Are we going to lay them down?"

"We shouldn't have to go out like that, but if we have to then we'll do what needs to be done."

"I'm not strapped. I was with my boo and didn't bring any heat with me."

Special smiled. "Don't trip, you know I got you. I got two nines out in the Beemer. Once we see how these fools are moving we'll get strapped and ready to do us."

Keli downed her beer. "Well, I guess it's time to get this shit cracking, because Pat Pat just came into the club followed by two high yellow niggas who gots to be those Seattle suckers, looking like they just came from a Jay-Z video shoot with all of that platinum they rocking."

Special calmly turned in her seat and stared at the three men as Pat Pat led them toward the VIP section of the club. "Let's wait for Pat Pat to spot us; then it will be show time. You ready, K?"

Keli smiled. "Always. Let's make it do what it do, girl."

The two women gave each other some dap. It was on.

When Twirl entered Papio's suite he saw Brandy looking absolutely edible sitting in the living room, watching television. "Damn, dog, you didn't tell me you had a lovely lady like this here with you." Twirl sat down on the couch opposite where Brandy was sitting.

"Yeah, dog, this is my *mami,* Brandy. She's from Oklahoma City. Brandy, this is my mans, Twirl."

"Pleased to meet you Twirl."

"Same here. Okay, what's the business, my nigga?"

"We're going to wait until I get word from the bell-hop that the occupants of suite 8556 have returned. We'll let them get comfortable and then we'll send Brandy to their suite. After she knocks and they see her through the peephole and start to open the door, we'll make our move."

"You're positive they're not strapped right?"

Papio smiled. "But of course. But like I said we'll play it like they are and watch our six at all times. Once we secure the room we tie they ass up with some of these plastic cuffs and break they ass." Papio held up four sets of plastic hand restraints.

"I thought you said it was only two of them. Why you got four sets of cuffs?"

"Never can have enough, my nigga. We can tie they hands and feet just to make sure we got they ass tied down right."

"I love how you don't miss shit, my nigga. Did I ever tell you that you're my hero?"

They both started laughing.

"You two are a hot mess. Daddy, I'm going to go take a shower real quick okay? I'm still sweaty from that damn basketball game. It was hot in there," Brandy said.

"You're good, go on and get fresh, *mami*. When we're finished with this move I'm gonna make sure you get right back sweaty."

"Humph. Don't make me no promises you can't keep, daddy," she said in a sassy tone as she stepped toward the bedroom of the suite.

"Since when have I ever sold a wolf ticket, Brandy?"

She smiled. "Never. And don't let tonight be the first time." She left the room laughing.

Twirl waited until the door closed behind her and then whispered, "Damn, my nigga, she is right! I thought you told me she was an older broad."

"She is. She's like in her late thirties, almost forty."

"No fucking way! Stop playing with me! She can't be no more than twenty-five or twenty-six years old, dog."

Papio smiled. "For real, my nigga, she just kept her shit nice and right over the years."

"Damn. One question, my nigga."

"What up?"

"This bellhop you got on your line, is he good or will he have to be disposed of after everything is everything?"

"Tip Toe is my man and he's good, peeps, he's already been broken off so you won't have to worry about him. He has my back one hundred percent."

"I should have known."

Papio laughed. "Yeah, you should have."

Twenty minutes after arriving at the Guys & Dolls Lounge Pat Pat stood in the VIP section and let his eyes roam all over the club until he spotted Special and Keli conversing at the bar. He never met Special before but he knew he had seen Keli around the way. They were looking so damn good that he knew instantly that they were the two ladies Poppa Blue told him to be looking for.

He spoke briefly to one of the Seattle guys and then stepped out of the VIP and headed toward the women. When he made it to the bar he asked, "Are you two ladies ready to make some serious decisions tonight?"

After hearing that question Special smiled at Keli and told Pat Pat, "All the time. But first I gots to call my Poppa."

The code had been given; now all he had to do was give the right reply and it would be time for the business to proceed.

Pat Pat said, "Poppa Blue has left you in good hands this evening."

"In that case, let's do this."

"Special, I assume?"

"That's right. And this sexy specimen here is Keli."

Pat Pat was a dark-skinned, slim-built brother who appreciated a dark-skinned woman. Special was sexy and pretty as fuck but Keli was damn fine! Black was definitely beautiful to him and he was loving what he was looking at. *Mental note: get with Poppa Blue to see if he can hook me up with this bad-ass bitch,* Pat Pat thought.

"All right, ladies, it's time to make it happen. These fools are chipped up and got mad ends at their suite. You're safe, so do what you need to do and make these jokers feel comfortable. They're some tricky-ass niggas so it shouldn't take too many drinks for them to be ready to take y'all back to their suite. Once that goes down it's on y'all. I'll drive them back to the Westin and then it's on. Any questions?"

Special looked at Keli, Keli shook her head no, and Special told Pat Pat, "We're ready."

He smiled. "I know that's right. Let go." He turned without waiting for the ladies and headed back toward the VIP. When they made it in front of the two men from Seattle, Pat Pat made the introduction. "You niggas are in for a hell of a treat tonight. Look at these two bad-ass females I bumped into."

Before Pat Pat could continue, one of the men stood and said, "I know that's right, homie. Ladies, please have a seat. My name is Caz and this is my homie, C-Nutt."

After they were seated Special took the lead. "Hiya, Caz. My name is Shelly and this is my girlfriend, Kamden."

Keli was smiling on the outside but on the inside she was like, *Kamden? That sounds so fucking white!*

"Please allow me the pleasure of buying the bar for you ladies this evening," Caz said conceitedly. "Whatever you want you can have tonight. We got y'all."

Keli smiled. "I already see something I want, Caz."

He laughed. "Is that right? And what's that, baby?"

She pointed directly at C-Nutt. "I want me some C-Nutt."

C-Nutt was a broad-shouldered brother with some real long hair. He looked as if he had some Samoan in him with his thickness. He smiled at Keli. "Baby, if you want some Nutt, then you can have all of me."

"Oh, I want some nut all right. How much you gonna give me?" she flirted shamelessly.

"All you need, baby. Now come over her and sit next to Nutt because you done already got me fired up."

"That's what I'm talking about right there, homie. Well, I guess, Shelly, you and I are the lucky ones tonight."

"Why is that, Caz?" Special asked with a smile.

"Because I'm a boss, and you have the look of a boss female, so two bosses might as well enjoy the night and have a boss-ass time."

How fucking corny is that shit? she thought, but to Caz she said, "I know that's right, daddy."

"Looks like y'all got it all mapped out then. Excuse me for a minute, because since y'all done took the best the club has to offer I gots to go see if I can find me a lovely honey to chill with." Pat Pat left the VIP.

"All right, my nigga, we're going to chill, but when we're ready to roll out we'll holla," Caz said as he wrapped his arm around Special and smiled. "Yeah, we're definitely going to have a good time tonight, baby."

"Hmmmm, what makes you say that, Caz?"

"'Cause I know how to treat a fine woman to the best of everything, baby. And I plan on treating you all night long."

"Seeing that you're outshining every other nigga in this spot tonight I have no doubt that you will be a man of your word and treat me right. But I have to be straight with you, Caz, so we won't have any illusions about what's going to pop off. I expect to have a good time with you, and I also expect to be compensated for making sure that you have an equally good time. Cool?"

"Baby, I'm a Hilltop Seattle nigga and nothing in this world is for free, no nigga understands this better than me and my homie C-Nutt. Don't sweat the formalities, ma, I got you. Now sit back and chill because tonight the world is yours, compliments of yours truly and my man C-Nutt. Hilltop in this bitch!" Caz yelled and started laughing.

Special smiled. "I like your get down, Caz; you're a boss for real." *You fucking lame-ass jerk, you're about to get got. Hilltop my ass. If Seattle is full of tricks like y'all I may need to make me a trip to that rainy motherfucker,* she thought as she smiled and continued to flirt with Caz.

Twirl checked his gold Rolex. "Damn, my nigga, still no word from your peeps huh?"

Papio was lying on the couch with his head on Brandy's lap, watching the highlights from the Lakers game five blowout of the Oklahoma City Thunder. "Not yet. Don't trip, it's all good, those fools are probably out getting their trick on. They should be back in a little while. I mean what else is it to do this late on a Tuesday night?"

"That's right. Shit, it's almost two in the morning. Those fools are most likely faded or some shit."

"Which will make our business even easier."

"Right," Twirl said as he once again thought about calling and checking on Keli. He was starting to worry if she was good, and those thoughts were fucking with him big time. There was no way in the world he could lose her now that she had become a part of his life. He was in love for the very first time and it felt good. Just his damn luck he had to go and fall in love with a down-ass female who was living the wicked life. *We're going to have a serious talk about changing some shit,* he thought as he once again looked at his watch.

Papio's cell chimed, informing him that he had a text message. He sat up and grabbed his phone and smiled when he saw that the bellhop, Tip Toe, just texted him, letting him know that the occupants of suite 8556 were entering the hotel. Papio got to his feet and stretched; it was time to get ready. He went into the bedroom of the suite and came back with a gym bag with the weapons he had chosen for the robbery.

He set the gym bag onto the table in front of the couch and pulled out four chrome H&K .40-caliber pistols equipped with silencers. After checking each clip, making sure that they were full, he tossed two of the pistols to Twirl along with two sets of the plastic hand restraints. He reached inside of the bag again and pulled out two more pistols; these were smaller than the .40s he pulled out first. He tossed Twirl one and put one in the small of his back. He wasn't taking any chances tonight; he was going to be on point in every way. He thought back to how he almost was killed by taking shit for granted back when he was in Oklahoma City making a move against a youngster from Dallas. He swore he'd never slip again. *Special taught me that lesson well,* he thought as he smiled at Twirl and asked, "You ready, dog?"

Twirl's answer to his question was to rack a live round into each chamber of the three guns he was going to use. He then put the backup pistol in the small of his back. "Yeah, my nig, let's make it happen."

Papio turned and faced Brandy. He expected to see some fear on her face but was surprised when he didn't notice any. *I guess she's finally gotten used to my get down. Good,* he thought. "You ready, *mami?*"

"Mm-hmm. Whenever you're ready, daddy. I'm good."

"Cool. Check it, let's give them like ten more minutes to get settled and then we'll take the stairs up to the either floor and make it happen. Remember, *mami,* all I want you to do is knock on the door. When you see some eyes at the peephole say, 'Damn, are y'all going to let me in or what?' That will give them pause but they should be comfortable enough to open the door. Once we hear the door opening, step away and head back down here. Don't do no waiting, Brandy, get to stepping and don't look back. You understand?"

She smiled. "You don't have to tell me that twice, daddy. And you damn sure don't have to worry about me waiting around!"

They all started laughing. Papio was about to say something when he heard his phone chime again. He picked it up and saw that the Seattle men were at their room and they weren't alone. They brought two females with them. After he finished reading the text from Tip Toe he folded his phone and turned toward Twirl. "Looks like they got some company: two broads, so those extra cuffs will be needed. Let's make it," he said as he led the way out of the suite.

***

Special was slightly buzzed from the liquor she drank at the club but she was good. She knew that once they got Caz and C-Nutt comfortable it was going to be on and popping. *This is going to be one easy-ass lick,* she thought as she stepped out of her Jimmy Choos and made herself comfortable on the couch. She smiled as Keli was walking around the suite, acting as if this was the most expensive hotel room she'd ever seen. *Go on and play that role, girl; get these suckers nice and ripe for the taking,* she said to herself as she watched Keli do her thing.

Caz's cocky ass was walking around the room like he was a big boss, bragging about how they come to the Westin every time when they come to L.A. to handle their business. Special shook her head and thought, *I bet you switch that shit up after tonight, nigga.* C-Nutt took off his shirt and she was impressed by all of the muscles that ripped all over his body. *Damn, that nigga is a big old sexy nigga. Humph, just one big sexy-muscled sucker,* Special said to herself as she watched Keli go over to C-Nutt and begin to rub her hands all over his body. She started kissing his chest and he moaned. *Good girl; let's get this party started,* thought Special as she stood and began to take off her blouse. Caz noticed that and smiled and quickly stepped to her and helped her out of her clothes. When she was stripped down to her bra and matching thong, she said, "Damn, daddy, y'all ain't got no music in this expensive-ass suite?"

Caz was mesmerized by her beauty and barely heard a word she said. He shook his head from side to side. "Damn, Shelly, you're one bad-ass broad. Yeah, we got some music in this piece." He turned and went to the entertainment center that was located in the middle of the living room and turned on the satellite radio. Keyshia Cole's "Shoulda Let You Go" came on and that put a smile on Special's face, because that music was just what she needed when everything went down. Keli was now kissing C-Nutt and making sure she got him nice and fired up. Special stepped over to them and pulled her from C-Nutt's embrace.

"Uh-uh, let's give these ballers a real show." She began to tongue kiss Keli tenderly. Caz and C-Nutt both had a shocked expression on their faces as they watched the two ladies as they kissed each other passionately.

"Damn, cuz, this is gonna be off the chain," C-Nutt said as he watched the women while fondling himself.

"You ain't lying, Nutt. The homies ain't gonna believe this shit when I tell them about this demo. Wish I'd brought the video cam for this one."

"Fuck a video camera, my nigga, we gonna remember this one for a real long time, Caz."

"I know that's right, cuz!"

Special pulled away from Keli and winked, letting her know that it was almost time for them to make their move. She turned and picked up her purse and told Keli, "Come on, girl. Let's go get in the shower so we can be squeaky clean for the fellas."

Keli scooped her purse from the table and followed her into the bathroom while both men sat there as if in a daze at what they were watching.

Special stood in the doorway of the bathroom. "Give us a few minutes and then we'll be back to blow the both of your minds." She stepped into the bathroom before either could respond.

"Damn, my nigga, we got to throw that nigga Pat Pat something extra for this shit! You see how bad these bitches are?" asked Caz.

"Yeah, loc, I do. That nigga looked out for real. But look, we should go take these ends down to the car while we're freaking these bitches; never can be too careful, cuz."

"Come on with that shit, Nutt. We're way out the way and it's after two in the morning, my nigga. We're good. Relax and get ready to flip these bitches real swell," Caz said as he began to take off his clothes.

Though he knew better the liquor overrode his first mind to protect their money. *Fuck it, we're good. We've done this shit too many times; ain't shit gone happen,* he thought as he too began to undress.

Special and Keli came out of the bathroom, both wearing nothing but a towel wrapped around their luscious bodies. They were still slightly wet from their quick shower and this only added to the men's arousal.

Just as Caz was stepping toward Special there was a knock on the door. Caz stopped and turned toward C-Nutt and gave him a quizzical look.

C-Nutt shrugged and wrapped his arms around Keli. "Probably that nigga Pat Pat."

That seemed to relax Caz as he smiled and went to open the door. When he peeped through the peephole and saw a gorgeous-looking woman on the other side he smiled.

"Damn, are y'all going to let me in or what?" asked Brandy.

Caz's smile widened as he thought Pat Pat had added another beauty to the pot. *Yes!* he thought but how mistaken he was. As soon as he opened the door Brandy was no longer standing there; in her place were two men, each with two pistols in their hands. *Damn, we're fucked,* was Caz's only thought as he quickly raised his hands in the air.

Papio put the barrel of his silenced gun to Caz's forehead. "Make one wrong move and your brains will be splattered all over this fucking room."

Twirl wasted no time and rushed right past Papio with his own gun aimed at the big Samoan who had his arms around Keli. When he focused and saw that it was in fact Keli who was being held by C-Nutt with nothing on but a large terry cloth towel, he lost it. Without thinking he pulled the trigger of one of the guns in his hands and shot C-Nutt twice in his right leg. The only reason he didn't go for the kill shot was because Keli was too close to C-Nutt and he didn't want to risk shooting her accidentally.

When Papio heard the two soft "phfft" sounds he knew that for some reason Twirl had to fire his weapon, so without any hesitation he did the same. He shot Caz in his right and left knees and watched as he dropped to the floor, grimacing in pain. He then closed the door to the suite and stepped into the living room and smiled. "Well, well look what we got here, a big old fucking freak party huh?" Papio stared at Special with a look of disgust on his face and continued. "You good, my nigga?"

All Twirl saw was red but he refused to lose it in front of his man Papio. "I'm good, dog, let's get what we came for and get the fuck." He then proceeded to place the plastic restraints on C-Nutt and Caz. After they were secured Twirl began going through the suite looking for the money and anything else he wanted.

He opened the closet inside of the bedroom and found a large Louis Vutton suitcase filled with money. He smiled and zipped the suitcase closed and tossed it onto the bed. After a few more minutes of searching for more loot he grabbed the suitcase and went back into the living room.

Papio had made Special and Keli get dressed; he had other plans for them. He didn't know exactly what the deal was with Twirl but he knew it was something. *The other female in the room has to be the broad he's feeling,* thought Papio as he continued to keep his eyes on Caz and C-Nutt, who were both sitting on the couch crying softly. Neither of them said a word as they watched Papio keep his guns aimed at them. All they wanted was to make it out of this madness alive. And they knew the only way for that to happen was for them to cooperate totally.

When Twirl came into the living room Papio nodded toward Caz and C-Nutt. Twirl understood what that subtle nod meant and stepped over to the two men from Seattle and snatched their jewelry. He took a pair of solid platinum and diamond earrings out of Caz's ear and set them onto the table in front of the couch. He removed several large diamond and platinum rings from Caz's fingers and a Cartier watch and heavy platinum and diamond bracelet from his wrist. He then relieved C-Nutt of all his jewels as well.

"Come on, man. Y'all got all of our shit. Please don't kill us. Let us make it, man," begged Caz.

Twirl put his index finger to his lips and said, "Shh-hhhhhhh." After placing all of the jewels inside of the suitcase Twirl stood and stared at Papio. Papio pointed his guns at the women and gave a nod for them to follow him. They stood without saying a word and did as

he motioned for them to do. Twirl picked up the suitcase and followed them as they left the room.

Both Caz and C-Nutt sighed with relief as they
watched as the door closed to their suite. They had just
been shot and robbed for over $2 million in jewelry
plus $3 million in cash. None of that seemed to matter
at that moment because they were both happy as hell
to still be breathing. Now they needed to figure out how
to get the medical attention they needed to stop the
bleeding from their legs.

Chapter 16

Papio didn't say a word until he had Special and Keli inside of his suite. Brandy came out of the bedroom when she heard them enter. "Did everything go okay, daddy?"

Papio laughed. "We're good. Real good, in fact. *Mami,* I'd like for you to meet someone. Special, this is Brandy. Brandy, this is Special."

Brandy put her hands to her mouth and thought, *oh my god!* She then stared at Papio to try to see if she could figure out how he was going to handle this situation. *I hope and pray that he doesn't kill Special,* she thought as she stared at Special, who, for some strange reason, seemed to be extremely calm.

Before anyone could say anything else Twirl spoke up. "Dog, this shit is fucked up and I want to apologize for tripping out up there. I tripped because this stupid mothafucka has my head fucked up. This is my girl, my nigga. You know, the one I told you about."

Papio gave him a nod in understanding because he didn't want to tip Keli off that Twirl had already put him up on her knowing Special.

Special finally spoke. "Ain't this a nice reunion. Girl, this is too fucking funny. Twirl is your boo you been telling me about?"

With a puzzled expression on her face Keli said, "You know him?"

Special stared at Twirl and pointed toward Papio and said, "He's Papio's good friend."

"Shit."

"Exactly." Special laughed.

"I'm glad you think this shit is humorous, Special. You do know that I'm not letting your ass out of this suite alive right?" Papio said in a tone that Brandy had never heard him use before.

Special stared at him with a challenging look. "Stop being so damn emotional, Clyde. I know you're hot at me but look at it from my side; you would have done the exact same thing if you was still on the grind as serious as I was. I did what I did. It may seem fucked up to you and I understand that. That shit was a year ago. Shit has gotten thicker and I got myself into some deeper shit by not letting those fucking Indians take you. You owe me for real."

"Owe you? Bitch, I don't owe your shysty ass nothing but a motherfucking bullet in your brain. Yeah, I do headshots, bitch, not leg shots," he spat angrily.

His words bounced right off of her. "Whatever, nigga. I need you, Clyde, and like I said, you owe. I have a way that will get you that one hundred million you want. If you help me get out of a monster squeeze with some majors in the game I'll make sure you get that one hundred mill before the end of the summer."

Papio smiled as he thought about what Fay had told him about the device they purchased. His mind began calculating how he was going to use Special to get that money as well as take her life in the process. Yeah, everything had fallen right in place perfectly.

"Unless you can give me a hundred mill right now I'm not even trying to hear anything your wack ass is saying, Special. I don't trust your skank ass and you already know I'm not believing anything you got to tell me."

"Just hear me out, and when I'm finished, if you're not feeling my words, then do what you got to do, nigga."

He looked at Twirl. Twirl shrugged his broad shoulders as if saying, "What else do you got to lose?" Papio smiled. "Speak."

"You already know about the device so there's no need for me to go into specifics," Special said as she turned and faced Brandy, who was still standing in the doorway of the bedroom.

"You can speak freely, she's good. She's my future wifey."

Special grinned at him. "Sure, whatever. Like I was saying, you already know about the device and how it gets down. I now am part owner of that device. With that in our hands we can get that one hundred mill you want plus way more in no time. I'm willing to get that to you if you can find a way to help me out of a serious jam."

"What kind of jam are you in, Special?"

"When I didn't let those Indians take you I not only crossed them but I crossed some major Cubans out of Miami. They got a hit out on me, Clyde. I got to either get right and get the fuck or get at them some way and bring an end to their hunt. I'm not built to get at them for real, you and I both know that. But I'm not scared either. If I got to go out I'm going out blasting. I was hoping that you could make something pop for me."

"Do you have a name of these Cubans?"

"The Suarez organization."

Papio whistled. "Damn, you fucked with some big ones for real. They ain't nothing to be played with."

"Tell me something I don't know. So, are you going to help me out or what, Clyde?"

He frowned at her. "Stop calling me that shit! The only way I'll fuck with you on this shit is if you put the device in my hand. I can make my own moves once I got it. I ain't trying to trust you with shit."

"I should be able to make that happen but you have to understand that I have two partners in this with me. You will have to get with them and set up something so everyone involved can get something."

Papio thought about Fay and smiled. "I'm cool with that. All right, I'll fuck with you and see what I can do to get you out of this jam with Mr. Suarez."

Special sighed with relief. "You know them, don't you, Clyde?"

He laughed. "You could say that. And I told your ass to stop calling me Clyde!"

Special shook her head from side to side. "Whatever."

"Okay, I have a few questions here," said Twirl. "First, what the fuck is this device you're talking about? Second, why the fuck was your ass stripped down to a fucking towel, looking like you was about to fuck the shit out of that fat-ass, Samoan-looking nigga?" he asked Keli.

Before Keli could speak, Papio told Twirl, "Dog, the device this scandalous motherfucka is talking about it the coldest shit in the game right now." He then went on and told him about how he helped rob those banks in San Diego with Kango and his crew.

"So you're telling me we can run into banks and shit and won't have a damn thing to worry about as far as security cameras and alarms?"

"That's right."

"And you're part owner of this shit?" he asked Special.

"Yep," she answered with a smile on her face.

"Damn. All right, now what's the business, Ms. Keli?"

"You already know the business, Twirl. We were about to hit those sucker-ass fools before you and your man came in and took over shit. I wasn't about to do no fucking, we were just about to make our move when y'all came into the suite. You know how I get down so I don't even know why you tripping out anyway. This shit is business and business only."

Twirl had heard enough. He didn't want to further discuss this topic in front of Papio. "Yeah, whatever, we'll get back to this shit later. What up, dog, how we gonna move this shit?"

"I guess I'm going to have to make a call to Mr. Suarez and see if I can get him to let this wack-ass female make it."

"Do you think he'll go for it?"

"It depends. This is something that's going to take some time. So in the meantime you need to be making some arrangements for me and my man so we can make a few moves with that device."

"Do what you do and get with me Friday. I should have it by then. Seriously, Papio, I know you're still fucked up with me for what I done. I understand that and I understand that the only reason you're doing this for me now is the money. I respect that. I knew that was the only way I could get you to even listen to me. Thank you."

"Don't thank me yet, ain't nothing guaranteed that Mr. Suarez will let me in on this shit."

"I know. But I also know how you get down, you want that hundred mill more than anything in this world."

"And?"

Special smiled. "You're going to make it happen, Pussy Monster. I know you will."

He smiled at the phrase she used: Pussy Monster. That's what she used to call him when he would sex her crazy. A Pussy Monster was a man who did the pussy so right it screamed as if it had seen a monster. He shook his head. "You are one nutty bitch."

"Compliments will get you everywhere with me, Clyde."

"Ugh!" Brandy rolled her eyes. "Okay, now what's going on, daddy? Is everything okay now?"

Papio turned and faced her. "Everything is good, *mami*." He then went and opened the suitcase and emptied the money all over the floor and smiled. "Can't stop, won't stop, *mami,* you know how I do it."

Brandy shook her head from side to side and said, "Yes, that I do. I'm going to sleep now."

"All right, after I get everything situated I'll be in in a little bit." He stepped to her and gave her some tongue. He gave her firm ass an extra squeeze for Special's benefit then let her go into the bedroom. Brandy had a smile on her face as she closed the door.

"Oh, how sweet, you done went and got yourself an older woman. Hope she takes good care of you, Clyde," Special said with a confident grin on her face.

"She gets me all right. Don't let the age fool ya ass, she's at the top of her game." *Wait a minute, how in the hell did she even know that Brandy is an older broad? She damn sure don't look no older than twenty-seven,* he said to himself.

Special smiled at him and shook her head. *This nigga is still so transparent, I can see right through his ass. He does still love me. But it's going to take some time to get him back to where he was,* she said to herself. "Mama Mia told me you were fucking with an older broad out of Oklahoma City, Clyde, that's how I knew about her age. She keeps herself right, I must say, because if Mama Mia wouldn't have told me I would have never guessed she was damn near forty."

"You've spoken to my mother?"

"Yeah. We had lunch and went and got massages a few weeks back. I had to talk to her to let her know what went down in my own way so she wouldn't hate me. Regardless of what you think, I love that woman and I would never do anything to hurt her."

"Bitch, are you serious? You were going to cross her and hurt her the worst ever if you would have let those Indians take my ass out! You must be stupid or some shit! Check it though, let's dead this convo before I forget about the deal we just made and blast your fucking ass right now."

Special saw that she hit a nerve and let things go. *Later for that shit,* she thought. *I'm not going to push him too hard right now. But I know one damn thing for sure: there's no way in hell I'm going to let him stay with that old hag with that fat ass. He's my Clyde, dammit, all mines!*

Chapter 17

Special and Poppa Blue were sitting in his office discussing what had taken place at the Westin. Poppa Blue rubbed his full white beard as he listened to Special as she told him how Papio and Twirl entered the suite and took complete control of the robbery. He smiled after she was finished. "I like this kid. From everything you've told me about him he seems serious when it comes to getting his paper."

"That's one thing I can say: when it comes to getting that money Papio don't be on no fake shit. He moves at a pace like no one I have ever seen before. Every move is calculated and planned to the tee. As soon as I saw his face I said to myself, 'damn, this fool done beat me to another lick.'"

"That's right, he did beat you out on that Italian clown huh?"

"Yep. Nicoli was my move and was going to get me a nice chunk of change. I was sitting on that clown for five months and then Papio and Twirl comes out of nowhere and snatched that away from me. Shit, he did the same thing with the Indians, too. It's like every time I get a line on a nice one he comes out of nowhere and beats me to the punch. That's some strange shit right there, Poppa Blue."

"Not really. All that means is he has some solid contacts in the game. It's not like the information I pass along to you is privileged, Special. Shit, any nigga with any type of street connects can come up with the same information I get for you; Papio is obviously well informed and has some solid people on his team. Now, what's the deal with the Suarez business? How is he going to make that business disappear?"

She shrugged her shoulders. "He said he's going to call in a favor and see what he can come up with and get with me. He's dealt with them before and has some serious ties to them."

"And how do you know this?"

"I know Papio, Poppa Blue. I saw it in his eyes. That nigga knows he can make it happen for me. That cocky, pretty-ass man knows he has the advantage by me needing his ass right now. And he plans to use that as best as he can."

"Do you think he'll try to bounce back and cross you later in the game for what you did to him in Dallas?"

Special smiled at her mentor and friend and answered honestly, "I'd bet my life on it that that's his plan as of right now. I know that man like a book and he thinks he's in the prime position to get money as well as get back at me for doing him dirty. But there's two things he doesn't know that tips everything back in my favor in all of this shit."

"I know one of them, please enlighten me of the second."

"He still loves me, Poppa Blue. I see it in his eyes. That love is going to make sure he does whatever he has to keep me breathing."

"You better be right about this, Special, 'cause if you're not you're a dead woman."

"Don't I know it. Let's get to business. I need that device so that nigga can get a move or two under his belt and feel comfortable so he can put shit in motion with the Cubans."

"Lance brought it to me yesterday, so whenever you want it it's on deck. But I want you to make sure you let Papio know that it never leaves your sight. If something has to go down then you have to be a part of it, period, no objections whatsoever."

Special laughed. "Poppa Blue, now I know you didn't think I was going to let his ass get all the money without me getting some of that shit. You gots to know me better than that. He's not going to like this one bit but he has no fucking choice."

"Also, let him know that your two partners expect a fair share of whatever move he puts down. Ten percent to be exact. We need some return on our money and every move he makes takes away from us making moves of our own."

"Understood. He shouldn't have any problems with that."

"Before the device touches his hand make damn sure that he understands this is not negotiable, Special. You have to maintain some control of this shit. This is a situation that can get real fucked up real quick if you don't. Too many emotions are involved in this and I don't like it when emotions are twisted with business. This is serious; your life is on the line, girl."

"I got you, Poppa Blue. Now give me that damn device so I can get with this fool. The quicker I get him started on those Cubans, the quicker this shit will be over with."

"I wish I could share the confidence you have in Papio. I just don't think he has that kind of pull, Special. This is some major shit here. Those Cubans won't easily go for crossing out someone they've dealt with for years."

"When it comes to the money and making shit that's impossible happen, Papio is the best in the business, Poppa Blue. On top of everything he loves me and that love is going to make everything all good, watch."

Poppa Blue smiled and shook his head from side to side. "I never thought I'd ever hear you speak on love so much. Your mother is looking down on you smiling right now, girl, God rest her soul."

Special frowned. "Kill that shit, Poppa Blue. It is what it is. That nigga loves me and I'm going to use that love to make sure I remain breathing, plain and simple."

"No, you kill that shit. You love that nigga just as much as he loves you. The sooner you admit that to yourself, the better off everything will be."

Special stuck out her right hand. "Gimme the device, Poppa Blue. I gots to go."

With a stubborn look on his face Poppa Blue asked, "Do you love him, Special?"

"Yes! Are you happy now? Gimme the damn thing! Ugh!"

Poppa Blue laughed as he reached inside of his desk and pulled out the small garage door remote–looking device and gave it to her. "Love is a good thing, Special, but never let love override your intellect. Your street smarts and instincts are among the best I've ever came across; never second-guess them."

She put the device inside of her Gucci bag and stood. "I never do, Poppa Blue. That's why I'm making these moves, not out of love, just plain old common sense. Talk to ya later, old man. Give you a holla in a few days."

Poppa Blue shook his head as he watched Special leave his office and home. He prayed that everything would be all right with her. If it wasn't he knew that his days were numbered, because there was no way in hell he was going to let those Cubans get away with hurting a hair on that beautiful head of Special's. "Come on, Papio, handle your business, young nigga," Poppa Blue said aloud as he sat back in his seat and thought about what moves had to be made for later in the game. Always trying to stay three moves ahead was how he got down; that's one of the reasons he'd been in the game this long.

"My God! I love you, baby! I love this dick! Don't you stop! Hit it harder, Twirl! Hit! It! Harder!" screamed Keli as she raked her French tips across Twirl's back. Twirl groaned loudly as he continued to pound away at Keli's soaking wet pussy. He gave a grunt and she knew that he was about to come. "Yes! Yes, baby! Let it go! Come with me, baby, let's come together!" she screamed as her juices started pouring out of her like a faucet turned high. The flood she was releasing triggered Twirl and he came with her in several large spurts, After their orgasms slowly subsided Keli laid her head on top of Twirl's sweaty chest and smiled. "Damn, baby, that was intense. You never gave it to me like that before. What got into you?"

Waiting until his breathing became even he told her, "For real, I think it was some jealous shit that made me give it to your ass like that, ma."

"Huh?"

"While we were going at it all I kept thinking about was you fucking that fool from Seattle and that shit got me madder and madder."

"Madder and madder huh? How about harder and harder! Your dick has never been that hard. You know what that means right?"

"What?"

"You get turned on by the thought of another man fucking me. You may be on some freaky shit, baby. We might have to get a threesome going with me, you, and another man. You will give me the best fucking I've ever had in my life. What'cha think?"

Twirl pushed her off of his chest and got off the bed. He turned and faced her. "I love you, Keli. I'm in love with your ass. That's why I got so damn hot behind seeing you with that nigga. This was some fucking bomb-ass makeup sex because you begged me to forgive you for doing you. Don't get it twisted and think I'm one of those kinky freak-type niggas who gets off on seeing his girl get flipped by another man. You said you love me and you wanted to be with me for the long ride."

"I do."

"Good. If it's real then you're going to have to fall back on making moves and doing that shit with Special. It's got to be about me and you exclusively. Never thought I'd be on this type of shit but it is what it is. Choose now. Is it me or the life?"

"What about you? What are you going to give up for this relationship?"

"I don't have a extreme amount of broads on my line or any extra shit going down. I make my money and I take care of shit. What you want from me, Keli? Whatever you want you will get. I want you to be mines, all mines, baby. The thought of another nigga touching you drives me fucking crazy. I could have killed that fool last night and made extra drama with the business and that's not cool at all. So either you make it be known right here right now what's what or I'm out. Your call. Make it."

Keli smiled and thought about how she had never in her twenty-seven young years of life ever wanted a man as much as she wanted Twirl. She not only was physically attracted to him; she knew without a doubt that she loved him. She was in love with him and she was not going to let him get away from her. But she also loved the carefree lifestyle she lived and wasn't sure if she was ready to give that up just yet. "Baby, I love you and yes, I am in love with you too. I will do whatever it takes to make you happy. I want to keep you happy, Twirl. I know you can keep me happy as well but there are some things I'm not ready to give up yet."

"Like what?"

"Making moves with Special and doing me." Before he could object she held up her small hands to stop him. "Wait, let me finish. I feel you on the fucking other nigga part because that's disrespectful and I would never want you to think that I would ever intentionally diss you like that, because I wouldn't. I'm a money-getting bitch and I get my own, baby, you gots to respect that as well. I have to remain a free spirit or I'm nothing. If I'm nothing to myself how can I be anything to you, baby?"

"All right, you still make your moves with your girl, but no way do you do any fucking any other niggas, Keli. You make damn sure that I'm aware of all moves and how shit is going to go down. I may not be in on your shit but I have to be on notice just in case some shit goes left. I have to be there to protect what's mines as well. Cool?"

She smiled brightly. "Cool. Now come here and give me some more of that bomb-ass dick!"

He shook his head from side to side as he happily obliged her request.

When Special made it back home she kicked off her shoes and went into the kitchen to make herself something to eat. While she was preparing her food she couldn't help but wonder if she was making the right decision about putting Papio in her mess. She shook those thoughts out of her head because she knew she was right. Papio was her best bet at keeping her life together. She knew it all along but it was confirmed when his cocky ass smiled that special smile of his when he spoke on asking the Cubans for a favor. *He knows them! That alone makes things easier,* she thought as she grabbed the plate of eggs and bacon and went into the dining room to munch on the small breakfast she just made.

Her thoughts switched to Brandy while she ate. She knew that there was no way in hell Papio was feeling that old bitch over her. She had to admit that Brandy was some eye candy, for real one bad bitch. That thought fucked with her tremendously. She tried to find a flaw in her but couldn't. Not only was she pretty; she had a body that was nice and tight. She even seemed down with the program and that gave her more reasons to feel threatened than anything else. Papio craved a woman who looked good and was down for him and the business; to him that equaled the perfect mate. *Shit, that was the main reason why he fell so damn hard for me in the first place,* she said to herself as she picked up her glass of apple juice and took a deep gulp. *No way can I afford to let that old bitch get in the way of my plans. She can have that nigga for real but only after my business is taken care of. Who the fuck am I kidding? She can't have him! Papio is my man! My Clyde and there was no way in hell I'm going to sit back and let that country bumpkin take him away from me. Once everything is everything I'm going to pull my ace in the hole out and get what's mine. That nigga loves me just as much as I love his fine ass. I know it's going to be hard to get him back like he was but I got to. I got to get my Clyde back,* she said to herself as she grabbed her plate and took it back in to the kitchen.

She grabbed the phone and called Papio. When he answered she told him, "I got that thang; we need to hook up. We got some more business to discuss before we make the first move."

"Yeah, whatever. When and where?"

"Why you being like this, Clyde? We gonna make a lot of money and all is going to be good. Ain't that what you want?"

"When I wanted it all to be good all you wanted was the ends. Now that you need a nigga to save your punk-ass life you want it to be all lovey-dovey and shit. You woke a nigga up, Special. Now that I'm woke you trying to rock me back to sleep. That's not gon' happen. Business is business and that's all it is between us. Business! So like I said, when and where?"

Special checked the time. "I wanna see Mama Mia, I'll be at your spot tonight at seven."

"No, we don't handle no business at my home. Some-place else, Special."

"Fuck you, Clyde! Seven at your place or it's a wrap, nigga. I don't really need you all that bad. Don't forget a bitch does have some millions in the vault. I can easily disappear and say fuck you and those Cuban motherfuckers! Then you getting that hundred million you've been working so hard to get will take that much longer. You know this device is the key to you getting that shit this year! Hell within the next two months! So stop fucking with me, you emotional-ass nigga."

"Seven it is." Papio hung up the phone.

Special smiled into the receiver. "Yes, seven it is, Clyde."

Chapter 18

Special didn't know for sure whether Brandy would be at Papio's home so she went and got a little extra with her choice of clothing for the evening. Not too dressy but clean enough to let Brandy know that she wasn't going to be the only five star in the house. A pair of loose-fitting slacks that showed off every sensual curve of her body, topped with a sheer white blouse with a lacy black bra underneath. Her shoe game was always up to par but for tonight's meeting she chose a pair of lace-up shoe boots by Pedro García and felt as if she was killing it as she pulled into the circular driveway of Papio's spectacular home in Riverside, California. Smelling good from her Glow perfume by Jada she was confident that she was on her A game as she stepped to the door and smiled as Mama Mia came outside and gave her a tight hug.

Mama Mia turned and led her into the house. Once they entered the living room Special almost felt sick. Brandy looked stunning to say the least. But what really ripped through Special was how comfortable the older woman seemed to be inside of Papio's home. Brandy was seated on the expensive leather couch with one foot tucked up under her firm ass, sipping a glass of white wine. Special didn't mean to stare but she just couldn't help herself. Brandy was looking fine and she knew it. She had her shoulder-length hair pulled back in a ponytail and the cream-colored hooded dress by Stella & Jamie fit her perfectly, Special noticed.

Brandy stood and said, "Hello, Special. Nice to see you again."

Special smiled even though she was seething on the inside. "Likewise. Hope you didn't get too spooked with all of that drama the other night."

Brandy laughed. "Girl, nothing can surprise me when it comes to Papio. Let me go see if he's finished getting dressed. I'll be right back."

Mama Mia waited until Brandy was all of the way up the stairs before saying, "Don't let her get to you, *mija*. Papio loved you and that won't change because he has a new friend. Don't make yourself crazy by her. That's exactly what they both want. Be real cool and you will win my son's heart back. Trust me on this, *sí?*"

Special smiled at the small woman and answered, "*Sí*, Mama Mia. I'm okay. She is pretty though huh?"

Mama Mia laughed as she pulled Special into the kitchen where she was preparing dinner of enchiladas, rice, and refried beans. "Brandy is indeed very pretty; she's smart, too. She is very nice, Special, I will never lie about that, but she's not the one for Papio. The age difference isn't the reason why either. She's just not the type of woman who can keep him happy."

"What makes you feel that way? She seems like she's ready, willing, and able to do whatever he tells her to."

"Exactly. See, Papio needs a strong woman. A woman who will not let him call all of the shots all of the time. That's why he was so much in love with you. You showed him that you were your own woman and he respected that. He respects Brandy and he cares for her, I can see this easily. But he doesn't want her for the long time, *mija*, he wants you."

Special sighed. "I'm glad one of us is confident about this because I sure don't feel like I'm the one he wants. Look how good she looks, Mama Mia,"

Mama Mia laughed again and shook her head from side to side. "It's not the look, *mija,* it's what inside of the heart. My son has you inside of his heart and in time everything will come out, you will see."

Before Special could respond Papio came into the kitchen with a smile on his face. "Well, well, glad to see you could make it on time. Come on, let's go, chop it up real quick while Mama Mia finishes dinner."

"That's what's up. Is your little friend going to join us while we discuss our business?" Special asked and wanted to slap herself the instant she spoke those words. *Ugh.*

"Nah. Brandy is going to chill outside by the pool until dinner is ready. I trust her but she doesn't need to be all in the mix, she knows what's up. Come on," he said as he led her out of the kitchen and into the living room.

He stepped behind the bar and asked, "Do you want a drink?"

"Some wine would be nice."

After pouring himself a glass of Hennessy he poured some of the same white wine that Brandy had been drinking and gave Special her drink. "So, where's the device?" he asked as he sat down on the opposite end of the sofa from where Special was sitting.

Special sipped her drink. "Damn, nigga, you scared of me or some shit? Why you sitting way down there? Come and sit next to me so I can look into those killer brown eyes, Clyde." She lightly tapped the side of the sofa right next to her.

Papio laughed. "You just don't get it do you? I don't want to be near your skank ass, Special. Just looking at your ass makes me want to do you something real fucked up. So don't push this because for real, baby, with the device or without it I will get mines. You already know this, so stop fucking with me. You want to do business, we can do business, but that's it and that's all. Fucking with you again is the last thing I would ever want to do. That shit is a wrap, feel me?"

"Yeah, sure, nigga, strictly business, Papio. This is how it goes down and this isn't negotiable so hear it and roll with it. The device never leaves my sight, so that means I'm in on all the moves you make with it." Papio was about to speak but she held her hands up to stop him and continued. "Next, my people expects ten percent of all earnings made from the device. We've spent a lot of money on this piece and we've got to start making our ends back ASAP. I'm in on the business so I'm not tripping on the ten percent; shit, a bitch like myself expects to get broken off fairly. Not asking to be given shit. You already know my get down. I'll earn my share. Either that or I fall back and collect the ten percent like my peoples. Either way the device never leaves my possession."

Papio downed his drink and went back to the bar and poured himself another before speaking. "I don't have a problem with the ten percent but for real I don't want to fuck with you, Special. I'm trying to keep my mind on the money but with you in the picture it's hard for me to remain focused on shit."

"You hate me that much, Clyde? You're letting a sound business decision stop you from making some serious money. Come on with that shit, you're not that fucking sensitive nigga." After she made that comment she saw the pain in his eyes and realized for the first time that yes, he was that sensitive. She really underestimated what she had done to him. Up until now she didn't realize the fucked-up effect her decision in Dallas had on him.

"Special, you hurt me in ways that I can't speak on because a nigga would sound too damn weak. Check it, it is what it is though. You say you made a sound business decision and I say you fucked over a nigga who would have given his life for your ass. That's a wrap, we're here now to talk business and business is all we got to talk about from this point on. I agree to your terms. Ten percent to your peeps and you can get down with us on the moves we make and earn your share. You cross me in any way, Special, and you die. Painfully."

"Understood. Now, how are you going to move with those Cubans? I need to know that you ain't playing me, Papio. I know you hate me and you would love for a bitch to get slaughtered, so you gots to do something to make me feel right about this."

He nodded. "I feel you. What I'm about to tell you is going to blow your mind and it's quite fucking funny to me really. But before I get at you I want you to know that since the trust issue between us is so fucked up some security measures has to be set in place. One: before I make the moves necessary to get the Cubans off of your ass I have to have made a substantial amount of ends. Once that has been taken care of I will then get them off of your ass completely. Then we can continue to make the rest of the moves with the device to get me that hundred million."

"Come on, Clyde, you gots to give me something in the be-gin to make me feel comfortable wit' this shit."

Ignoring her statement he said, "Two: I'll show you that I am indeed serious about being in with the Cubans well enough to get them to dead the issue they have with you."

"How? How will you show me this?"

"Easily. See, I'm the man they paid to find your dumb ass."

"What? Stop fucking with me."

"Do I look like I'm fucking playing with your ass? Remember when we were in the MIA and I left the suite to go take care of some business?"

"Yeah."

"I went to go put some ends on a serious debt I had with the Suarez organization, namely Mr. Suarez himself. If you think back to when I told you about those fools I crossed in order to get out of the Feds you will be able to put it all together rather easily."

She thought back to when he told her that story about him and realized that he was telling her the truth. "Okay, but how did they choose you to come after me?"

"Mr. Suarez knows my get down and by me being from out this way he figured he'd be able to kill two birds with one stone. If I bring your head to them he will squash my debt plus they gave me a million dollars in advance for my time and efforts."

"You're telling me that you could have took me out and got your debt clean as well as made a cool million?"

"Yep."

"Why haven't you did it then, Clyde? Why not just go on and smoke my ass and get your debt clear and keep it pushing? I mean, after all, you do hate me right?" she asked with a hint of a smile on her pretty face.

"Don't go patting yourself on the back too fast, bitch. Money. Money is the only reason why I haven't smoked your skank ass. You said it yourself: that hundred million is all I want and if it means dealing with your skank ass a few more times then so be it. I'm not worried about shit else but getting my ends and getting out of this life. I'm in the right position to make all of my dreams come true. I hate it that I have to fuck with you to make this happen but fuck it, it is what it is. The best thing about this deal is simple for me: you cross me again I get to kill your ass and get paid for doing it. Sweet!"

"Fuck you. I got these Cubans on my ass for not letting those Indians smoke your ass, nigga. If I would have remained the coldhearted bitch I am we wouldn't even be having this conversation right now. You owe me this, Papio. You owe me for saving your life."

"You didn't do that shit for me, bitch, you did it for my mother! If it wasn't for Mama Mia you would have let those fools take me. Let's not go back and forth with this shit, what's done is done. I am in the position to make things good for you as well as for me. So, are we going to do this or what?"

"As long as you keep to the agreement, we're good."

"All right then, here's the proof you need." He pulled out his cell phone and quickly punched some numbers. When the other line was answered Papio said, "Let me speak with Mr. Suarez please."

While he waited for Castro to give Mr. Suarez the phone, he pressed the speaker button on his cell so Special could hear the conversation. When Mr. Suarez came on to the line Papio said, "Good evening, sir, how are you?"

"I am fine, *Señor* Papio. Tell me you have some good news for me regarding that Special lady."

Papio stared at Special and smiled because the look on her face was priceless. *Fear. Good, you deserve to be scared, you trifling bitch,* he thought as he told Mr. Suarez, "It looks as if she's got word of the hunt for her. She slipped through my nets, sir. Don't worry though, I got an idea where she's headed. I just wanted to let you know that it may be a few more weeks before everything is everything."

"As long as you're on top of things, Papio, I understand. Thank you for the call. Please continue to keep me posted, *sí?*"

"*Sí,* sir. I'll be talking to you again soon." After he hung up the phone Papio smiled at Special and asked, "Are you satisfied?"

"You proved to me that you're real with this, but tell me something: how are you going to get them off my ass permanently?"

"Like I told your ass, once I got me a nice chunk of ends from that device I will make everything go away. I have it already planned, you just make sure I get my ends quick like. When it's time for you to die you will die and I will give the confirmation to Mr. Suarez and everything will be everything."

"So all you have to do is tell them I'm done and they'll take your word for it? Come on, you gots to do better than that, Clyde."

"My word is good with them but in this case it's different because of the chief. We're going to doctor up a little something something and make it look all proper like, that shouldn't be too hard. Once I send a confirmation photo of your dead ass then everything will be good."

"That means that you're going to cross the Cubans again. You'd do that for me, Clyde?"

"I'm doing it for my fucking money! I never had any intention of paying those fucking Cubans back all of that fucking money any-damn-way. This way I get to get that debt off my ass, plus a nice, easy-earned million. On top of all of that I will get my hundred million. It's a win-win all the way around for me. That is, as long as your ass don't fuck with me and try to cross me again. 'Cause if you do I swear on everything I love I'm going to bury your skank ass."

"But what if they find out you gave them the fifty-two fake out on all of this shit?"

"How can they? The hunt for your ass is off because I told them to fall back before you got word that they were looking for you. Nobody is hunting you but me. When I give the green light and send the flick of your body with one to the head everything will be good. All you will have to do is lay it down and chill and you will be good. It's not like they'll still be looking for your ass."

Special smiled. "You are something else, Clyde. I knew you could get me out of this shit. Let's get this money and make this shit happen."

Papio couldn't help himself; seeing her smile like that touched him in ways he didn't want to face. *I hate this bitch, don't forget that shit, Papio. I hate this bitch,* he told himself over and over. "Yeah, whatever. Check it, Twirl is working on this credit union down the way. If everything is good I want to knock that bitch off this Friday. Until then I'm going to finish showing Brandy a good time out here in L.A. I'll give you a call Thursday if everything is everything, cool?"

"Yeah, that's straight. Tell me something, Clyde, and tell me the truth, nigga, no fronting."

"What, Special?"

"Are you in love with old girl?"

With a serious expression on his face Papio told her, "After loving your ass I can honestly say that I'll never love another bitch. You fucked that up for any other woman and that's on everything."

"Okay, answer one more thing for me and then we can go eat some of Mama Mia's enchiladas."

"What, Special?"

"Are you still a Pussy Monster?" she asked with a smile on her face.

Papio couldn't help but smile too. "Your ass will never find out. Now come on, let's go eat." He was acting hard but his heart was beating extra hard at that very moment. And that's when he realized that he was still very much in love with Special. *Damn.*

Chapter 19

Brandy was so mad at Papio she was literally steaming. Even though he had shown her a wonderful time she was still upset with him. She couldn't believe he was cutting her trip short because of business.

This just isn't fair, she thought as Papio pulled in front of the American Airlines departure terminal at LAX. *Oh, no, he isn't! I know this man doesn't think he's going to drop me off in front of the airport and leave me,* she thought as she folded her arms across her chest with a defiant look on her pretty face.

There was no need for her to speak a word; her body language told him that she was pissed off with a capital P. Papio sighed as he put the car in park. "I know you ain't feeling this shit, *mami,* but I gats to get ready for this move and I just won't have the time to finish off this trip. Give me a few weeks and I'll fly down to Dallas and we'll spend a week out there relaxing and sexing, cool?"

"But, daddy, I was having so much fun out here. Why can't I stay and spend some more time with Mama Mia until your business is finished? I took two weeks off of work just to be here with you. Don't end it so abruptly, daddy, please?"

Shaking his head no he told her, "This business is going to be too hectic for you to be this way, *mami.* If I thought I could handle my BI and give you some attention you know I would. Let it go, Brandy. I'll see you in a few weeks in Dallas."

"Is this really all business, daddy, or does that wench Special have anything to do with me leaving?"

"Stop playing. You know it's a wrap with her so don't go there. Don't turn this into anything else other than what it is, baby. Strictly business. Now you already know what the play is with her as far as that device goes, other than that it's a wrap for real." He smiled and continued. "Plus, it's all falling just how I want it to with that bitch. She really thinks she's gotten away with fucking me over, but believe me, baby, she is in store for a big surprise. I told you I was going to do that bitch and I meant every single word. Come on, let's get you and these bags checked in."

Seeing that she had no win with this one she gave up reluctantly and got out of the car. Back to boring Oklahoma City it was. *Ugh!*

Twirl, Keli, and Special were all waiting for Papio inside of his suite at the Westin. They were in the final stages preparing for the robbery of the C&C Credit Union in Inglewood. The plan was to pull in front of the credit union exactly at one P.M. and use the device to dead all of the alarms and security cameras before entering and robbing the place for all of their money. Papio had confirmed from Q that there should be at least $7 million or more inside of the credit union. Now that was a nice come up. Even after dumping 10 percent to Fay and Poppa Blue they would all clear a couple of million easy.

Twirl was with it as always but he was more eager to be putting something down with his wifey. He wanted

Keli to see that she could move with him and they would be able to get money together. He didn't want her having to be way out there with the sex thing. Keli was loving it because she was excited about being with her boo too. Special was just happy to be able to be near Papio. Hopefully after this move she would be able to get him alone. She was even happier when Twirl told her that Papio was sending Brandy back to Oklahoma City. *Good, one less problem to worry about,* she thought after Twirl gave her the good news. Now as they waited for Papio's return Twirl decided to go over things again.

"We have another SUV parked about three blocks away from the credit union just in case we have to make an emergency switch of vehicles."

"Why is that, baby? I mean with the device thingy I thought everything was going to be super smooth," said Keli.

"We can never be too careful with this shit, baby. This is purely a precaution but a necessary one. What if we come out of the credit union and the police just happen to be passing by and notice us getting inside of the truck or some shit? You never know exactly how things are going to fall so we gots to be prepared for anything. That's why we're going in so heavily armed. You have to understand that if shit does go left we will have to blast our way outta that bitch. No hesitation at all, you feel me?"

"Oh, I feel you all right. You won't have to worry about that, baby. I'm not trying to do no time at Cybil's house." Keli was referring to the short stay she had at Cybil Brand women's prison.

"Yeah, we got that part of the business. While me and you keep everyone under watch, Papio and Keli will hit the tellers and the vault. After they got all of the ends we watch their backs as they get inside of the truck, then we follow with me first and you bringing up the rear. It's so simple, just like taking candy away from a baby," said Special.

"It's not candy, it's a whole lot of damn money and we have to make sure that we have our eyes alert and on everybody inside of that credit union. Papio and Keli will be blind except for us so it's on us to make sure they're good."

"I got it. Damn, what's taking Clyde's ass so long? What, he had to walk that old bat to the gate or some shit?"

Twirl laughed. "Stop hating, Special. If your ass wouldn't have tripped out Brandy wouldn't even be in the picture right now. Blame it all on your greed."

"That's what you think it was, Twirl? You're so far off base that it don't make sense."

"Straighten me out then."

Special thought for a minute. "When we first hooked up I told Clyde that we could never work but he kept insisting that we were meant to be and all of that lovey-dovey shit. I won't lie to y'all, after a while I started feeling that shit too. But I knew what it was. It was another move as far as I was concerned. I had to set it up so I could get those ends from the Indians and do me. It was strictly business."

"If that was the case then why didn't you finish the play and let them take my nigga?"

"Two reasons for real. One: I just couldn't let anything happen to Mama Mia behind my moves."

"And the second?"

She smiled at the couple. "I fell in love with that pretty-ass nigga. I didn't know it until I saw the pain in his eyes when he realized that I had crossed him out. I never seen so much pain on a man's face in my life. When I saw how he was hurting I knew right then and there that I loved him. But it was too late; how could we be together after that? So I smoked the Indians and shot him in his legs so I could have enough time to get away from his ass. I knew one day we would have to face each other again, I just didn't expect for it to be like this."

"Tell me, do you still love my nigga, Special?" Twirl asked as he stared directly at her so he could see if she was lying to him.

Before she could answer Twirl's question the door of the suite opened and Papio entered with a smile on his face. "All right, it's time to get this fucking money. I hope y'all ready because it's about to go down." He turned and faced Twirl. "Is everything ready, dog?"

"Yeah. I got the other truck in place and everything is here. All we have to do is suit up and go make it do what it do."

"What about them. Have you gave them the run-down on how we're going to move?"

"Yeah. They know the business. It's all about making it happen now, my nigga."

"That's what's up." He turned and stared at Special. *Damn, she still is one fine-ass female. No, don't look at her like that; that bitch is a snake and she will cross you out again, nigga. Don't be a fool twice,* he warned himself and frowned at her. "So, are you ready?"

"Mm-hmm. I'm good to go, Clyde."

"What I tell your ass about calling me that corny shit?"

She gave a slight shrug of her shoulders. "You're still and always will be my Clyde, nigga, so kill that shit."

Before he could say a word she turned toward Twirl. "The answer to your question is yes, Twirl. Why it's yes is beyond me though. But it is what it is and I know I have to make it right one way or the other."

"That's what's up. For what it's worth, I believe you."

"Believe what? What the fuck are y'all talking about?" Papio asked as he sat down and began going through the duffel bag he brought. He started pulling out the weapons they were going to use for the robbery.

"Just chopping it up on some other shit, my nigga, it's all good."

Papio raised his eyes from the bag and smiled. "Don't go and get all mushy on a nigga now that your ass done fell in love, Twirl. You got to hold me down while dealing with this one over here. Your girl may be righteous but that skank right there can't be trusted. Feel me?"

Twirl laughed. "Damn, my nigga, you sound like a woman scorned for real."

"In other words you sound like a real bitch, Clyde. Kill that shit and let's get the business handled. The quicker we make moves the quicker we can be away from each other. I'm not trying to keep hearing you dissing me and shit."

Papio laughed. "Oh, excuse me if my disses has hurt your fucking feelings. Who gives a fuck how you feel? Not me. So sit your ass there and shut the fuck up."

"You two lovebirds kill all of that shit. We're about to make some serious moves. Let's get along until after we've made it back and have counted all that damn money." Keli sat down next to Special.

"What. Ever." Special frowned at Papio.

"Yeah, whatever." Papio checked the time. "All right, suit up. After we're dressed we're going to bounce and roll around the wood until we're miked up and ready to make it go down."

He went into the bedroom to change into his black army fatigues and boots. He decided that they all would wear the same thing as far as clothing just as he did when he was with Kango's crew back East. They were all going to put on some baggy sweatpants and sweatshirts over their army fatigues and walk out of the hotel dressed as if they were about to go do some serious working out. Once they were inside of the Ford Explorer they would pull off their sweats and get ready for the robbery.

Special came into the bedroom just as Papio was pulling off his pants, and stood in the doorway, smiling.

He frowned at her. "What the fuck do you want, Special?"

She pulled off the baby tee and pants she was wearing, stepped to him, and put her hands on his chest. "I want you, Clyde. I want to feel you inside of me again. After this move is over later I want you to show me you're still that Pussy Monster I fell for in New York. I know you think you hate me, nigga, later for that though. I'm talking about some serious fucking, that's it and that's all. I can see it in your eyes, Clyde, you miss this pussy. Yeah, you're still salty at me but you still miss this," she purred as she ran her fingers over her freshly shaved pussy. Before he could say a word she turned and left the room.

He stood there smiling because she was so right; he missed that pussy like crazy! After they got that money from the credit union he was definitely going to get at that pussy. *Might as well, because after everything is everything she is still going to be one dead bitch. Why not enjoy her ass while she's still breathing,* he thought as he finished getting dressed in his work clothes. It was time to get money. *Roger that!*

***

Everything was set. Papio pulled in front of the credit union on the corner of Century Boulevard and Yukon Avenue at exactly 1:00 P.M. He was confident that everything was going to go as planned, though he was slightly nervous about not having a driver inside of the SUV while they were inside of the credit union. That was the only wrinkle in their plan and it bothered him more than he originally thought it would. *Fuck it, we'll be straight,* he said to himself. "Check it, it's about to be on, everybody make sure your ear mikes are on now. Mike check one, two."

They all answered back with the same phrase.

"All good. Stay in constant contact with the time while me and Keli are cleaning that bitch out, dog. Also, you gats to make sure you keep an eye on the door, Special. That way you can watch the Explorer; that's our only way out and if something goes left that way we're fucked. If you see anything, and I do mean anything at all concerning the truck, let it be known and deal with it as best as you see fit."

"Gotcha. Let's do this shit, Clyde." Special pulled the device out of her purse and gave it to him.

Papio smiled. "Yeah, let's get this fucking money. Strap up and check all weapons." He flipped the switch and turned on the device and waited for the green light to flash. Two and half minutes after he flipped the switch the red light on the device turned to green and Papio smiled. "We're ready. Y'all good?"

"Ready," said Twirl.

"I'm good," said Keli.

"Fucking right!" said Special.

"Once we're inside pull down your ski masks and watch your six! Let's do this shit!" Papio said as he

opened the door and stepped out of the truck, quickly
followed by his three crew members. As soon as they
entered the credit union a calm came over Papio and
the takeover began. He pulled down his ski mask
over his silky long hair and yelled, "Everybody put
your hands where we can see them and you won't be
hurt! Y'all know what this is! Hands up!" The credit
union was slightly crowded, Papio observed as he went
straight toward the counters where the tellers were
staring at him wide-eyed and scared. Keli had her
weapon aimed at the small crowd in the bank as she
followed him. Special went straight to the middle of
the credit union and started pushing people, yelling for
them to hit the floor. She knew the best way to control
this crowd was to have them all down. Twirl gave her
a nod as he watched her back. When everyone was on
the floor Papio gave them a nod and whispered into his
mike, "We're going in."

"Roger that. We're forty-five seconds in and everything is good," said Twirl.

"The ride?"

Special looked toward the door. "We're clear, do
you."

Papio and Keli proceeded to empty each of the three
tellers' drawers of stacks and stacks of money. After all
three drawers were empty they took the manager and
led him to the back of the credit union where the vault
was located. Keli gasped when she saw all three walls
of the vault filled with money. *My God, that has to
be way more than seven to eight million dollars!* she
thought as she started to fill up one of the three duffel
bags she had on her.

As Papio helped her he too thought that that was
way more money than they originally expected. It took

nearly four minutes to fill all six of their duffel bags. Once they were full Papio turned and told Keli to start taking the three bags out to the others. The bags were too heavy for her to carry all at once so she dragged two of them and left the third. Papio noticed this and quickly came behind her with his bags and grabbed the one she left behind.

When they made it to the other side of the counter Twirl saw the difficulty they were having, and told Special through his mike that he was going to help them with the money and to watch his back. When Special told him that she had him he quickly went and took two of the bags from Keli and told her to get out to the truck; she would be the driver. Papio came next with all of the bags and they made their way out of the credit union. Once they were inside of the truck, Keli eased away from the curb and drove into the neighborhood. She made a right turn on 104th Street off of Yukon and drove the half mile to Prairie Avenue and then made a left. Two minutes later she made a right turn on to Imperial Boulevard and turned on to the 105 Freeway headed west toward LAX. She switched to the 405 Freeway headed north and got off on the Manchester Boulevard exit and pulled into the Best Western hotel.

During the seven-minute drive everyone but Keli had changed clothes. When she stopped in front of their hotel room Papio climbed out of the SUV and opened their room door. He then stepped back to the truck and started grabbing the duffel bags as Twirl grabbed two and Special grabbed the others and they quickly entered the room. Keli pulled out of the parking spot and went to get rid of the truck.

Once they were inside of the room Papio sighed with relief. Everything had gone smoothly. His adrenaline was pumping so hard he felt as if his heart was going to explode. He took a look at Special and Twirl and could tell they shared how he was feeling by the looks on their faces. "Damn, putting that takeover down is one hell of a rush huh?"

"The ultimate high!" Twirl started laughing as he began to relax.

"That shit was crazy! A bitch can get addicted to that type of high for real!"

"True. But for real the only thing I can get addicted to is that fucking money!" They all started laughing as they heard Keli pull back in front of their hotel room in her own car and blew the horn to let them know she was back. After Special let Keli inside of the room Papio said, "Check it, let's count this money and relax for a few hours and then we'll go back to my suite and celebrate."

"Celebrate?" Special asked with a smile.

Papio returned her smile. "Yeah, celebrate, Bonnie."

Twirl and Keli shared grins. Papio shook his head as he started to empty one of the duffel bags onto the bed.

Twirl laughed. "Making moves with you, dog, is a true honor."

"Yeah, yeah. I know, fool, I'm your hero!"

"You're not only his hero, Papio, you're mines too!" Keli started laughing as she grabbed another duffel bag and emptied it onto the bed as well.

Special grabbed the third duffel and emptied it onto the bed too. "You already know you've been my hero, Clyde!" They all laughed as they began to count all of that damn money!

Chapter 20

It took them close to four and a half hours to count it all and when they were finished none of them could believe that they were all staring at forty-four million. Forty-four million! No way in the world were Papio and the three members of his newly formed robbing crew prepared for the astounding amount of money they seized from the credit union robbery. By far it was the largest amount of money any of them had ever seen in their lives.

Papio did some quick calculations and, after a few minutes, figured they would all clear eight million apiece. That would be the split of thrity-two million even. Fay and Poppa Blue would get their 10 percent, which would be four million even, because he planned keeping it simple. He didn't think they would trip too much. Then the last four million would be given to Q. He earned his 10 percent by putting Twirl on to the credit union. *So all in all this will be another perfect caper,* Papio thought as he sat back on the bed and smiled. *Damn, a few more nice licks like this and I'll be able to take Mama Mia somewhere real nice and say good-bye to the game forever.*

He stared at Special, who was smiling from ear to ear. *A damn shame that snake bitch had to cross me. She could have been wifey and everything would have been all good.* He quickly shook that thought out of his head. "Check it, let's get this shit bagged back up and get back to the suite so we can chill and start that celebration we were talking about."

"Yeah, let's do that." Special was ready to sex.

Twirl stared at his future wifey and smiled. "You ready to do some celebrating, baby?"

"Mm-hmm. What about you, you good?"

"We gon' chill and split this loot up and have a chilly time with our folks, but when we leave and get back to my spot the real celebrating will begin."

The very thought of his touch gave her goose bumps as she smiled lovingly at him. "Hurry up and get that shit bagged up. I'm ready to get the fuck outta here!" They all laughed.

Poppa Blue was sitting down in the living room watching television when the program he was watching was interrupted by a news bulletin. Poppa Blue smiled as he listened to the news reporter give a report about a robbery of a credit union in the city of Ingelwood:

"So far what we've been able to learn is this robbery at the C&C Credit Union here in Inglewood seems very much the same as the robbery of two banks in San Diego that happened a few weeks ago. The federal authorities have spoken to us briefly but refuse to release any other information except that it seems as if this robbery was similar to those in San Diego. I was able to learn from a source that it seemed as if the robbers were extremely calm and didn't seem to be rushed at all. Almost as if they knew that they had a certain amount of time. This seems to hint toward an inside job of some sort. When I asked the authorities about this I received a stiff 'no comment.' So it remains to be seen what will come from this. We have been told that well over fifty-five million dollars has been stolen here today from the C&C Credit Union. Back to you, Sherry."

Fifty-five million dollars! My God! Special, what the fuck have you and that damn fool Papio done? Poppa Blue thought as he lifted his heavy frame from his couch and went into his office. He grabbed the phone and quickly called Special. When she answered the phone Poppa Blue said, "Please tell me you're good."

"Okay, I'm good."

"Stop being slippery at the lip, girl; are you all right?"

"I guess you've been watching a little TV huh?"

"You damn right I've been watching TV! And it seems like all they're talking about is a certain credit union getting took for over fifty-five million dollars!"

"Wow! They sure do know how to put extras on that shit. I'd say more like forty-four mill to be exact."

"Shut the fuck up, Special! You know better than that to be talking on this damn line!"

"Well, what the fuck you call me for?" she said defensively because she knew he was right; she was slipping by speaking on the phone about the business they handled. "Look, I'll be getting with you in the morning; right now I'm in relax mode and I'm about to get me some."

"TMI, Special! You just make sure you have your hot ass here at nine A.M. sharp!"

"I will, and I'll be bringing that change for you and our partner."

Poppa Blue had to smile at the thought of all that money coming his way. "Yeah, whatever. See you in the morning." Before she hung up the phone he asked, "Hey, I'm curious, who's giving you some? I know not Papio?"

"Fuck you, Poppa Blue!"

"Ahhh, I see. Enjoy yourself and tell your man I said job well done on both accounts!" Poppa Blue was laughing as she gave him a few choice expletives. After he hung up the phone with Special he called Fay.

Before Poppa Blue could say a word to Fay she said, "Ahh, mon, I see your people move quickly. Damn, mon, the heat from this is going to be wicked."

"I know. I have something that can keep our people out the way so everything should be good."

"I hope so, mon, because tis ting may get out of hand if we don't keep control of it."

"I was thinking the exact same thing. Get down here tomorrow, say by noon, and I'll have a nice treat for you."

"Ooooh, you nasty mon. I didn't think you still wanted Fay that way. Mi come earlier as possible for a romp with you, mon."

Poppa Blue laughed. "Stop playing! Just have your ass down here by noon and we'll do lunch and you can get some shopping money."

"I see. See you by noon then, mon," Fay said, laughing as she hung up the phone.

Poppa Blue sat back in his seat after he hung up the phone and thought about this robbery. *Damn, it's about to get real fucking hot. Shit.*

Papio and Special were sipping some rosé with Keli and Twirl when he received a call from his money man, Q. "Dude! Have you seen the fucking news? They're going fucking ape shit behind this thing. Every snitch in the West is about to have pressure applied behind this move. I think it's time for you to start using that nice piece of land you bought last year. At least for a little while. This is too much right now, dude."

"I feel you. For real I was thinking the exact same thing a few minutes ago. I could make some noise out that way while I'm down there chilling. Check into it and see what you can put together for me, Q."

"Aww, dude, what's the use for you to go out that way to chill if you're going to make some moves when you get out there? Come on, Papio, let's chill for a minute and exhale, you know. This shit is spooking me big time, dude."

Papio laughed. "Calm down, white boy, and listen. You won't be spooked after I drop this nice chunk on your ass. Relax and see what you can see for me. It's not like I'm going right down there to get busy. Fuck, I haven't been there since . . ." He paused and stared at Special as she was conversing with Twirl and Keli. "Never mind. Just get me something lined up for the next few weeks or so. I'll get at you tomorrow before I bounce."

Q sighed with relief that Papio was at least taking his advice and going down to Dallas to chill at the home he purchased last year. With Papio out of town he didn't have to worry about him getting caught up by the authorities. Everybody who had any kind of criminal history was going to be sought during this federal investigation and Q knew that the heat was going to be tremendous. He loved money but he was terrified of jail. He had to make sure that his number one money maker remained free at all costs. Even though he knew Papio would never snitch he didn't want to leave anything to chance. *There's always a first time for anything.* "All right, dude, I'll talk to you tomorrow." Q hung up the phone.

"Looks like the town is on fire. It might be wise if we all shook the spot for a nice stretch. I'm going to bounce down to Dallas and relax out that way for a few weeks. I got my man making some moves to see if he can set up something down that way for me. When he gets at me and it looks right I'll holla at y'all, cool?" Papio said to his crew.

"No doubt. I was just thinking how I need a vacation anyway. We might as well hit Hawaii for a few weeks and enjoy the islands. You with that, baby?" Twirl asked Keli.

"Mmmmmmm, that sounds like a damn good plan, baby. Me, you, and the ocean all day and night equals one hell of a vacation!" They laughed.

"What's up with you; what are you going to do?" Papio asked Special.

She shrugged. "Most likely chill at my house and relax. Not really in the mood to do any traveling. Get at me when you have something lined up. I'll be out here shopping and spending some money. Lots of it!"

He smiled. "I know that's right. I'm going to do the same thing when I get down to Texas. They got some nice shopping spots down there. I got me a tailor I haven't seen in a minute who has a exclusive spot in the Grapevine Mills Mall in Fort Worth. Yeah, I'll drop a few pennies while I'm chilling, too."

"I'll bet you can even have your old broad come down from Okie land and y'all can do it real big," Special said as she sipped some more champagne.

Papio stared at her for a minute. "Why would I have Brandy come down there when I can have you?"

Before Special could answer his question Keli fanned herself and told Twirl, "Damn, baby, don't it feel as if it has gotten hotter in here all of a sudden?"

Twirl smiled and watched as Special and Papio stared
at one another. "Yeah, baby, real hot. Come on, let's go to
the house and make some heat of our own."

Keli emptied her flute of champagne. "I'm with you!"

Papio stared at Special. "So what, your ass speech-
less all of a sudden? You trying to join me in Dallas or
what, Bonnie?"

"Are you sure you want me to, Clyde? Don't play with
me here. I mean you know when we get there what kind
of memories are going to come into that head of yours.
Can you really deal with that shit?"

"If I couldn't deal with it I wouldn't be able to deal
with sitting here next to your ass. Special, I hate you.
I mean that. But for real I love your ass more than I
could ever hate you. That shit don't make no damn
sense, but it's how I feel. Making this move with you
today showed me what I knew last year: we're meant to
be together, Bonnie. We can win big time side by side,
baby. I want you. I want that bomb-ass body but most
of all I want you. I love you. I'm in love with you. I can't
fight it, it's how I feel, it's how I always felt. It is what it
is. So, what up?"

Special could tell by the way he was staring at her
that he meant every word he was telling her and it
touched her in ways that she couldn't put into words.
Her dream had come true; she had her Clyde back.
She looked from Papio to Keli and smiled when she
saw the tears brimming in her lover's/friend's eyes. A
single tear slid from her right eye as she grabbed his
hand. "I love you too, Clyde. But before we make this
next move together please let me apologize for fighting
what I knew was right all along. I should have gotten at
you from the gate and let you know the business. I was
greedy and I was fighting love, Clyde. I was wrong. I am

so sorry, baby. I give you my word on everything that I love I will never cross you again in any way. I know with you there's nothing I can't have in this world. I want it all, Clyde. I want it all and that includes you. I love you. I'm in love with you." She stepped to him and gave him a tender kiss that turned passionate instantly.

They were so caught up kissing that neither of them heard Twirl and Keli as they grabbed their share of the robbery money and left the suite. The sex that followed was hot. So hot that Papio felt as if he could go on and on all night long. Special wrapped her legs around his waist and held on for dear life as he gave her all of his girth. Deep, long strokes; slow, long strokes; and hard, fast ones were what he gave her over and over. She moaned and screamed out his name as she came. Her body was trembling when he scooped her from the floor and carried her into the bathroom so they could shower and cool off some. But cooling off was the furthest thing from her mind.

As soon as the water was turned on Special dropped to her knees and began to suck Papio's dick. She gave him her tremendous head game and made his knees feel as if they were made of Jell-O as he tried to stand there and accept the superb mouth game of hers. When she put his balls inside of her mouth and began to hum as she stroked him slowly he knew that he was about to come any second. Sensing this she quickly reinserted his dick inside of her mouth and caught all of his sperm as he came long and hard.

When he finished she didn't give him any recuperation time; she stroked him a few more times to ensure that he was still hard and then turned around in the shower so her back was to him and gently guided his stiff member right inside of her piping hot pussy from the doggie-style position. She groaned loudly as he filled her up from behind. "Yes! Damn you, Clyde! Yes! Fuck me, Pussy Monster! Smash this pussy! Please! Please give it to me hard!"

Her words drove him crazy and seemed to make him even harder as he gave her exactly what she was begging him for. She worked her pussy muscles and gripped that dick as if her life depended on it. This was the best sex she had ever had and she was enjoying it thoroughly. Her third, fourth, and fifth orgasms were proof of that.

When they were finished they showered slowly and then took turns drying each other off as they went back inside of the bedroom and fell onto the bed and went to sleep wrapped in each other's arms. Papio was thinking about how he was lying to himself. *I hate this bitch. I gots to get her ass back for fucking over me. Fuck! I love this bitch too! I don't think I can be that cold and take this bad motherfucker out. What a fucking mess,* he thought as he drifted off to a satisfied sleep.

Special's thoughts were similar. *I love this nigga, but can I really trust this man? Is our love strong enough for him to truly forgive me? I can't let this fine-ass nigga rock me to sleep like I did his ass and then let him smash me. Ugh! Watch this nigga, Special, before you go head first. You'll know if this love is real with him. He's too emotional not to slip and show he has other plans; at least, I hope he is. If not then he's got me. Damn,* was her last thought as sleep overtook her. They held on to each other tightly as if neither ever wanted to let go. The love they obviously had for one another was apparent by their embrace. Their love was for real.

Chapter 21

Special felt something soft and wet between her legs and sighed when she realized Papio was down there licking her pussy. "Mmmmmm, damn, Clyde, what you doing to me this early in the morning?"

"What I forgot to do last night. I was so caught up with being inside of you again I forgot how good you taste. Now shut up and relax while I get my eat on," he said as he returned to sucking and licking her real good.

"Yes, baby. Please, eat on," she panted as she squeezed her legs tighter on the sides of his head. She came, screaming as if she were being punished painfully instead of being pleasured.

After Papio finished eating her he slid himself inside of her and brought her to another satisfying orgasm by penetrating her deeply. They came together and fell back to sleep, completely sated.

Special woke up a little after 8:00 A.M. and realized she had to get moving if she was going to make it on time to Poppa Blue's. She climbed out of bed and ran into the bathroom to shower. Ten minutes later she returned to the bedroom and quickly got dressed. Papio opened his eyes and saw that she was getting dressed. "Damn, where are you going so early?"

"I got a meeting with my mans and I have to drop off the device. After I take care of a few things I'll come back and we'll finish getting reacquainted, cool?"

"That's what we're doing huh, getting reacquainted?"
She smiled at him. "Yeah, corny huh?"

"Very. All right, baby, do you. I have to get with my mans and check some shit too. Are you serious about coming to Dallas with me, Bonnie?"

"Yeah. I just want you to be sure you're with it."

"I'm good. I'm going to hit Oklahoma City and take care of a few things, and then I'll be down there ready to chill and relax. When do you think you'll be able to come down?"

She shrugged. "I'll know for sure after I get with my mans. We have some issues to talk about and then I'll be able to put things together."

"That's what's up. Give me a call when you're done and we can do lunch or something."

She stepped to the bed and gave him a kiss. "Ugh, you need to go brush, Clyde, kinda tart there."

He laughed. "So what, you love this tart shit, it's your pussy that's on my breath anyway."

"Now that is like really nasty. But I guess you're right. Come here." She pulled his face to hers and gave him another kiss, this time longer and with much tongue. She pulled back. "Umm not really bad, my pussy always tastes good!" She was laughing as she turned and walked out of the suite.

Papio laid his head on the pillow and once again wondered if he was going to be able to kill Special. He knew he should, but he wasn't sure if he would when the time presented itself.

Thirty minutes after leaving the Westin, Special pulled into Poppa Blue's home and smiled when she saw his wife Bernadine carrying an absolutely gorgeous little boy out to her car. Special stepped to them and said, "Hello there, how are you guys this morning?"

After giving Special a hug and a kiss on each cheek Bernadine said, "We're just fine, young lady. Aren't we, little Pee?"

The fourteen-month-old toddler smiled a single-tooth smile at Special and waved. That gesture almost broke her down as she bent and gave the little guy a kiss. She looked at Bernadine, who was watching them with a smile. "I know what you're thinking, and believe me when I tell you some things are about to change for the better."

"I have never passed judgment on any decisions you or my husband have made, Special. All I ask of you is to do what's right."

"I will, promise." She gave Bernadine another hug and kiss before entering the house, where Poppa Blue was sitting at his desk talking to someone on the phone, shaking his head from side to side at the same time. He said a few more words after Special was seated and then hung up the phone loudly.

"Stupid bastard!" screamed Poppa Blue.

"What up?" Special asked as she set her large Dooney & Bourke bag on top of his desk.

Poppa Blue eyed the bag and smiled when he realized what was inside of it. His smile quickly turned back into a frown when he told her, "Your friend Dena was found murdered in Denver last night."

Special put her hands to her face and cried, "How? Who did that shit to her, Poppa Blue? Was it her punk-ass husband?"

Poppa Blue shook his head no. "Nah, they don't have a clue, but it definitely wasn't the husband. Me personally, I think it was that fat fuck Jolly. He still felt y'all beat him out of those ends and maybe he got it out of Dena before laying her down."

"If he did get it out of her you think he may be trying to come look at me and Keli?"

"Don't worry about it. I'll get at that bitch-ass nigga and set him straight."

"Set him straight? Nah, fuck that, Poppa Blue, I'll set his fat ass straight my damn self! Fuck Jolly! For doing Dena he's got to die, it's as simple as that! I was planning on taking a little trip anyway; before I do I'll make a stop in Colorado and lay that fat bitch down and be on my way."

"Where are you going?"

She smiled. "Dallas. I'm going to fall back and go kick it with Papio down there while shit this way cools down."

"Good. I was going to suggest some shit like taking a vacation because shit is really smoking. The Feds know it's something fishy cracking but they ain't been able to figure out what yet and it's driving them fucking crazy. I'm meeting Fay later on and she wants the device for some moves out East with her peoples. That's just what we need to throw shit off track. When the shit goes down East they will be fucked up for real," Poppa Blue said with a huge smile on his face.

"You love fucking with the Feds huh?"

"Not really, but shit why not? It's really rare in this game when we can get the upper hand on those bitches. Mind-fucking them right now gives me pleasure, but nothing beats getting this motherfucking money, so don't you ever get that twisted, young lady."

"No doubt."

"What's the business with you and Papio? You seem to be really comfortable with him now. Was he that convincing?"

She thought about the lovemaking she had the night before. "He was very convincing but that don't change shit. I'm still the coldest bitch in this game, Poppa Blue. I love that nigga and I will give this love a chance to shine, but the first time I even think that pretty nigga is trying to cross me he's dead. That's why I want you to make a call for me and have some weapons available for me in Dallas. So when I get out there I can go scoop them and be ready."

"That's my girl. Stay ready so—"

"I won't have to get ready," she finished the sentence for him.

"Exactly. When will you make it to Texas?"

"I don't know exactly, after I leave here I'm going to go get with Papio and see what his plans are and then I'll let you know. I'm going to hit Colorado tomorrow though. I'm catching the first thing smoking that way and take care of that fat prick, Jolly. After that I may come back here or make that move to Dallas, it all depends on Papio."

"I'll make the calls and get everything ready for you down in Texas. I got a man out in Garland—that's a small city right outside of Dallas—who can strap you nice and right. His name is Jimmy, Jimmy Ross. A old head like me who will definitely try to fuck as soon as he sees your pretty face. He's a horny old fool but dependable."

"That's cool. I'll handle his old ass if he gets out of line, so let him know I'm not to be fucked with. I don't have time for no horny old fart drooling all over me," she said.

"How are you going to move on Jolly?"

"Painfully."

"I wouldn't expect anything less. Be careful."

Special stood, grabbed her purse, and emptied its contents on top of the desk. Poppa Blue smiled as he watched all of that money pour out of her bag. Special was special indeed. She stared at him for a few seconds and said, "I'm going to tell him, Poppa Blue. After I see that he's really serious about what he's talking about I'm going to tell him that he has a son."

"Whoa. You are really feeling him huh?"

"That's right. If everything goes as planned I'm going to help his ass get that hundred million he wants so badly and we're going to leave the game and go somewhere and live happy ever after: me, him, and our Little Pee. Our child."

"What if he is on some grimy payback shit?"

"Then it's going to be either him or me. If it's me, you and Bernadine will have all of my ends and I know you two will continue to take the very best care of my son. If it's him then I'll continue to live and let it be at that."

Poppa Blue sighed. "You've done everything your way so far and haven't made a misstep yet so I have no choice but to roll with whatever you decide. Just be careful, Special."

"I'm always careful, Poppa Blue. Always."

Papio was sitting in the dining room of his suite, eating some grapes, talking to Q. He had come over to retrieve his 10 percent from the robbery of the credit union. "Dude, I can't believe you got your hands on that damn thing you told me about. Do you know how much fucking money you can get with that piece?

Geesh, you're actually going to get that hundred mill, dude. Fucking A! I thought it would take at least another couple of years but now it looks like you will have that shit by the end of the summer! That is if you don't go off and get caught."

"How in the hell can I get caught? As long as I take care of my business and plan properly this shit is in the bag. Yeah, the heat is on right now; that's why I got to bounce and make a few moves out the way. I won't have no set plan nor any type of pattern that the Feds can try to pick up on. I'll make my move in Dallas, then fucking bounce way to the East Coast somewhere. After that I'll hit the Midwest and then hit Dallas all over again. They will be kept in left field the entire time. As long as you can find me the right spots to hit so I can get the maximum amount of ends this shit is in the bag. That device is a fucking goldmine."

"You got that right, dude. I'm on top of some things now and hopefully in a week or so I'll have everything for you out in Dallas."

"That's what's up. I'll be down there chilling and getting my vibe of the town. Do you and I'm gonna make you richer than you already are, you greedy-ass white boy." They both laughed.

There was a knock on the door and Q damn near jumped out of his white skin. Papio laughed at him. "Relax, you scary-ass fool. That can't be nobody but Special," he said as he stood and went to the door. After taking a look through the peephole to confirm it was in fact Special, Papio opened the door and let her inside. He could tell by the determined look on her face that something was wrong.

After introducing her to Q he said, "All right, my man, get at me and let me know when everything is right. I got to take care of some shit with my girl. I'll holla at you later."

Q stood. "That's cool, dude. Be safe." When they were both standing at the door of the suite, Q asked, "Is that the same Special who—"

"Shut up, Q. Yes, that's her, and don't worry about shit. I gats this. I'll hit you before I leave for Oklahoma City."

Q rolled his eyes. "Whatever, dude. Later."

"Yeah, later." Papio closed the door behind his man and quickly stepped back toward Special, who was sitting in his seat eating some of his grapes. He grabbed her free hand. "What's the problem, Bonnie?"

She sighed and gave him the entire rundown on what took place out in Denver and how they took those high-denomination bills from Dena's husband and fucked over Jolly in the process. She didn't see the need to tell him about Rico so she left that part of the trip out. By the time she got to the part about spending the weekend in Las Vegas with Dena she broke down and began crying so hard she could barely finish the story. She regained her composure long enough to tell him how she had just found out that Dena was dead and Jolly was responsible. She started crying again as she swore how she was about to get with Keli and they were going to go out to Denver to take care of Jolly's fat ass. "I gats to get his ass, Clyde; that fat bitch has to die."

Papio gave her a nod of his head in understanding and said, "No question. Do you need any help wit' this one, or are you good with Keli?"

"Nah, Clyde, me and my girl gats to handle this one. We got to do this for Dena. I'm going to get with Keli and we're flying out in the morning to Denver to deal with that fat bitch," she said with venom dripping from every word.

He saw the fire in her eyes and once again admired her for her gangster side. *Damn, if I could only trust this broad, she could be the one for me.* He shook his head from side to side. "All right, then, I'm going to go kick it with Mama Mia for a few days and then I'll hit Texas. Hit me after you've done your thing and we'll meet out that way."

"That's cool."

"My man Q is setting up something nice for us out that way so make sure you get at Keli and keep her ready. I'll get at Twirl so he'll know the business as well."

"I have to get at my mans and let him know we'll be needing the device in a little while so he can get at our other partner." Papio smiled at that. "What are you smiling for? What's funny, Clyde?"

"I know Fay is your other partner, Special. Me and Fay are good with each other. She put me up on her going in with you and Poppa Blue for the device."

The shocked expression on her face passed quickly. "Humph. You fucked her old ass, too, didn't you, Clyde?"

Papio laughed. "Mind ya business, Bonnie! But on the serious side I want you to be careful while you're dealing with that fool Jolly. Don't be faking; handle that shit and bounce."

"Are you concerned for my well-being because you really care about my safety or you just want to keep me safe because I'm your meal ticket to get that hundred million dollars, Clyde?"

Papio stared at her and didn't hesitate to give his answer. "I love you and I want you. It's going to be hard for me to totally trust you again but I'm willing to try. If we take it slow we can make this right again, As for the ends, yeah, you know what it is that plays a huge part in my get down. But my priority is seeing if we can be the coldest couple in the game. If you do right there is nothing that can stop us, Bonnie. You feel me?"

She smiled at him. "Yeah, I feel you. We're going to make it work, Clyde. I'm not playing any games with you. I really want us to make it. I love you."

"I love you too. So like I said, be careful out there."

She smiled lovingly at him. "I'm always careful, Clyde. Always."

Chapter 22

Keli's anger had her in serious danger mode for real. After Special gave her the news about Dena's murder she went ballistic. After twenty-five minutes of ranting and raving Keli settled down and began to cry. Once the tears dried, murder entered her eyes and heart.

She stared teary-eyed at Special and asked, "When are we going to Denver to slaughter that fat pig Jolly, Special?" When Special told her that she already reserved them a flight for the next morning she nodded her head and started crying again. "Damn, she's dead because of us. We should have never let her go back out there, Special. We should have set her up so she could bounce from Vegas and move on with her life."

"Come on, baby, don't put that kind of pressure on yourself," Twirl said as he gently rubbed her back.

The look she gave him made him feel like a chump but proud but all at the same time. She was a gangsta and that shit excited the hell out of him. "Why don't y'all let me roll out there with y'all? I may be needed."

Special shook her head no but Keli was the one who spoke. "Nah, boo, this here is between us girls and, believe me, we won't need any help handling that fat bitch, Jolly. I'll be back in a day or so and then we can go on that Hawaii trip and get some much-needed rest, okay?"

He smiled at her. "Yeah, you got that, ma. Be careful."

"I will."

Twenty-four hours after having such an enormous emotional breakdown Keli was smiling as she pulled out of Hertz Rent-a-Car in a black 2010 Camaro. She loved speed and power and the Camaro had both. Special shook her head as she watched her girl punch the rental car to the max. She pulled her cell out of her purse and called Poppa Blue back in Los Angeles.

"What's up, Poppa Blue, we're here."

"Head toward Park Hill. There's a Pizza Hut delivery-only spot on the corner of MLK and Colorado Boulevard. My man Preacher Willie will meet you there. I just got off of the phone with him."

"What will he be in?"

"Ain't no telling. Don't worry about all of that, you'll know him when you see his crazy ass. Just get what you need and go handle your business and get the fuck outta Colorado. You're playing with fire as it is with that fool Rico looking for you. If one of his peoples happen to spot you two it's a wrap, so remain shaded and handle up."

"You don't have to tell me that shit, we're good. What's up with Jolly?"

"Preacher Willie will give you that information after he gives you what you need." Papa Blue didn't want to say too much on the phone.

"All right, I'll give you a call when we're on our way back home."

"Do that. Oh and tell that fat fuck Jolly I said bye bye!"

"Roger that!" Special hung up the phone and told Keli to head toward Park Hill, a small neighborhood in Denver that was well known for its violence and drugs.

Thirty minutes after arriving in Colorado, Special and Keli were ready to handle their business by getting their revenge against Jolly for killing Dena. Keli pulled the black Camaro into the parking lot of the Pizza Hut delivery restaurant and said, "What the fuck?" She couldn't believe what she was looking at as she put the car in park. There was a huge Winnebago RV parked in the parking lot with a pimp-looking guy dressed flashier than the famous pimp Bishop Magic Don Juan standing next to it actually screaming at anyone who would listen.

"Live! Laugh! Love! That's what life is all about, world! Be happy and enjoy everything that God has given us! He gave us air to breathe and life to live! Be happy and let no man stop you from living life! Believe Preacher Willie! I know what was planned for us and I am living life the way God wants me to and you should too! Woooooooooo! I love God! Yes, I do!"

Special laughed. "Well, I'll be damned, this gots to be some way-out shit right there. Come on, girl, let's get this over with before this clown gets us spotted by some of Rico's people."

"I can't believe Poppa Blue would put us out there like this by dealing with a nigga like this."

"I'm not tripping, let's go." Special got out of the car and quickly stepped to Preacher Willie. "Excuse me, can I speak with you for a second, Preacher Willie?" she asked in a serious tone.

The flamboyant and loud self-proclaimed preacher smiled. "Mmmmm, you must be Special, because you have that glorious, special look about yourself, young lady."

"Yeah, I'm Special. You got something for me, Preacher Willie?"

Preacher Willie's smile widened. "Yes, I do have something for you, Special. Please step into my world." He pointed toward the huge Winnebago and led the way.

Special turned toward Keli and motioned for her to wait for her. Once they were inside of the RV Preacher Willie made a complete transformation right before her eyes. His high-pitched voice became low and calm and smooth as he took off the long fur coat he was wearing. "Damn, it's hot out there. I'm glad you got here when you did. I was just about to call Poppa Blue and tell him to set up another meeting." While Special stared at him with a shocked look on her face he went into the back of the RV and grabbed a medium-sized gym bag and brought it to her. "Here's everything you need: four pistols each with two extra clips fully loaded, all equipped with silencers." Preacher Willie smiled and continued. "Don't look like that, Special; you have been in the mix long enough to know that not everything in this game is what it appears to be. My little act is the reason for my longevity out here in the land of thin air."

With respect for his get down she smiled. "I know that's right. You had me like what the fuck?"

He laughed. "Exactly. That's how it's supposed to be at all times. I respect the game and I play this game to keep everyone who's not knowing out in left field completely shook. Feel?"

"Yeah, I feel you. You're good, I mean really good." They both laughed.

"Thanks."

"The information?"

With a serious expression on his face Preacher Willie said, "The Aladdin's Lamp is a restaurant out in Montebello. The setting is dark and grimy. This is where Jolly handles most of his late-night activities. He normally gets there between ten and eleven P.M."

"How long does he stay?"

"Depends, some nights he leaves before two A.M. and some he has stayed as late as four in the morning."

"So it would be best to take his ass when he arrives?"

"That, my dear, is up to you. I'm only here to provide information, not advice."

"That's right. Thanks." Special stood and reached out and shook his hand. "I understand and respect your get down, Preacher Willie. But you might want to tone it down a bit; you're a little loud."

"That's the plan, baby girl. The louder the better. On the serious side though, it would be better to take Jolly when he first arrives at the spot. The later you wait the more dangerous it becomes because of the late-night laws. Denver PD tends to crawl around that area more in the wee hours."

"I thought you weren't here to give advice."

He smiled as he reached for his loud hat and fur coat and screamed, "Preacher Willie only gives what God wants him to give! God wants you to be happy, Special! So be happy, baby! Go and be happy!"

Special was laughing so hard that tears were sliding down her face as she went and got into the car with Keli.

"What's so funny?" Keli asked as she started the car and pulled out of the parking lot of the Pizza Hut.

Special grabbed her cell phone and dialed Poppa Blue's number. While she waited for him to answer she said, "Girl, you wouldn't believe me if I told you." When

Poppa Blue answered the phone she told him, "Just got with your man and, wow, what a experience."

"I figured you'd like the show. There's more to that than you would ever imagine though."

"I'm knowing, he kind of broke that down to me in one of his calmer moments."

"He did? Wow, that's a first, he must really like you if he came out of character in front of you."

"We're straight. All right, we got what we need so we're about to go get a room and relax until this evening."

"No extra shit with this, Special, make your moves and get out," warned Poppa Blue.

"Roger that." She hung up the phone.

"What time are we going to make it go down?" asked Keli.

"We're going to go sit on this club called the Aladdin's Lamp after we get showered and some rest. This is supposed to be Jolly's late-night hangout where he makes his evening moves. When he rolls up we have two options: either we blast his ass right there and bounce or we snatch his fat ass and take him somewhere to handle the business."

"I want to snatch his fat ass."

Special smiled. "Yeah, I figured you would. If it can do down like that we will; if not we run up on him and unload everything we got into that fat belly of his. If we can snatch his ass I got a way we can make that move just as smooth." Special then proceeded to tell her how she planned on kidnapping Jolly.

Back in Los Angeles Papio was having lunch with his mother at a nice steak house that had just opened out in Riverside. While they were eating their salads Papio told his mother about how he and Special came to a sort of truce.

Mama Mia smiled. "I knew you still loved her, *mijo.* It was just a matter of time before you came to your senses. She's the right woman for you. Brandy is nice and I can see that she truly cares for you, but it wouldn't work with you two."

Papio laughed. "Why do you think that, *Madre?*"

"You like the younger woman, the woman who make you feel excited all the time. She has that now because she's kept herself up nice over the years. But that won't last too much longer. Father Time will catch up to her eventually, *mijo,* and that's when you will leave her high and dry. Why waste your time? Go on and be with the woman who has your heart right now and be happy. You can start a family and leave all of the rough living you two live alone. I know that's what you want, *mijo,* so go make it happen."

He smiled lovingly at his mother and then frowned. "You do know that I was mad at you for talking to her behind my back. Why would you do that to me, *Madre?*"

"Bah! Go on with your foolish talk. You know how I feel about Special. I wanted to see her face to face to see if she really loved you like I felt she did. When I saw her face to face and heard her version of what happened in Texas I knew without a doubt that her love for you is genuine. You know that I would never betray you, *mijo,* so there's no need for you to even think I would. I love you and only you. You are all that I have in this world."

He smiled at his mother. "I feel exactly the same way, *Madre.* You mean the world to me. I hope you're right about me and Special. I care about her more than

I ever thought but I still worry if I can trust her. There are a lot of things you don't know about her, *Madre*. If she crosses me or makes me even think she's up to something tricky I'll kill her. I love her but I won't hesitate to take her life, *Madre*. I know that sounds crazy but that's just how it is until I can know for sure that she has me and my best interest at heart. Special is so much like me that it's scary. I've already learned that first-hand, *Madre,* that girl don't play fair. I'm not falling for the goofy a second time."

Mama Mia smiled at her only child. "Don't worry, *mijo*. She won't cross you no more. She wants a life with you and only you. Trust me."

"You're the only woman I've ever trusted, *Madre*. I love you."

"I love you too, *mijo*. Now, where are those steaks? I'm hungry!" They both laughed as they sipped some wine and waited for their orders to arrive.

Keli was lying on the bed in their room at the DoubleTree Hotel, talking on the phone with Twirl while Special was taking a shower. "Everything is good right now, baby. We're just chilling, getting some rest, waiting for the sun to set before we go make those moves. What up with you?"

"Shit. Just chilling, waiting on my man to come drop me off some ends so I can go get with my peoples to get right for next weekend. After that I'm going to sit back and be waiting for your call to let me know that you're good."

"That's what's up. Have you made our reservations for Hawaii yet?"

"Yep. I got with this travel agent and she hooked us up with a nice suite at this fly-looking hotel in Honolulu. We're going to have fourteen days of chilling in the sun and having the time of our lives."

"Chilling in the sun? Uh-uh, I'm talking about getting my freak on the beach, baby. That sun shit is a wrap. I'm dark enough already!"

"You are too damn silly. You know what I meant, baby. I got us all kind of stuff to do other than just freaking. I signed up for a helicopter ride and—"

"Wait a minute, Twirl, did you say a helicopter ride?"

"Yeah, we ca—"

"Hold the hell up! I don't do nobody's helicopter, Twirl! So you can do that one by yourself. I'll go get my shop on while you're all up in the air looking down at the water or whatever."

"Come on, Keli. You got to live life, baby, it will be exciting."

"Live life huh? That's funny because me and Special saw this preacher dude today and he was preaching that same shit. Live life! Ha! But look at this, baby, I'm living my life and as long as I got you in it I am enjoying it to the fullest, please believe that. I don't need no damn helicopter ride because that is something that I won't enjoy at all."

"Whatever you want, baby. I ain't mad at ya because for real I can get me a break while you're shopping because I'm not into walking around no damn mall all day anyway."

She laughed. "See, there you have it: a simple compromise. I shop, you ride in the helicopter, and when we meet back up we get real freaky and everybody will be happy!"

"You are crazy. All right then, let me go. My mans just pulled up. Time to go handle my BI. You make sure you stay safe and get at me after everything is everything."

"I will. I love you, Twirl."

"I love you too, Keli."

After she hung up the phone with her man she was wearing a smile that only a person in love could have. Special was drying herself off, shaking her head at her lover/friend because she knew the feeling. She just hoped that the feelings her friend was feeling at this very moment would last forever. She knew that nothing lasted forever but she wanted for Keli to have happiness for as long as she could. The life they were leading was wild enough and so damn unpredictable that a little bit of happiness was rightly deserved. These thoughts made her smile as she put on her thong and told Keli, "Get dressed, K. It's time for us to make a move. We got to hit Montebello and peep the area so we can have a lay of the land before that clown-ass nigga Jolly hits the club."

"Are you sure we can pull off that snatch move?"

"I'll know for sure when we peep out the spot. If it don't look right then we'll do Plan B and run up on his fat ass and dump him right as he gets out of his truck. Now get dressed."

Forty minutes later they pulled up in front of a record store across the street from the Aladdin's Lamp nightclub. Special was checking out the area as Keli kept a trained eye on the front of the club. After twenty minutes of this Special told Keli that she was going to go across the street to check out something and she would be right back. She got out of the car and strolled across the street. She wanted to see if she would be able to hide herself enough so when Jolly arrived she would be able to ease out on him and catch him totally off-guard. If she could do that then they would take him to the east side of Denver, where she knew a good spot where they could have a little privacy with Jolly before they took his life.

She walked by the entrance of the club and saw that it was perfect. There was basically a blind spot for any-one who pulled in front of the club. And since Jolly's fat ass would have it no other way she knew she would be able to make her move when he pulled directly in front of the club.

She returned to the car and told Keli, "Yeah, we're going to make the snatch move. It should go real easy. If you see anything that looks fucked up, come out blasting and get my back. If not, then watch my work and follow us over to east Denver. That's where it will go down."

"That's what's up. Now what? It's only eight-some-thing. What are we going to do for another two to three hours?"

Special gave Keli her cutest smile. "Well, we can go get a bite to eat first. After that it's back here so we can wait on that buster-ass Jolly."

"That's cool. But I had something else in mind before eating."

"What?"

"While you were checking shit out I made a few calls and found out that Dena's body is being held at this mortuary in Montebello and—"

Special held up her hands to stop her. "Say no more. Let's go."

"I'm glad you're with it because the mortuary closes in about fifteen minutes," Keli said gloomily as she started the car and pulled away from the curb.

Seven minutes later they pulled in front of Williams Mortuary. They both inhaled deeply as they got out of the car. After looking around to check and see if Dena's husband was around they entered the mortuary silently. They checked a bulletin board that had the names of the bodies that were being held there at Williams and saw that Dena's body was being held in viewing room D in the back of the building. Without either of them speaking they turned and went in the direction of viewing room D.

When they made it to the door-less viewing room they both stood in the doorway with tears sliding down their faces. Dena was lying peacefully in a soft pink casket with gold trimmings. Her hair was done in a long, expensive weave and that brought sad smiles to both of their faces as they thought back to when they first met Dena. Once they were all the way inside of the room they stood in front of the casket and cried. The tears just wouldn't stop while they looked down on their friend.

After a few minutes of this Special wiped her eyes and whispered to Keli, "Come on, K, let's go." Keli nodded her head in agreement and bent over and kissed Dena's cold cheeks. Special did the same and they turned and left the room.

Once they were back inside of the car Keli was so mad she began to tremble. "I don't know about you but I'm not hungry no more."

"Me neither. Head back to the club so we can wait on that fat fuck and take his ass," Special said angrily.

As she pulled the car into traffic Keli started crying again. "Why he have to do her like that, Special? It wasn't her fault, that shit was all on us! Why that bitch-ass nigga have to hurt Dena?"

Special was rubbing Keli's right leg while she drove. "I don't know, K. I really don't. But I do know we can ask that fat bitch before we kill his ass."

"Those were my exact same thoughts. I can't wait to shoot that bastard."

When they made it back to the same parking spot right across the street from the club Special told Keli that she was going to chill in the car for an hour or so. Once it got close to 10:00 P.M. she was going to go across the street and get into the cut and start her wait for Jolly to arrive. If everything went their way they wouldn't have to wait too long for his fat ass.

While they were waiting Special pulled out her phone and sent Papio a text message. She wasn't in the mood to do any talking so they texted back and forth, talking about nothing in particular. When he texted that he missed her and couldn't wait to see her, she smiled and texted him back, telling him that she felt exactly the same way. Before she realized it it was ten minutes after ten. She sent one last text, telling Papio that it was time for her to go handle her business and that she would get back with him after she was finished.

She then grabbed two of the silenced pistols that they got from Preacher Willie and checked to make sure they were loaded and ready to fire. After securing one in the small of her back and the other in the front of her jeans she got out of the car silently and went across the street to start the wait for Jolly.

Fate was on their side because Special hadn't been waiting longer than forty-five minutes when she saw

Jolly's Ford Excursion cross the light on Sheridan headed directly toward the Aladdin's Lamp. She took a quick glance in Keli's direction and saw Keli give a nod of her head, letting her know that she saw Jolly also. *Time to get this fat fuck,* Special said to herself as she inhaled deeply to calm her nerves. Jolly pulled his SUV right in front of the club, and was reaching in the back seat for something when Special stepped quickly from her blind spot to the passenger's side of the truck and opened the door and jumped inside with her gun aimed directly at Jolly's head.

"If you move your brains will be splattered all over this fucking truck, nigga. Now start this bitch up and put both of your fat hands on the steering wheel and drive, Jolly," Special said in a deadly tone.

Jolly knew not to try her because he knew her work first-hand. He'd watched her do some serious damage to niggas over the years. *Damn, I knew I should have got them bitches before I got that bitch Dena. Fuck!* he thought as he eased his truck into traffic, followed closely by Keli. When he saw Keli's smile through his rearview mirror he knew that he was dead for sure. *Fuck!*

"Come on, Special, y'all did me dirty. I know you didn't think I was gonna sit back and stand for that type of shit."

"At least your soft ass ain't trying to deny how you got down, that's a pleasant surprise, nigga. But still, your punk ass was wrong for getting at Dena like that. That move was on us, not her."

"Yeah, I know, she told me just before the bitch bit the bullet."

Special didn't think about her next action; it just happened. She slapped Jolly hard across his head with her pistol and blood from the wound gushed all over the front of the truck. Jolly took one of his hands off of the steering wheel to hold his head and Special shot him in his thick thigh. He was screaming so loud he could barely hear her when she instructed him where to drive. When they made it to east Denver, right across Colorado Boulevard down the street from where they had met Preacher Willie, she told him where to park. After parking the truck in the driveway of a vacant house, Special aimed her gun at his head and said, "What you got in the back of the truck, Jolly?"

"I got like seven pounds of meth and four hundred Gs. Take it all, Special, just don't do a nigga huh? Let me make it please?" he begged.

"Now you know damn well I'm not doing no shit like that. You're about to bite the bullet, bitch. Ain't that what you said you made Dena do? Huh you punk-ass coward? But you know what, if Keli wants to let your punk ass make it then I'll be with it. You never know, she might be in a forgiving mood. I doubt it though. We'll see, 'cause here she comes now."

Before he could say a word Keli got into the back of the SUV right behind the driver's seat. She smiled when she saw all of the blood inside of the truck. "Glad you saved me some." Without saying another word she put her gun to the back of Jolly's head and blew his brains out.

"Damn! Girl, I was gonna have some fun with his fat ass."

"Fuck that shit, let's get the fuck."

"All right, but grab that bag right there: ends and some meth. We came up too."

Keli snatched the bag and took a peep inside and frowned. "Now, what in the hell are we gonna do with some fucking meth?"

"Sell that shit. What else you think we gone do with it?"

"How are we gonna get this shit back home?"

Special was smiling when she said, "Looks like we got to make another road trip back to Cali!"

Keli shook her head as she pulled out her cell and called Twirl to let him know there was a change of plans. She wouldn't make it back to California when she said she would. She wasn't mad though because she had just come up $200,000 plus, and on top of that she had her revenge for her girl Dena.

Rest in peace, Dena, she said to herself as she drove the Camaro toward their hotel room so they could get their things before they started their trek back to sunny California.

Notes

Notes

Notes

ORDER FORM
URBAN BOOKS, LLC
78 E. Industry Ct
Deer Park, NY 11729

Name: (please print):_____

Address: _____

City/State: _____

Zip: _____

QTY	TITLES	PRICE

Shipping and handling-add $3.50 for 1st book, then $1.75 for each additional book.

Please send a check payable to:

Urban Books, LLC

Please allow 4-6 weeks for delivery

ORDER FORM
URBAN BOOKS, LLC
78 E. Industry Ct
Deer Park, NY 11729

Name: (please print):_____

Address: _____

City/State: _____

Zip: _____

QTY	TITLES	PRICE
	16 On The Block	$14.95
	A Girl From Flint	$14.95
	A Pimp's Life	$14.95
	Baltimore Chronicles	$14.95
	Baltimore Chronicles 2	$14.95
	Betrayal	$14.95
	Black Diamond	$14.95
	Black Diamond 2	$14.95
	Black Friday	$14.95
	Both Sides Of The Fence	$14.95
	Both Sides Of The Fence 2	$14.95
	California Connection	$14.95

Shipping and handling-add $3.50 for 1st book, then $1.75 for each additional book.

Please send a check payable to:

Urban Books, LLC

Please allow 4-6 weeks for delivery

ORDER FORM
URBAN BOOKS, LLC
78 E. Industry Ct
Deer Park, NY 11729

Name: (please print): _____

Address: _____

City/State: _____

Zip: _____

QTY	TITLES	PRICE
	California Connection 2	$14.95
	Cheesecake And Teardrops	$14.95
	Congratulations	$14.95
	Crazy In Love	$14.95
	Cyber Case	$14.95
	Denim Diaries	$14.95
	Diary Of A Mad First Lady	$14.95
	Diary Of A Stalker	$14.95
	Diary Of A Street Diva	$14.95
	Diary Of A Young Girl	$14.95
	Dirty Money	$14.95
	Dirty To The Grave	$14.95

Shipping and handling-add $3.50 for 1st book, then $1.75 for each additional book.

Please send a check payable to:

Urban Books, LLC

Please allow 4-6 weeks for delivery